The Beacon Best of 2000

Edwidge Danticat, guest editor

The Beacon Best of 2000

great writing

by women and men

of all colors and cultures

Beacon Press

Boston

Beacon Press
25 Beacon Street
Boston, Massachusetts 02108-2892
www.beacon.org

Beacon Press books
are published under the auspices of
the Unitarian Universalist Association of Congregations.

Printed in the United States of America
ISSN 1525-173X
ISBN 0-8070-6244-8 (cloth)
ISBN 0-8070-6245-6 (pbk.)

This book is printed on acid-free paper that meets the uncoated paper
ANSI/NISO specifications for permanence as revised in 1992.
Text design by Julia Sedykh Design
Composition by Wilsted & Taylor Publishing Services
05 04 03 02 01 00 8 7 6 5 4 3 2 1

contents

introduction

On January 1, 2000, I woke up to the very sobering realization of being a writer from another century. But as I jumped out of bed, the thought seemed far less important than the waiting pot of squash soup that I would soon share with my family, something that we have always done on the first of the year, to commemorate Haitian Independence Day. My mother and I had spent the morning of the day before shopping for all the ingredients, just the right kind of meats and noodles, the correct spices, and of course the perfect squash. Even with the looming threat of the world caving in under the constant menace of Y2K, we scoured supermarket aisles for cabbage, vegetable oil, and broth, then spent the whole day cooking so that our soup would have enough time to boil and simmer while we waited for a new millennium to begin.

Thankfully unscathed by Y2K, three generations of our family gathered the next morning to enjoy our soup: my mother and father, myself and my brother, who stopped by with his five-month-old daughter, Nadira, the elder of the two youngest members of our clan (the youngest being my three-month-old nephew Karl). As we all sat around the table, we were often interrupted by phone calls from friends and family members both from Haiti and the United States, wishing us a "Bonne Année," or a "Happy New Year." Between these telephone conversations, we took turns recalling memorable moments from the past year, naming my niece's and my nephew's birth, and my return trip to my father's birthplace in the mountains of Léogane, a three-hour drive and ten-hour walk from the Haitian capital. We remembered my father's three-story plunge from a broken staircase in the back of the building where he works in East Flatbush, Brooklyn, and the subsequent surgeries on his disjointed ankles. My mother recalled vividly the first few days after my father's accident, how the doctors had told him that he was lucky to be alive. I confessed to being extremely angry that my mother and brother had kept the news of my father's fall from me during the whole time I was in Haiti, sleeping in the house where my father was born, visiting the graves of his parents and grandparents.

Halfway through the reminiscences and regrets, however, it occurred to me that the most cohesive aspect of our family life had survived the transition from one century to the next: our stories. My parents, my brother, and I were collecting these fragments of our wonders and losses now on the other side of this new century, like the soup ingredients that my mother and I had so carefully gathered the day before. We were sharing all this now with one another, with a new kind of resolve, almost as if to remind ourselves that we were the same, and that both individually and as a family we were still hauling these important moments with us along the unpredictable continuum of time.

However, as we talked, and laughed, and then fell silent to entertain our own thoughts, I wondered why bother to tell these stories now when shifting to another millennium would bring with it its own sets of events and new voices to recount them? What would my niece, for example, who was looking up wide-eyed, drooling and smiling at us, what would she have to add two years, five years, ten years from now? Would she emerge as the loudest or the most silent of the talebearers among us? Would she resent or welcome the place she had inherited around the large steaming pot of soup on our dining room table? How significant would our stories remain for her? For us?

These questions seemed as relevant to an immigrant family celebrating a homeland holiday in America as to a writer crossing a pivotal period of time. They needed to be asked to shield us from irrelevance—irrelevance to the world from which we had come and the one in which we were now living. On the first day of the new century, we did what survivors have always done. We got up, went out into the world and gathered our food. Then we called our flock together to eat it, performing a family ritual, and in the process creating another story to tell at a later congregation of our tribe.

I see these pieces gathered here in *The Beacon Best of 2000* as a similar type of congregation. This is only the second year of the Beacon Best series, but it is already beginning to feel like a loving tradition. And this time I have the wonderful honor of being the family member who is asked to open the ceremonies and say the few words of thanks (or grace). This honor feels to me like a distinction that has always been reserved for my mother at our New Year's Day soup feast—it feels as if I am being asked to pour the soup. Making this particular soup, however, took a whole year. Every once in a while a wonderful bundle would arrive from Beacon Press filled with some amazing pieces of writing that they thought I should look at. And more frequently, almost once a week, I would go to a bookstore where I would use being *The Beacon Best of 2000* guest editor as an excuse to indulge in buying literary magazines and to search for that one essay, short story, or poem, that might come together along with the other pieces to form a crucial component of our book.

Of course the selections are subjective. There are so many wonderful things that might have been included, but one hopes for the best and picks from the heart, almost as if choosing guests for a cherished occasion. I hoped to bring together voices that might echo or question each other, works that have a greater impact on the reader when aligned or juxtaposed. What ultimately won me over in all of these pieces is that even while written on the threshold of one century and the next, they feel timeless, as timeless as life, love, joy, and pain; timeless because we might be able to share these words with men and women of all "colors" and catch a glimpse of recognition in their eyes; timeless because when we read well or listen closely that look of recognition may never leave our own eyes.

"My life has always been too large for me," Nicholas Samaras writes in his poem "No Countries but the Distance of the World." This book is full of large lives and the ways they are balanced and reclaimed.

Persistence is always an admirable trait in any life, but particularly in the lives of story people, who with their tenacity heighten our curiosity and interest. For example, that morning of January 1 when over my bowl of soup I asked my father if he, like the doctors who treated him after his fall last August, believed that he was going to die, he answered, "Yes."

"Then why didn't you die?" I asked.

"Because I was waiting for you to return," he said. "I had a desire to see you return."

Perhaps it is a similarly blatant wish, the same type of forceful desire, that constant yearning to affirm our lives, that keeps us all telling our stories, writing against the constraints of absolute realities and predetermined truths, against negative reactions and changes in place and time.

We were all told that the closing of the century was the time before the storm, pre-annihilation, pre-world chaos, and pre-Y2K. However, a few months into this century, from the other side of the millennium threshold, I am joyful, and exhilarated, not only to have survived, and to have seen my father survive, but to have been a part of the joining of these tales, the making of this book. This volume brings together a phenomenal group of poets, essayists and fiction writers, both emerging and established, in what Nicholas Samaras calls "a place of no fences"—or at least a place of fewer fences. Having read and lived with these pages for a year now, there is no longer any fear in my mind of being a writer, or a person, from another century, another millennium. I know that I am on a journey with many brave and talented souls, some of whom, in this place and time, have been gathered here to recount these exceptional tales.

Edwidge Danticat

Nicholas Samaras

No Countries but the Distance of the World

From *The Kenyon Review*

And the smoke of the incense rose
with the prayers of the saints
from the hand of the angel before God.
—Revelation 8:4

My life has always been too large for me. Deep in the heart of darkest
America,
no country was sufficient. Only air became enough and able to speak to
me in its

transparent, fleeing vowels moving me out of myself, to a place of no
fences,
a horizon that spans the circumference of zero, this distance with
everything

yet in front. I wanted to find the physical, the rooted place of least walls
where we can
approach ending or the expanse of ending. In a place of earth and spread
of ocean,

emerald to olive to blue in the brace of light, I stood on the edge of a
sunlit cliff,
and it was enough to stand—the sun on my face uplifted, the sun in all
its benevolent

fury warming the outstretched splintered sea. Here where I stood
rooted and
reaching, I spoke of reality and reality came in its moment. Oh, look and
see.

In the space of this earthen wall and this sea that changes color but does
not
change, this light and this light, the white and gold dissolve of all ahead
of me,

what was the word within my breathing chest? Not the barbed words of
those
who ever cut me, the wounds I still carried for comfort. And here, my
wise father

beside me forever, who said whatever happened to me personally was
nothing, for it
all happens to everyone, as well. I was never hurt more than anyone else
was ever hurt.

I bless him forever for that gift. Through his sainted breath and his
words, it was never
myself alone. It was myself wanting containment, but wanting
exhalation more.

I wanted both parts of the contradiction. I wanted to read of last things
for a while—
and move beyond. After hurt, I found I can still love the world because I
can still

imagine the world. Past words that may praise or scold—through
language and
breath, then, I am getting to the world. My purpose has always been the
world.

What could be the word? When all I ever wanted then was three chords
and the truth.
Not the lie that begins everything wrong. There is only the simple, only
human dignity

and we must bear the quiet witness. What is language but consciousness? If I am
alive, then I am alive to the world. If I write, then I write for the world. I
am writing

to meet the world. So, I came to stand in this place of light, looking for a
country
autocephalous, a soul rising like vapor, giving my words to the one wide
chasm.

If language can wound, it can also redeem. Then, I choose redemption
and the language of redemption, walking forward, eyes focused ahead

to this moment and then, this moment. Look back and History doesn't
justify.
It is a sin to love someone else's tragedy because it is exotic. If we say

Dachau and Golan, if we say Belfast, Cyprus, Aberfan: no privilege.
If we say holocaust and holocaust: no privilege because oppression is
oppression,

no matter the circumstance or degree—public or personal. If the world
is broken,
it doesn't mean permanently as long as there is time. What is optimism

but the ability to work with time and the world in time? In air brine-
heavy,
I breathed out the beginning holocaust of the lie within me, and
inhaled

the salted *Yes* of the world, the smoke-cured ascent, the feel of distance growing
near. In a twilight, I stood responsible in my body. I looked out over the curving

geography of the globe, *and the smoke of the incense rose with the prayers of the saints*
from the hand of the angel before God. It was moving, that foggy blue and gray,

and it was enough for the equal moment I remained in. Oh, light and spiraling
waft of light, it was a quiet witness that did not speak but was enough to just

be there, a body in time, a testament of silence that said more. And that
was the hand and that was the prayer. And there is always a kind of response.

Sherman Alexie

The Toughest Indian in the World

From *The New Yorker*

Being a Spokane Indian, I only pick up Indian hitchhikers. I learned this particular ceremony from my father, a Coeur d'Alêne, who always stopped for those twentieth-century aboriginal nomads who refused to believe the salmon were gone. I don't know what they believed in exactly, but they wore hope like a bright shirt. My father never taught me about hope. From an early age, I was told that our salmon would never come back, and though such lessons may seem cruel, I learned to cover my heart in a crowd of white people.

"They'll kill you if they get the chance," my father said. "Love you or hate you, white people will shoot you in the heart. Even after all these years, they'll still smell the salmon on you, the dead salmon, and that will make white people dangerous."

All of us, Indian and white, are haunted by salmon.

When I was a boy, I leaned over the edge of one dam or another—perhaps Long Lake or Little Falls or the great gray dragon known as the Grand Coulee—and watched the ghosts of salmon rise from the water to the sky and become constellations. Believe me, for most Indians stars are nothing more than white tombstones scattered across a dark graveyard.

But the Indian hitchhikers my father picked up refused to admit the existence of sky, let alone the possibility that salmon might be stars. They were common people who believed only in the thumb and the foot. My father envied those simple Indian hitchhikers. He wanted to change their minds about salmon; he wanted to break open their hearts and see the future in their blood, because he loved them.

Driving along one highway or another, my father would point out a hitchhiker standing beside the road a mile or two in the distance.

"Indian," he would say, and he was never wrong, though I could never tell if the distant figure was male or female, let alone Indian or not.

If that distant figure happened to be white, my father would drive by without comment. That was how I learned to be silent in the presence of white people. The silence is not about hate or pain or fear. Indians just like to believe that white people will vanish, perhaps explode into smoke, if they are ignored enough times. Perhaps a thousand white families are still waiting for their sons and daughters to return home, and can't recognize them when they float back as morning fog.

"Indian," my father would say again as we approached one of those dream-filled hitchhikers. Hell, those hitchhikers' faces grew red and puffy with the weight of their dreams.

"We better stop," my mother would say from the passenger seat. She was one of those Spokane women who always wore a purple bandanna tied tightly around their heads. These days, her bandanna is usually red. There are reasons, motives, traditions behind the choice of color, but my mother keeps them secret.

"Make room," my father would say to my siblings and me as we sat on the floor in the cavernous passenger area of our blue van. We sat on carpet samples because my father had torn out the seats in a sober rage not long after he bought the van from a crazy white man.

I have three brothers and three sisters now. Back then, I had four of each. I missed one of the funerals and cried myself sick during the other one.

"Make room," my father would say again—he said everything twice —and only then would we scramble to make space for the Indian hitchhiker.

Of course, it was easy enough to make room for one hitchhiker, but Indians usually travel in packs. Once or twice, we picked up entire all-Indian basketball teams, along with their coaches, girlfriends, and cousins. Fifteen, twenty Indian strangers squeezed into the back of a blue van with nine wide-eyed Indian kids.

Back in those days, I loved the smell of Indians, and of Indian hitchhikers in particular. They were usually in some stage of drunkenness, often in need of soap and towel, and always ready to sing.

Oh, the songs! Indian blues bellowed at the highest volumes. We called them "49s," those cross-cultural songs that combined Indian lyrics and rhythms with country-and-Western and blues melodies. It seemed that every Indian knew all the lyrics to every Hank Williams song ever recorded. Hank was our Jesus, Patsy Cline was our Madonna, and Freddy Fender, George Jones, Conway Twitty, Loretta Lynn, Tammy Wynette, Charley Pride, Ronnie Milsap, Tanya Tucker, Marty Robbins, Johnny Horton, Donna Fargo, and Charlie Rich were our disciples.

We all know that nostalgia is dangerous, but I remember those days with a clear conscience. We live in different days now, and there aren't as many Indian hitchhikers as there used to be.

Today, I drive my own car, a 1998 Toyota Camry, the best-selling automobile in the United States, and therefore the one most often stolen. *Consumer Reports* has named it the most reliable family sedan for sixteen years running, and I believe them.

With my Camry I pick up three or four Indian hitchhikers a week. Mostly men. They're usually headed home, back to their reservations or somewhere close to their reservations. Indians hardly ever travel in a straight line, so a Crow Indian might hitchhike west when his reservation is back east in Montana. He has some people to see in Seattle, he might explain if I ever asked him. But I never ask Indians their reasons for hitchhiking. They were Indian, walking, raising a thumb, and I was there to pick them up.

At the newspaper where I work, my fellow-reporters think I'm crazy to pick up hitchhikers. They're all white and never stop to pick up anybody, let alone an Indian. After all, we're the ones who write the stories and headlines: "HITCHHIKER KILLS HUSBAND AND WIFE," "MISSING GIRL'S BODY FOUND," "RAPIST STRIKES AGAIN." If I really tried, maybe I could explain to them why I pick up any Indian, but who wants to try? Instead, if they ask I just give them a smile and turn back to my computer. My co-workers smile back and laugh loudly. They're always laughing loudly at me, at one another, at themselves, at goofy typos in the newspaper, at the idea of hitchhikers.

I dated one of them for a few months. Cindy. She covered the local courts: speeding tickets and divorces, drunk driving and embezzlement. Cindy firmly believed in the who-what-where-when-why-and-how of journalism. In daily conversation, she talked like she was writing the lead of her latest story. Hell, she talked like that in bed.

"How does that feel?" I would ask, quite possibly becoming the only Indian man who has ever asked that question.

"I love it when you touch me there," she would answer. "But it would help if you rubbed it about thirty per cent lighter and with your thumb instead of your middle finger. And could you maybe turn the radio to a different station? KYZY would be good. I feel like soft jazz will work better for me right now. A minor chord, a C or G-flat, or something like that. O.K., honey?"

During lovemaking, I would get so exhausted by the size of her vocabulary that I would fall asleep before my orgasm, continue pumping away as if I were awake, and then regain consciousness with a sudden start when I finally did come, more out of reflex than passion.

Don't get me wrong. Cindy was a good one, cute and smart, funny as hell, a good catch no matter how you define it, but she was also one of those white women who only date brown-skinned guys. Indians like me, black dudes, Mexicans, even a few Iranians. I started to feel like a trophy, or like one of those entries in a personal ad. I asked Cindy why she never dated pale boys.

"White guys bore me," she said. "All they want to talk about is their fathers."

"What do brown guys talk about?" I asked her.

"Their mothers," she said and laughed, then promptly left me for a public defender who was half Japanese and half African—a combination that left Cindy dizzy with the interracial possibilities.

Since Cindy, I haven't dated anyone. I live in my studio apartment with the ghosts of two dogs, Felix and Oscar, and a laptop computer stuffed with bad poems, the aborted halves of three novels, and some three-paragraph personality pieces I wrote for the newspaper.

I'm a features writer, and an Indian at that, so I get all the shit jobs. Not the dangerous shit jobs or the monotonous shit jobs. No. I get to write the articles designed to please the eye, ear, and heart. And there is no journalism more soul-endangering to write than journalism that aims to please.

So it was with reluctance that I hopped into my car last week and headed down Highway 2 to write some damn pleasant story about some damn pleasant people. Then I saw the Indian hitchhiker standing beside the road. He looked the way Indian hitchhikers usually look. Long, straggly black hair. Brown eyes and skin. Missing a couple of teeth. Bad complexion. Crooked nose that had been broken more than once. Big, misshapen ears. A few whiskers masquerading as a mustache. Even before he climbed into my car, I could tell he was tough. He had some serious muscles that threatened to rip through his blue jeans and denim jacket. When he was in the car, I could see his hands up close and they told the whole story. His fingers were twisted into weird shapes, and his knuckles were covered with layers of scar tissue.

"Jeez," I said. "You're a fighter, enit?"

The hitchhiker looked down at his hands, flexed them into fists. I could tell it hurt him to do that.

"Yeah," he said.

I pulled back onto the highway, looking over my shoulder to check my blind spot.

"What tribe are you?" I asked him.

"Lummi," he said. "What about you?"

"Spokane."

"I know some Spokanes. Haven't seen them in a long time."

He clutched his backpack in his lap like he didn't want to let it go for nothing. He reached inside a pocket and pulled out a piece of deer jerky. I recognized it by the smell.

"Want some?" he asked.

"Sure."

It had been a long time since I'd eaten jerky. The salt, the gamy taste. I felt as Indian as Indian gets, driving down the road in a fast car, chewing on jerky, talking to an indigenous fighter.

"Where you headed?" I asked.

"Home. Back to the rez."

I nodded my head as I passed a big truck. The driver gave us a smile as we went by. I tooted the horn.

"Big truck," said the fighter.

I haven't lived on my reservation for years. But I live in Spokane, which is only an hour's drive from the rez. Still, I hardly ever go there. I don't know why not. I don't think about it much, I guess, but my mom and dad still live in the same house where I grew up. My brothers and sisters, too. The ghosts of my two dead siblings share an apartment in the converted high school. Believe me. It's just a local call from Spokane to the rez, so I talk to all of them once or twice a week. Smoke signals courtesy of the U.S. West Communications. Sometimes they call me up to talk about the stories they've seen that I write for the newspaper. Pet pigs and support groups and science fairs. Once in a while, I used to fill in for the obituaries writer when she was sick. Then she died, and I had to write her obituary.

"How far you going?" asked the fighter, meaning how much closer was he going to get to his reservation than he was now.

"Up to Wenatchee," I said. "I've got some people to interview there."

"Interview? What for?"

"I'm a reporter. I work for the newspaper."

"No," said the fighter, looking at me like I was stupid for thinking he was stupid. "I mean, what's the story about?"

"Oh, not much. There's two sets of twins who work for the fire department. Human-interest stuff, you know?"

"Two sets of twins, enit? That's weird."

He offered me more deer jerky, but I was too thirsty from the salty meat, so I offered him a Pepsi instead. It's a little-known fact that Indians can be broken up into two distinct groups: Pepsi tribes and Coke tribes.

"Don't mind if I do," he said. He was obviously a member of a Pepsi tribe.

"They're in a cooler on the back seat," I said. "Grab me one, too."

He maneuvered his backpack carefully and found room enough to reach into the back seat for the soda pop. He opened my can first and handed it to me. I took a big mouthful and hiccupped loudly.

"That always happens to me when I drink cold things," he said.

We sipped slowly after that. I kept my eyes on the road while he stared out his window into the wheat fields. We were quiet for many miles.

"Who do you fight?" I asked as we passed through another anonymous small town.

"Mostly Indians," he said. "Money fights, you know? I go from rez to rez, fighting the best they have. Winner takes all."

"Jeez, I never heard of that."

"Yeah, I guess it's illegal."

He rubbed his hands together. I could see fresh wounds.

"Man," I said. "Those fights must be rough."

The fighter stared out the window. I watched him for a little too long and almost drove off the road. Car horns sounded all around us.

"Jeez," the fighter said. "Close one, enit?"

"Close enough," I said.

He pulled his backpack closer to him, using it as a barrier between his chest and the dashboard. An Indian hitchhiker's version of a passenger-side air bag.

"Who'd you fight last?" I asked, trying to concentrate on the road.

"Some Flathead kid," he said. "In Arlee. He was supposed to be the toughest Indian in the world."

"Was he?"

"Nah, no way. Wasn't even close. Wasn't even tougher than me."

He told me how big the Flathead kid was, way over six feet tall and two hundred and some pounds. Big buck Indian. Had hands as big as this and arms as big as that. Had a chin like a damn buffalo. The fighter told me that he hit the Flathead kid harder than he ever hit anybody before.

"I hit him like he was a white man," the fighter said. "I hit him like he was two or three white men rolled into one."

But the Flathead kid would not go down, even though his face swelled up so bad that he looked like the Elephant Man. There were no referees, no judge, no bells to signal the end of the round. The winner was the Indian still standing. Punch after punch, man, and the kid would not go down.

"I was so tired after a while," said the fighter, "that I just took a step back and watched the kid. He stood there with his arms down, swaying from side to side like some toy, you know? Head bobbing on his neck like there was no bone at all. You couldn't even see his eyes no more. He was all messed up."

"What'd you do?" I asked.

"Ah, hell, I couldn't fight him no more. That kid was planning to die before he ever went down. So I just sat on the ground while they counted me out. Dumb Flathead kid didn't even know what was happening. I just sat on the ground while they raised his hand. While all the winners collected their money and all the losers cussed me out. I just sat there, man."

"Jeez," I said. "What happened next?"

"Not much. I sat there until everybody was gone. Then I stood up and headed for home. I'm tired of this shit. I just want to go home for a while. I got enough money to last me a long time. I'm a rich Indian, you hear? I'm a rich Indian."

The fighter finished his Pepsi with one last swallow, rolled down his window, and pitched the can out. I almost protested, but decided against it. I kept my empty can wedged between my legs.

"That's a hell of a story," I said.

"Ain't no story," he said. "It's what happened."

"Jeez," I said. "You would've been a warrior in the old days, enit? You would've been a killer. You would've stolen everybody's goddam horses. That would've been you. You would've been it."

I was excited. I wanted the fighter to know how much I thought of him. He didn't even look at me.

"A killer," he said. "Sure."

We didn't talk much after that. I pulled into Wenatchee just before sundown, and the fighter seemed happy to be leaving me.

"Thanks for the ride, cousin," he said as he climbed out. Indians always call each other cousin, especially if they're strangers.

"Wait," I said.

He looked at me, waiting impatiently.

I wanted to know if he had a place to sleep that night. It was supposed to get cold. There was a mountain range between Wenatchee and his reservation. Big mountains that used to be volcanoes. Big mountains that were still volcanoes. It could all blow up at any time. We wrote about it once in the newspaper. Things can change so quickly. So many emergencies and disasters that we can barely keep track. I wanted to tell him how much I cared about my job, even if I had to write about small-town firemen. I wanted to tell the fighter that I always picked up every Indian hitchhiker, young and old, men and women. Believe me. I pick them up and get them all a little closer to home, even if I can't get them all the way. I wanted to tell him that the night sky was a graveyard. I wanted to know if he was the toughest Indian in the world.

"It's late," I finally said. "You can crash with me, if you want."

He studied my face and then looked down the long road toward his reservation.

"O.K.," he said. "That sounds good."

We got a room at the Pony Soldier Motel, and both of us laughed at the irony of it all. Inside the room, in a generic watercolor hanging above the bed, the U.S. Cavalry was kicking the crap out of a band of renegade Indians.

"What tribe you think they are?" I asked the fighter.

"All of them," he said.

The fighter crashed on the floor while I curled up in the uncomfortable bed. I couldn't sleep for the longest time. I listened to the fighter talk in his sleep. I stared up at the water-stained ceiling. I don't know what time it was when I finally drifted off, and I don't know what time it was when the fighter got into bed with me. He was naked and his penis was hard. I could feel it press against my back as he snuggled up close to me, reached inside my underwear, and took my penis in his hand. Neither of us said a word. He just continued to stroke me as he rubbed himself against my back. That went on for a long time. I had never been that close to another man, but the fighter's callused fingers felt better than I would have imagined if I had ever allowed myself to imagine such things.

"This isn't working," he whispered. "I can't come."

Without thinking, I reached around and took the fighter's penis in my hand. He was surprisingly small.

"No," he said. "I want to be inside you."

"I don't know," I said. "I've never done this before."

"It's O.K.," he said. "I'll be careful. I have rubbers."

Without waiting for my answer, he released me and got up from the bed. I turned to look at him. He was beautiful and scarred. So much brown skin marked with bruises, badly healed wounds, and tattoos. His long black hair was unbraided and hung down to his thin waist. My slacks and dress shirt were carefully folded and draped over the chair near the window. My shoes were sitting on the table. Blue light filled the room. The fighter bent down to his pack and searched for his condoms. For reasons I could not explain then and cannot explain now, I kicked off my underwear and rolled over on my stomach. I could not see him, but I could hear him breathing heavily as he found the condoms, tore open a package, and rolled one over his penis. He crawled onto the bed, between my legs, and slid a pillow beneath my belly.

"Are you ready?" he asked.

"I'm not gay," I said.

"Sure," he said as he pushed himself into me. He was small but it hurt more than I expected, and I knew I would be sore for days afterward. But I wanted him to save me. He didn't say anything. He just pumped into me for a few minutes, came with a loud sigh, and then pulled out. Believe me. I wanted him to save me. I quickly rolled off the bed and went into the bathroom. I locked the door behind me and stood there in the dark. I smelled like salmon.

"Hey," the fighter said through the door. "Are you O.K.?"

"Yes," I said. "I'm fine."

A long silence.

"Hey," he said. "Would you mind if I slept in the bed with you?"

I had no answer to that.

"Listen," I said. "That Flathead boy you fought? You know, the one you really beat up? The one who wouldn't fall down?"

In my mind, I could see the fighter pummelling that boy. Punch after punch. The boy too beaten to fight back but too strong to fall down.

"Yeah, what about him?" asked the fighter.

"What was his name?"

"His name?"

"Yeah, his name."

"Elmer something or other."

"Did he have an Indian name?"

"I have no idea. How the hell would I know that?"

I stood there in the dark for a long time. I was chilled. I wanted to get into bed and fall asleep.

"Hey," I said. "I think, I think maybe—well, I think you should leave now."

"Yeah," the fighter said. He was not surprised. I could hear him softly singing as he dressed and stuffed all of his belongings into his pack. I couldn't tell what he was singing, but I wanted to know. I opened the bathroom door just as he was opening the door to leave. He stopped, looked back at me, and smiled.

"Hey, tough guy," he said. "You were good."

The fighter walked out the door then, leaving it open, and walked away. I stood in the doorway and watched him continue his walk down the highway, past the city limits. I watched him rise from earth to sky and become a new constellation. I closed the door and wondered what was going to happen next. Feeling uncomfortable and cold, I went back into the bathroom. I ran the shower with the hottest water possible. I stared at myself in the mirror. Steam quickly filled the room. I threw a few shadow punches. Feeling stronger, I got in the shower and searched my body for changes. A middle-aged man needs to look for tumors. I dried myself with a towel too small for the job. Then I crawled naked into bed. I wondered if I was a warrior in this life and if I had been a warrior in a previous life. Lonely and laughing, I fell asleep. I didn't dream at all, not one bit. Or perhaps I did dream, but I can't remember any of it. Instead, I woke early the next morning, before sunrise, and went out into the world. I walked past my car. I stepped onto the pavement, still warm from the previous day's sun. I started walking. In bare feet, I travelled upriver toward the place where I was born and will someday die. Believe me. At that moment, if you had broken open my heart you could have looked inside and seen the thin white skeletons of a thousand salmon.

Henry Louis Gates, Jr.

Rope Burn

From *The New Yorker*

The link between the sacred and the profane is a tenuous one, but never more so than at Debra Damo, the oldest monastery in black Africa. The monastery sits at the edge of a fifty-foot cliff, right on top of a mountain in the Ethiopian highlands. For the past fifteen hundred years, the only thing that has connected it to the secular world below is a couple of leather ropes that dangle from its gatehouse.

Not long ago, I found myself at the base of the cliff, peering up and asking myself just how badly I wanted to make it up there. I'd had a lifelong fascination with Africa—I had spent a year in rural Tanzania when I was a college student, had studied African cultures as an adult, and had recently begun making a series of documentaries about the continent. This time, I thought I'd explore some of Africa's less visited corners, and that's how I ended up contemplating the doubtful integrity of an extremely elderly piece of leather.

According to legend, the monastery was founded by Za-Mikael, one of the Nine Saints who spread the doctrine of Christianity through the region. Since there was no way to scale the mountain, he decided that its top would be a perfect place for worship, meditation, prayer, and penitence. But how to get there? God conveniently commanded a snake to coil its tail around Za-Mikael and lift him to the pinnacle. God also commanded the Archangel Gabriel to stand guard with a drawn sword as Za-Mikael ascended and insure that the snake would do him no harm, because—well, you never know with snakes. The monk shouted "Hallelujah!" when he arrived at the mountaintop, and thus the monastery gained one of its bynames, Debra Hallelujah.

Za-Mikael's miracle soon attracted the attention of a great king of the region, who granted the saint's request that a church be built on the site where the serpent had deposited him. In order to build the church, the king first had a ramp constructed. Then, once the church was completed, Za-Mikael uttered the word *dahmemo*, which means "take it off," and the ramp was destroyed. *Dahmemo* was eventually shortened to "*damo*," thereby giving the monastery its most common name.

As I stood at the base of the cliff—and just to get that far had taken a twenty-minute climb past huge boulders and gnarled, ancient-looking tree roots—all I could see at the top was a doorlike frame. Before me were the two ropes, one made of plaited leather and the other of sewn-together strips of cowhide, swaying gently in the breeze. What I wanted was a little chair, strapped securely to a failsafe rope-and-pulley mechanism, and a few robust, youthful monks at the top, pulling me smoothly up the face of the mountain. But there was no chair; no harness; no system of pulleys; no robust monks at the top waiting to welcome the pilgrim home to Mother Africa. There was only one old monk, about my father's age, pretending that he could pull me up by that cowhide strap, which was so frayed and discolored that it might have dated back to the sixth century. He looked like a bronzed elf as he peered over the edge of the cliff, his snow-white goatee framed by what I imagined was the door to eternity.

The end of the strap was formed into a loop, and it slipped easily over my head and settled around my chest. Suddenly, I felt it go taut. My instructions now were to grasp hold of the plaited leather rope and, hand over hand, to walk my way up the precipice, my body parallel to the ground. My feet found their way into crevices worn into the cliff, and I began to scale it, like the human fly, or a cat burglar, or, anyway, someone who knew his way around the Ethiopian highlands. Then, when I was about halfway up, my feet lost their grip and, as the craggy, nearly vertical incline gave way to a sheer, smooth rockface, slipped off the side of the mountain. I was now dangling from the line, unanchored, like a side of beef. The strap constricted my chest like a noose, and I could scarcely breathe.

My abject terror settled on a question: Which vista would be less sickening—the view down or the view up? Should I contemplate the twenty-five-foot drop to the rocks below or the equivalently daunting distance that separated me from the sanctuary in the sky? It was onward and upward for me, and, with considerable difficulty, I summoned my breath to urge on the wizened monk: "Pull ... pull ... pull!" I couldn't swear he'd heard me, but I could see his face, and the strain of my dead weight was showing.

In Ethiopia, a monk has the legal status of a dead man. Monks pay no taxes, do not appear in censuses, and cannot vote. They are, in fact, known as "the Living Dead." They read scripture in the ancient ecclesiastical language of Geez. They dedicate their lives to preparing for Heaven. All in all, I wasn't convinced that this monk would handle what I now considered my lifeline in entirely the right spirit. If the rope snapped and I fell to my death, he might think I'd been done a favor. That wasn't the kind of salvation I was hoping for. Besides, the holy geezer scarcely seemed strong enough to raise me, and my body hung uselessly in midair, legs pumping like Wile E. Coyote's just before he realizes that he has overshot the cliff.

Then I noticed that I'd begun to move—slowly, inch by inch, but steadily, until the wooden stump to which the rope was tied came into my view. I reached out and grabbed it, and soon found myself dragged through the open door to safety. Hallelujah.

"You saved my life," I gasped pathetically. I was winded by the grip of the leather around my chest, marks from which would be visible for several days. For a brief while, I lay there on the sacred earth, promising God and myself that I would try to be a better person, and wondering what grand act of charity I could embark upon to make things right with the order of the universe. Only then did I realize that within a few hours I would have to go through it all over again: there was no other way down. What if I stayed where I was—dedicating myself to the hereafter, taking a vow of poverty, joining the Living Dead in an existence of communal holiness? That prospect was, just at that moment, more pleasing than the alternative. My beard would grow snowy, my skin leathery from the highland rays, and my arms sinewy and strong. My eyes would acquire the faraway serenity of the truly sanctified. I wondered how long it would take me to become fluent in Geez.

Derek Walcott

Pissarro at Dusk

From *The New Republic*

I

I suppose I should have told you about Louveciennes
and the other villages where he took a house

with his brood of seven, shown where this street ends
and that lane forks, those walks of a Pontoise

I have never seen except as his accompanying
shadow on leaf glued autumn pavements, or

crunching bright piebald snow, but I kept seeing
things through his eyes: a gate, a rusted door,

since all our radiant bush, a road, a hill
with torches of pouis, a shade-stayed stream

made joy recede to memory, our provincial
palms, bowing, withdraw before his dream,

as History's distance shrank a crescent fringe
of rustling yellow fronds on a white shore,

a house, a harbour with its mountain range
to a dot named by its cartographer

the name longer than the dot. In Trinidad,
there was one painter, the Frenchman Cazabon

whose embalmed *paysages* were all we had,
our mongrel culture gnawing its one bone.

Cazabon and Pissarro; the first is ours,
the second found the prism that was Paris,

rooted in France, his dark-soiled ancestors;
no matter, cherish the conviction their work carries.

II

Affliction: inflammation of the eyes
that often stops him painting. The tears run,

but older than tears is the paralysis
of doubt, unchanged from when he first began,

since man is a small island who contains
cisterns of sorrow, and drought that absence dries,

and doubt; St. Thomas hazing as it rains
and love, the mist-bow bent on paradise.

In his life's dusk, though hand and eye grow weary,
his concentration strengthens in its skill

some critics think his work is ordinary,
but the ordinary is the miracle.

Ordinary love and ordinary death,
ordinary suffering, ordinary birth,

the ordinary couplets of our breath,
ordinary heaven, ordinary earth.

To watch the moving sea, heavy and silver
on a mid-August afternoon, then turn

his catalogue of views of the great river
dragging its barges, so little time to learn,

you are taken there, though, by his brush's
delicate frenzy, by all his tenderness

even for winter scenes when the snow hushes
the rasping surface and a boulevard's noise.

My Paris comes out of his canvases
not from a map, and perhaps, even better

than Paris itself; they fill these verses
with their own light, their walks, their weather

that will outlast me as they outlast him,
their hustling crowds, their carriages in strokes

fresh, fast and trembling, as in a film
where wheels stop and run backwards, silver spokes

of drizzle down this boulevard, that park
where I can gaze at leisure, taking time

to loiter at each stroke, at the faint arc
of a white bridge; so modest, so sublime!

III

Paint a true street in Anse La Raye, Choiseul,
the roasting asphalt, the bleached galvanise roofs

grooved like these lines, paint the dark heat as well
inside the canted shacks, do the blurred hooves

of a boy whooping a white mare near a lagoon
for gone Gauguin, paint the violet bruise

of reef under water wiry at noon
paint the Cathedral's solace, the canoes

resting in the almonds, always the same
canoes resting under the almonds, and next you could

paint the thick flowers too poor to have a name,
that couple entering a shading wood

for something no longer your business,
mix the light's colour with that pliant knife

that is your plasterer's trowel. It would be nice
to do this in deep gratitude for your life,

just as its hallelujahs praise their giver
the chalk white chapel portals of La Fargue

before L'aouvière Doreé the sun-gilt river
whose missal shallows recite your epilogue.

IV

Our tribes were shaken like seeds from a sieve.
Our dialects, rooted, forced their own utterance,

and what were we without the slow belief
in our own nature? Not Guinea, not Provence.

And yet so many fled, so many lost
to the magnetic spires of cities, not the cedars,

as if a black pup turned into the ghost
of the white hound, but a search that will lead us

where we began; to islands, not the busy
but unchanged patronage of the empire's centre,

guests at the roaring feast of Veronese,
or Tiepolo's Moors, where once we could not enter.

Camille Pissarro must have heard the noise
of loss-lamenting slaves, and if he did,

they tremble in the poplars of Pontoise,
the trembling, elegiac tongues he painted.

Swivel the easel down, drill it in sand,
then tighten the canvas against vaps of wind,

straddle the stool, reach for the brush with one hand
then pour the oil in trembling sacrament.

There is another book that is the shadow
of my hand on this sunlit page, the one

I have tried hard to write, but let this do;
let gratitude redeem what lies undone.

Julia Alvarez

Planting Sticks and Grinding Yucca: On Being a Translated Writer

From *Zoetrope: All Story*

For years I told my North American friends who were reading Pablo Neruda, Gabriel García Márquez, Nicolas Guillén, and Gabriela Mistral in translation that they were missing out on so much. I suppose that it was my way of feeling important in the culture of the United States. So often I felt left out in the margin as a "minority writer," like a character in a novel who comes in only to serve the heroine her breakfast of toast and tea. But by being able to read Spanish, I had access to treasures my mistress did not even know about!

I admit I was proud to claim excellent writers as my own literary *padrinos y madrinas.* But in fact, by writing in English, I had joined the tradition of another language, and if I were to apply my argument to my own work, my Spanish-language readers would miss a great deal if they did not read me in English. As with most self-serving arguments, however, I did not explore the fine print of what I was saying, no doubt suspecting that were I to do so, I would not be able to agree with myself.

I remember when my agent told me that she had sold foreign rights to my first novel in Spanish. "Great!" I told her, wanting to sound grateful. I was flabbergasted that after years of writing, anyone wanted to read, much less pay for my writing. But I was also terrified. I had already had enough problems with the reactions of my immediate family to the English version—phones hung up, a book party boycotted—and now I was taking on the whole extended *familia,* who did not know any English, but would now be able to read my work in Spanish. Gone were the days when I could step into the houses of my Spanish-speaking *tias* and find my book of poems proudly displayed on their coffee tables. How could they know that the book contained poems to lovers? What would they have said if they had read the sonnet that begins, "My gay friends ask, so are you gay or what?" or the title poem that describes one uncle as "fondling my shoulder blades . . . as if they were breasts"? As I sat there, listening to my aunts gush at the fact that I, their niece, had written a book, I used to say a silent prayer to *la Virgencita.* No matter what She thought of me, She had been most kind to ensure that my poetry had not been translated into Spanish.

But now my novel was going to be translated into Spanish, and I would lose the protection of writing in a language the majority of my relatives couldn't read. After some sleepless nights, I decided I would call up my agent and give her my earlier, self-serving argument about how I didn't believe in translations. Too much would be left out. "*Traduttore traditore,*" as the Italians say. Translators are traitors.

Of course, I was forgetting that many of the great classics that form the foundation of my thinking and understanding as a human being, I had read only in translation. From Homer's *Odyssey* to the Bible, Tolstoy's novels to Dante's *Divine Comedy,* Sappho's poetry to Basho's haiku. Anyhow, I did not call my agent and back out of the Spanish publication of my novel. I realized that to be a writer, I had to have the courage to be read as well as to write honestly. And one of the advantages of having a large, extended *familia* is that I can always find someone to agree with me. Predictably, my family divided into two camps: family members who thought the novel was very good and family members who thought the novel was not so good because the characters who reminded them of themselves didn't sound very smart or had been described as "tedious" or as having "a smile bought on sale at a discount store." One uncle, so I heard, was upset because he could not find his counterpart anywhere in my book.

My second novel, *In the Time of the Butterflies,* did well in foreign sales. Suddenly, I was being read in Norwegian, Italian, Greek! My best friend's daughter, who married a Dutch man, told me during her visit to Vermont that she was reading *In de Tijd van de Vlinders.* She had a wink in her eye as she said this. "Oh," I said, wondering if this was a work I should have heard about. When she saw the baffled look on my face, she burst out laughing. She had already read my novel in English but was now reading it in Dutch in order to practice her new language. "How's the translation?" I asked her, because of course, except for Spanish, I couldn't read myself in another language. "Very good!" she said. A few years later, I met a bilingual reader who told me he thought the novel was much better in the Spanish translation than in the original. I did not know whether to feel complimented or not.

How does it feel to be in another language, especially one that I don't read? It must be akin to having your children traveling in far-off countries and wondering how they are faring and how strangers are responding to someone who is so much a part of you but who is not you. When I went on a foreign tour with *In the Time of the Butterflies*, one of the treats was meeting my translators and asking them what was most difficult to take from one culture to another. "The smell of guavas!" was one wonderful response from the German translator of *How the García Girls Lost Their Accents.* There is an atmosphere, a sensual presence that a language creates just in its sounds and rhythms that is bigger than the sum of its parts or the specifics of what is being translated. And the truth is that certain authors move into a new atmosphere better than others. I've always felt that Neruda translates much better into English, with his playfulness and plainspokenness, than Lorca, with his reliance on the blood-pulse and the rhythms of Spanish to enchant his readers.

How exactly my books are changed by being in German or Italian or Swedish or Dutch, I'll never know. On the other hand, I do know all about the process of translation. While I write in English (and read and dream and make love in English—my husband is American), I am constantly doing a little internal translation between my native being and the self I've created out of immigration and experience, chewing gum and guavas. My older sister has told me that she doesn't know how English-only readers can appreciate my books. For instance, she noted, when I have the *papi* say that he has been working hard all day grinding yucca, my American readers probably picture a man with a grater and a manioc root, working away. But in fact, the expression "grinding yucca," in our Dominican Spanish, is a colloquial way to say "working very hard." I remember my French translator faxing me with a question on how to translate "All my little sticks fell down." It makes no sense in English, she noted. She was right. The expression is a direct translation of the Spanish "*Se me cayeron los palitos*," which is a way of saying "I've had some bad luck." Since the character in my novel was a Dominican man playing the lottery, he would express his loss in this way. An American would probably say, "The shit hit the fan!" or "I'm up a creek without a paddle."

I am constantly going back and forth over borders with my work, so translation is natural for my characters and stories. But thank goodness, the work of translating from the imagination to paper stops for me once I've written my books. Then other translators take over, and for that I am glad. Translating is, like grinding yucca, hard work! As Mark Musa, who has translated Dante into English, once observed, "A translator has to be faithful without seeming to be, a type of faithfulness that is akin to being a good lover." I am grateful that my work has found so many good lovers. To think that my novels have crossed so many borders fills me with happiness. Every writer is greedy for more readers. We want to reach everyone with our books, no matter where they live or what language they speak. As Nikki Giovanni once observed, "I am speaking, not in English, but through English to reach you." We all share the same human body, the same vocabulary of feelings, the same baffling experience of being alive on this fragile planet, and successful translations affirm that basic human fact.

So how do I feel these days when my agent calls me up to tell me one of my books will soon be translated into another language? I feel supremely lucky. I feel as if all my little sticks are not just standing, but sprouting new leaves and opening new flowers.

Jaime Manrique

From *Señoritas in Love*

From *Global City Review*

> *Those who try to come near it are insane*
> *and those who reach it are shaken by grief.*
> —Anna Akhmatova
> *(trans. by Jane Kenyon with Vera Dunham)*

I

THE WILLA CATHER OF BANK STREET

This season, five years after Ramón's death, his face has been conspicuous all over town, appearing in many newspapers and magazines. With the posthumous publication of his autobiography, Ramón has finally made it and even those who despised him while he was alive have to acknowledge him now.

Nowadays I live on Bank Street in Greenwich Village. But the other night, feeling nostalgic for those days when I met Ramón and we became lovers, I went back to visit my old Times Square neighborhood.

Walking down 42nd to 8th Avenue, I noticed that the most notorious sex joints had been closed, that there were more cops than criminals on the street. I ambled along 8th Avenue in the direction of O'Donnell's bar which—in typical gentrification manner—had been renamed O'Donnell's Camp.

This was the year, too, when the old Times Square had finally closed down; when the fashion police, wearing Donna Karan uniforms, had been replaced by cops in Mickey Mouse hats, the year when 42nd Street—that erstwhile Grand Canyon of seediness—had become a Disney amusement park, metamorphosing the old sleazy grotesquerie into a soulless mall. Yet the main difference between then and the present was that back then I thought of myself as young and light-hearted; back then I had already experienced sadness and disappointments, but my life had not been touched by tragedy.

I'm getting ahead of myself. The story I want to tell begins shortly after I published my Christopher Columbus epic poem and I still lived above O'Donnell's bar. When the tome was published, the only essential missing from my life was love. Like every single person on the isle of Manhattan between the ages of 8 and 80, I became seriously interested in finding a mate. I had turned thirty-five the year I became a published author, and a middle-aged gay man has fewer chances of finding a boyfriend than a Washington politician has of entering the kingdom of heaven.

Despite the lack of romance, I was happy at last. With the publication of my epic poem, life in Times Square seemed rosier than ever. Yet, try as hard as I could, I couldn't get away from the subject of love because all my single friends, and even my septuagenarian mother, were desperately looking for their other half.

I tried to pretend that I was above all that. When Mother called to complain about the lack of appropriate, and available, men in Jackson Heights, or on the Scandinavian cruises she patronized, I'd say, "Mother, remember you're not American. You are Colombian, and love is not at the top of the Colombian agenda."

Happiness is fleeting, as we all know. One day my sainted landlady died of a heart attack; her greedy children took over the management of the building, and tripled my rent. I took the money I had received from a grant given by the Colombian Civic Center in Jackson Heights (it was rumored the money was put up by the Cali cartel to launder dollars into this country—though my mother vehemently denied it). "People who live in glass houses, Santiago," she said, "shouldn't look inside the horse's mouth." I knew what she meant so I decided to move to a less hectic neighborhood than Hell's Kitchen, one more befitting an aging homosexual.

That's how I came to move to Bank Street. I fancied Bank Street for two reasons: the American author Willa Cather had lived very productively at 5 Bank Street for almost two decades. And I liked looking out of my window and feeling that I lived in what looked like a set for a Merchant/Ivory production. Instead of hookers and junkies, I saw mainly neurotic gay men, walking their neurotic little dogs. The unpleasant aspect of an otherwise enchanting street was the neighborhood psychopathic homophobe who walked his huge Doberman without a leash, taunting homosexuals. Another annoying part of living on Bank (which is as white a street as exists in Manhattan) was that often, on my way home, or as I exited the building, some little old lady would come sprinting after me and asked me questions like, "Mr. Super, where do I put the newspapers?" Other times, some arriviste, and unctuous yuppie, would approach me with a hand in his pocket and say, "Excuse me, Super, if you can help me get an apartment on Bank I could make it worth your while." Racism aside, the loveliness of the street was quite soothing. It was, I knew, a great place for me to become the professional writer I'd always wanted to be.

My apartment was on the second floor of a three-story townhouse. My friend Manolo, who helped me move into my new digs, had warned me, "Watch out, Santiago, the nicer the building, the meaner the people."

Fall arrived and, for the first time in my years in Manhattan, I was fully aware of it as a real season because there were actually trees on Bank Street. As soon as the weather cooled, I began using the fireplace in my living room and spending my evenings at home reading. Boyfriend or not, I was determined to enjoy my life. Besides, since I had enough savings to last me several months (if I was careful with my money) I decided I'd start another epic poem, this one about pre-Columbian life on the savannah of Bogotá. For years, I had been reading about the Chibcha culture that inhabited the savannah and I found myself often daydreaming, trying to reconstruct their world. Before I got started, I thought it would be a good idea to give Tim Colby, my agent, a call.

I hesitated before calling him. Last year, after twenty-five years in the business, one of Tim's authors had become a huge best-seller in the United States and all over the world. It turns out that his Salvadorean cleaning lady, Juanita Chuchimurringi, who had been cleaning Tim's office for over a decade, had been taking home and reading all the books Tim agented. She had written an autobiography spanning her seventy years, beginning with her life in the jungles of El Salvador to her trek on foot to the United States. The book, each chapter written in the manner of a famous Latin American author, had been hailed as one of the most avant garde autobiographies ever written. I was jealous, very jealous. To make matters worse, the old Tim Colby I knew—the man who brought me bagels with cream cheese when he came by to see me and to talk about great books—had suddenly turned big-shot agent. I decided to make the call anyway and inform Tim of my plans.

"Before you get started," he said, "let's get together for lunch. How about tomorrow at one?" Tim gave me the name of a Chinese restaurant near Cooper Union.

Tim had been after me to write a thriller about Colombia. A literary thriller, of course. He had tried to hook me up with an important editor at a major house. For a while I wandered about the city looking at every situation to see if it had the potential to be turned into a thriller. But finally I came to the conclusion that I had no access to the worlds in which thrilling things took place. In the days when I had been an interpreter, I had worked one afternoon for a Peruvian middle-aged roly-poly man who asked me to accompany him to places all over town where he bought literature about explosives. But even if he had been a member of the now defunct Shining Path, what did I know about that stuff? God knows lots of thriller-like things took place in Jackson Heights, but for the sake of making some bucks I wasn't willing to run the risk of going underground, getting a new identity as well as total reconstructive plastic surgery. I had met a man who had done that, and he looked like a plastic Disney creature broiled in a microwave. I decided I simply did not have what it took to write a thriller, literary or not, and Tim was disappointed when I shot down the idea for good.

I hadn't seen Tim in months. Since he was not known for his punctuality, I meandered on my way to the restaurant. Tim was usually between a half hour to two hours late. In this respect, he was the perfect agent for a Colombian author: Tim lived on Colombian time. But when I arrived at the restaurant five minutes late, Tim was not only there (this was the first sign of how corporate he had become) but he was also sporting an Armani jacket and tie. It took me a while to get used to Tim's new look. For many years he had supplemented his agenting working as a messenger on Wall Street, but now he looked like a banker.

We ordered lunch. As we ate, Tim entertained me with stories about Juanita Chuchimurringi, the author who had made him a millionaire. One story was about how the day he had given Juanita a check for a million dollars, in the same restaurant, for the sale of her paperback edition, Juanita had fainted. "Can you imagine, Santiago," Tim laughed, "I wanted to give her a nice surprise, but instead I almost killed her. She is seventy-five years old now."

I was sick of hearing about Juanita Chuchimurringi. I knew very well he found anything she did charming. He had to—she had made him a millionaire. His only complaint was that he had not been able to find another cleaning lady who did as thorough a job, though Juanita had offered to continue doing it. But he was my agent too, though now I seemed to have become merely a friend to whom he could brag about his star's innumerable triumphs: meeting Brad Pitt, appearing on Oprah, being invited by García Márquez to teach in his journalism school in Barranquilla, receiving a nobility title from the Kings of Spain.

Tim sipped his wine. "Look, Santiago. Her success is good for you, too. It means that, as your agent, I have a lot of clout. I can get you a really good deal now. What happened for her, I can make happen for you."

I was ashamed of my envy, but more than anything else, I was ashamed of revealing myself as another jealous author, mortified by someone else's good fortune. It could be, too, that since Juanita had gone through the roof, my relationship with Tim had changed. I missed the old days when we'd get together to dream of great accomplishments. What irked me, I suppose, is that his turn had come whereas I was still completely unknown outside of the circle of my mother's "literary" girlfriends in Jackson Heights.

"There's somebody I want you to meet. I think the two of you would be a great match. Her name's Carola Terry and she's very interested in Latin American writing."

I must have looked unimpressed because Tim said, "And she doesn't want you to write a thriller. She's looking for young new novelists she can launch."

"But I was thinking of writing another epic poem."

Tim put down his fork. He looked at me with a focus I had never seen in him before. "Santiago, look, you're not a kid anymore. The only reason I can afford to keep you as a client is because of Juanita's success."

I squirmed on my seat and swallowed a large chunk of spicy tofu. Could he utter one sentence, I wondered, without mentioning Her name?

"Let me put it this way, how many copies did you sell of 'Christopher Columbus on his Deathbed'?"

"I don't know," I said, although I knew quite well.

Tim stared at me, and with one hand motioned the waiter to approach the table. "Check," he said.

"Okay, 380 copies." Three hundred of which had been purchased by my mother to give to her friends in Jackson Heights, to the people in the soup kitchen where she did volunteer work one night a week, and the remainder for our relatives in Colombia.

"I rest my case," Tim said, as he took the bill and deposited a crisp hundred-dollar note on the plate. "Look, I have to go now. I have to meet with the people at Paramount. They want to make Juanita's next three books into movies."

"She's written three more books?" I asked, stunned.

"Of course not. But that's how you do it nowadays—I don't sell a book unless there's a movie attached to it. They'll make the movies from her outlines as she's writing her memoirs."

I sighed. Tim must really like me, I thought. Otherwise, why would he bother with me. He's running on a track too fast for me.

"Look, on my way to the meeting, I'm going to call Carola Terry," he said pulling his cellular out of his breast pocket. "I'm sure we can arrange a meeting in the next twenty-four hours. We've got to strike while the iron is hot. But be ready for that meeting, *amigo.* I know you can rise to the occasion. By the way," he said, as he rose from his chair, "make sure you cast the book before you come to the meeting."

"Cast it? I don't even know what the book is all about yet."

"It doesn't matter, Santiago. This is book biz in the new millennium. Just make sure you get bankable stars—I've got all the connections. When I call from this phone," he said, shaking his cellular, "Disney answers. I'll call you later today. So be there or be square. Think big names.

By the way, the change is yours," he concluded, referring to what was left of the $100. "Live a little while I go out there to make you rich and famous."

I walked home. I was too disturbed to sit in a taxi. I knew that success made people crazy, but I didn't know that entirely new personalities could emerge. I had barely made it through the door of my apartment when the phone rang. "Santiago, what's up?" Tim said. "We're meeting tomorrow at Carola's office. Ten o'clock sharp. Don't be a minute late. Remember, the cast is everything. *Ciao,* baby. By tomorrow at this time, I hope to have made you a millionaire."

I spent the rest of the day obsessing about the meeting. I couldn't think of a novel I was ready to write yet and I certainly couldn't cast it before knowing what it was about. I decided the best thing to do was to go to bed early, get a good night's sleep, and wake up early and perky for my important meeting.

As I was getting ready for bed, I heard what sounded like my downstairs neighbor yelling, "Get in that closet, you dirty dog." This was followed by a door slamming shut, and my neighbor's voice bellowing, "Stay there til morning. You're punished for the night." My neighbor was a young, attractive blonde living on the ground floor, whom I often saw going in and out of the premises in a lavender spandex jogging outfit. I hadn't realized that she had a pet. Still, whatever the dog had done, the punishment sounded excessive. Thinking no more of it I went to sleep, but awoke at dawn, too wired about my meeting to be able to sleep. I found myself listening for the noises coming from downstairs to see if I could hear any barking or yelping. Getting along with my neighbors has always been one of my mottos, but if this woman was torturing her pet, I would have to report her to the authorities.

By eight o'clock, after several cups of coffee and a hot shower, I was ready for my meeting. As absurd as the whole thing sounded, I wondered whether this was going to be the turning point in my life as a novelist.

The publisher's swank offices were located in midtown, right in the middle of the theatre district. My Christopher Columbus book had been published by Spirit of the Underdog Press, a one-man operation run by a

Colombian friend of mine in Jackson Heights. This publisher was definitely a step up for me. When I arrived at the 28th floor, I noticed the walls were decorated with book jackets of many authors I recognized, along with show biz types and corrupt politicians. A young assistant came out promptly to greet me, leading me to the office of Carola Terry, where Tim was already seated on a comfortable chair, sipping a cup of cappuccino.

Carola Terry's office overlooked The Great White Way. She sat behind an imposing desk. Carola was a still young, attractive woman dressed in a well-cut suit that screamed money and power. She was smallish, slender and her blond hair was cut short. Her alert blue eyes were precision tools used for appraising anything that came in their path. As she shook my hand with her firm grip, and looked me up and down, I felt as though she was totalling my whole worth. At that moment I was hoping I passed her test as a potential money object. Santiago, I thought, you'd better get your act together in the next five seconds.

We chit-chatted pleasantly for a couple of minutes, and just when I was beginning to relax, she said, "Tim tells me that you're writing a romantic novel set in Latin America, about three powerful women. I take it the book is set against a glamorous background of corruption and drugs. I tell you, Santiago. You know the success we had with Juanita Chuchimurringi, and, to be quite frank with you, I'd like to find her male counterpart. A man who can write well about women. A man with a muscular, yet seductive, voice."

I smiled at her while thinking of what to say. When nothing came to mind I looked in Tim's direction.

"Tell Carola who you have cast for the roles ... the three actresses we discussed."

I did a double take. What if I said the wrong thing?

"Go ahead, the two young actresses we agreed upon," Tim said. "The older one we haven't really decided on."

"I can't wait!" Carola salivated, now looking at me as if I had turned into a mountain of gold.

"Well... Winona Ryder," I ventured, to see what reaction I'd get.

There was no reaction from Carola or Tim.

"And then . . . Gwyneth Paltrow," I added, though I detested her; but she seemed to be in every recent movie I saw.

"And, well, you know . . . ," I intoned as slowly as I could, hoping to be rescued by one of them.

"I've got it!" Carola said, jumping up from her chair. "For the older woman, Michelle Pfeiffer. Oh what a brilliant cast—though it may be a little too close to 'The Age of Innocence.' And we may have to change Winona Ryder for a Latino actor, you know. Perhaps Jennifer Lopez? We do have to take these things into consideration—although, don't get me wrong, I am not politically correct. Now we need the male lead. Someone sexy and hot at the box office."

"Antonio Banderas," I offered.

"That's perfect," Carola Terry exulted walking to her window and looking down at Broadway. "I see it already," she said, pointing down to the Great White Way. "In big letters. . . ." She was casting about for a title but was having trouble finding one.

"How about . . . One Hundred Years of Spirits?" I offered.

"Oh you're wicked, Santiago," Tim said, blushing.

"I like that," said Carola. "I like my writers to have a sense of humor. But seriously. We need an evocative title. Something grand like 'Gone with the Wind.' Something rich . . ."

"How about Rich Ladies of the Andes?" I said.

Tim got up from his sofa. "Of course," he said pointing to me, "we want to retain all movie, CD-ROM, foreign and paperback rights."

Carola paced slowly back to her desk, sat down and said, "We'll discuss all that tomorrow at lunch, Tim, you and I. We don't want to burden the author with all these details. We want Santiago to worry about nothing except his creative decisions."

Tim sat down, so it was my turn to get up; I walked over to the window. Broadway was hopping. It wasn't too long ago that I had been like one of those people down there, often passing this building and totally oblivious to what went on here.

"Santiago," Carola said, bringing me back to reality. "Is two okay with you?"

"Three," Tim came back quickly.

"Three . . . novels?" I asked.

"No, I can only sign you up for one."

"She's offering you three hundred thousand dollars," Tim said, as if we were talking about ice-cream scoops. "Though I personally think that idea is worth three million. You're lucky you're getting it for practically nothing, Carola. The next one will be three million. You mark my words."

"The sky's the limit," Carola enthused, "if this one works out. Now, Santiago." She turned and gave me a hard look. "Remember what I want. Something big, romantic. Something with a lot of scope. Preferably with lots of magic realism, which is what people like. Can you write it in six months? 400 pages? It will be one of our big books for the spring season, year after next. I'll get our lawyers to write the contract and it'll be ready in a couple of weeks and . . ."

"Santiago wants most of it upfront," Tim said, getting up again, a fighting cock ready to draw blood.

Carola stood too, her chest full-blown, her hands splayed on her hips. "We'll talk about that at lunch." Then she turned to me. "I'm going to call Peter Weir this afternoon and run it by him. He could do a great job. I've been longing for a movie like 'The Year of Living Dangerously' for a long time. Is Peter Weir okay with you?"

"Oh sure," I said. "Since we can't bring D.W. Griffith back, Peter Weir will have to do."

Downstairs, outside the building, Tim turned to embrace me and kissed me on both cheeks. "You're a great negotiator," he said. "Watch out, Santiago. I'm going to make you as rich and famous as Juanita Chuchimurringi. We won't stop until you're a count of Spain."

At that moment I felt like saying, "Tim, I'll give you the whole three hundred thousand if you promise never to mention Juanita's name to me again."

"I gotta go meet Madonna," Tim said. "I can't be late. Maybe I'll put her in touch with you. You like the idea?"

"How about Madonna for the older woman in the movie?" I suggested.

Tim shook his head. "No, Michelle Pfeiffer, Sigourney Weaver. We need older actresses for that role." Then he hailed a taxi and left me there on Broadway and 45th, $300,000 richer. I decided I'd walk home. I needed to exhaust myself to calm the thoughts racing in my brain.

2

9000 YEARS AGO

For the next couple of days, looking for ways to distract myself until I found out whether the deal had been finalized, I decided to investigate about my downstairs neighbor a little more. But as hard as I tried, I never saw her walking a dog, nor did I hear any animal noises coming from her apartment. I did notice that she went jogging around noon each day, regardless of the weather. I decided that she must have been keeping care of a pet for a friend who was away and had returned it to the owner. Now and then, however, my Colombian imagination got the best of me and it crossed my mind that in a rage my neighbor might have killed her pet and stored it in her closet, or her fridge. Just to make sure, whenever I passed her front door, I'd pause ever so slightly taking a deep whiff to try to detect the rotting pet. The only thing I noticed was that just about every night, around the time I was getting ready for bed, her bell would ring.

And then, as I was about to start obsessing about the mysterious young woman, Tim called. The deal had gone through. He apologized for not being able to get me more than three, but he said he hoped I'd be happy with the deal; he assured me that next time he would get me seven. "Seven hundred thousand?" I asked. "No, no, Santiago. Seven figures. And I'm not talking any seven figures." It would be a few weeks before the contract would be ready for signing and the check would follow soon after. "If you need some dough to tide you over, just yell," he said. "I'd be happy to advance you whatever you need." Overcoming my astonishment, I thanked him for everything he had done for me, promised I'd deliver a knockout manuscript, and reassured him that I still had some money left from my grant. "So, then just go for it, Santiago. Don't wait for the contract or the check. Let's get this book done within the year. I have big plans for you. Next year, by now, I want you living next door to us in

Connecticut. There's a great place I know where you can get fabulous horses. I want people to start calling you Don Santiago. From now on, every two years, I want a Santiago Martinez novel out there, outselling Stephen King."

When he hung up I realized that, for the first time in a year, Tim hadn't mentioned Juanita Chuchimurringi, not even once. I was so grateful to him for this that I decided not to disappoint him and to begin my novel the next day. But what, exactly, was I going to write about? I knew that it would take place in Colombia, that there were three main women characters and at least one major male romantic figure. I also knew that Carola wanted politics, revolution, glamour, and romance. Did this mean that I was selling out? Would writing something like this kill my poetic soul? I punched my friend Herbert's digits. I told him about what had happened and that now I was concerned about whether I would ever be able to take myself seriously again. Herbert was in his sixties, a trust lawyer who lived on Park Avenue. We had met one day at the Film Forum, watching a horrendous avant garde film that consisted of the screen turning red, redder, reddest. At one point, unable to contain myself, I uttered, "This is too boring for words." "Pretentious piece of crap," said the man sitting next to me. I got up to leave and Herbert followed me. Outside the theatre, bonded by our hatred of the movie we had seen, we started a conversation and struck up a friendship that centered mainly around going to the movies once a month. Whenever I was in a quandary, I would go to Herbert for advice. He seemed to be the soul of practicality, and was the only successful American I knew. My mother's friends in Jackson Heights were richer, but at least Herbert had made his money without breaking the law.

"Will people ever accept me again as a good writer?" I asked, tormented by this doubt.

"What people?" he said. "Nobody knows who you are, so forget about that. And what do you want with 'good,' Santiago? In this country, if you have money you're good. Half of those people out there who've made it were born with a diamond rattler in their hands. Listen to me, if you make lots of money, if you're a success, you'll immediately become 'good.' That, trust me, is the American way. So, don't even think twice about it. Anyhow, it doesn't sound like they asked you to write crap. A poetic 'Gone with the Wind,' that's what you have to think about. I've got to go, but there are a bunch of new movies I haven't seen so call me next week and we'll make plans."

"It's settled, then," I thought. "When my grant money runs out I don't want to go back to interpreting. I want to be a writer. To stay home and write."

Now that I had a deal, I called Mother to tell her the news. When I finished explaining about the novel I was going to write, the movie, the advance, I distinctly got the impression she didn't believe a word I had said. So I decided to go visit her in Queens and try to explain in person what had happened and how my life had changed.

"Come right over," she said. "I made the most delicious *mondongo,* and I made so much I was just going to take the leftovers to my Church."

A big steaming bowl of tripe soup with *picante* sounded like what the doctor had ordered. I grabbed my coat and left for Times Square, to transfer there to the Number 7 train. I never went to my mother's hoping to be comforted, or understood. Just as ostriches stick their heads in the sand to escape from reality, I went to visit Mom because once there, my life in Manhattan seemed so far away that I could put everything on hold. Visiting her in Jackson Heights was like taking a trip to another galaxy that offered different kinds of life forms than the ones I am accustomed to.

My mother was living alone once more. My sister Wilbrajan had moved to Miami, where she had a thriving singing career, and she had taken her son Gene with her. All the reports we got from them were that they were happy and had no intentions of returning for a long while, though with Wilbrajan one never knew. Mother, who never ceased to surprise me, had turned over a new leaf. She didn't seem to miss Gene at all. She had taken to traveling alone or with the Urrutias, and recently had returned from a pilgrimage to the Holy Land. Although she had always been interested in spirituality (meaning *santería*), lately she had become extremely active in her Church, becoming a member of many committees, going on retreats, and cooking huge *sancochos* for their soup kitchen. The other, and most remarkable, change in her life was her interest in the commodities market, where she was making piles of money. It all had started when Paulina Urrutia had given Mother a computer for her birthday. Since Paulina and Claudia were always traveling (running from the DEA was more like it), she was on the Internet. Now that they both had computers, they could E-mail each other every day, no matter where Paulina was. And then, maybe because Paulina was such a whiz making money, Mother started playing the commodities market.

When I let myself in through the door, Mother was in the living room, temporarily away from her terminal, reading *Business Investors' News.* She had a towel wrapped around her neck, to protect herself from Simón Bolívar's shit. The hideous parrot was perched on her shoulders.

"Hi, Sammy," she said, in her usual cheerful manner. "You look like you haven't had a good meal in days. Go to the kitchen and pop the *mondongo* in the microwave. Three minutes. And I just made some cheese *arepas* for you."

I was more than happy to leave her alone with Simón Bolívar, who, as soon as he saw me, started squawking. I was finishing a delicious bowl of soup, with the scrumptious *arepas,* when Mother came into the room, startling me.

"Please sit across the table, I don't want that bird shitting on my food," I demanded.

"You're such a baby, Sammy. You're just jealous of him. A grown-up man jealous of a parrot! Who ever heard of such a thing?"

To my relief, she put the bird on his perch, but she kept the shit-spattered towel draped over her shoulders.

"And to what do I owe the honor of your visit? I thought I only heard from you when you need a loan, but apparently you have plenty of money now."

Why *had* I come to visit? Why did I think this time around she would understand me any better than before?

"I wanted to see you. I thought it would make you happy that I'm a success," I said, knowing how important money was in her eyes, and how she saw me as a failure because I hadn't made lots of it.

"Well, I hope you've made plans to invest that money," she said, seeming to concede that my deal was not a product of wishful thinking. "You know, the thing about money is that you need to keep making it all the time. If you don't, you run out of it. Have you decided how to invest it yet?"

I shook my head.

"Santiago, you don't seem happy. Something's bothering you. You seem as lost as ever. Oh, I see.... You're having trouble writing your book? See, I told you. You should move back to Queens. This is where your roots are. What are you doing living with those Wasps? Is that what you want to be—one of God's frozen people? How do you expect to write about this place if you are a stranger to your constituents?"

"Who said I am not happy? And who said I'm blocked writing my book? And anyway... constituents. Where do you get such words? I'm a writer, not a politician. For God's sake, stop trying to make me feel like a traitor to Jackson Heights. In any case, it has nothing to do with my writing either; my writing's going fine," I boasted, lying through my teeth since I hadn't written the first line of my book yet.

"Hum... I think you need to see Matilde."

"What for? There's nothing wrong with me! No way I'm gonna go consult any witches."

"She'd be really hurt if she heard you calling her that. She likes you a lot, Santiago. Besides, I don't know how many times I have to tell you she's not a witch. She's an intuitive consultant."

"That's some fancy pc name for Voodoo," I snorted. "I really don't want any chickens sacrificed in my name. Thanks, anyway."

"Well then since you're here, would you like to learn how to multiplicate your money? Because knowing you, if you do get that money, it wouldn't surprise me if you go through it in no time. I'm gonna show you how to make your money grow."

"If you mean the commodities exchange, no thanks. I have other faults, but I'm not a gambler."

"May I remind you that I've made more money in the last year than in all the other years of my life put together. You should at least be happy. When I'm gone all that money will go to you and your sister and Gene. You know, what if you get writer's block and you're not able to write your novel? You'll have to return all that money. I'm not going to bail you out."

"I wouldn't expect you to, Mother."

"Anyway, I think you should let me teach you a few things. You know, I may not be around much longer to teach you everything like you are still in kindergarten."

"Wait a minute—what are you trying to say? Is there anything wrong with you? Do you have any health problems I don't know about?"

"Do I look sick to you, Santiago?" she said, sitting up straight, her chin thrust out, her shoulders back, her surgery-enhanced bust sticking out.

The truth was she looked great. Stunning. Of course she'd always be a beautiful woman even if she lived to be 100 years old. But what made her attractive was not her physical gifts—which were considerable—but something, some strength, a kind of power—that she radiated from within. "I've never felt better in my life."

Could she be hinting about moving back to Colombia, as she threatened every so often? Something *was* up then. But what? Whatever it was, she was not about to let me in on it.

Getting up from her chair, she announced, "Come and see how I do it." Whereupon she walked to Simón Bolívar's perch, installed the bird on her shoulder and left the room.

I had no choice but to go into her office where her terminal was set up, complete with state-of-the-art software. The screen was flashing the latest stock market quotations as Mother sat at her chair, put on her glasses and waited. I stood behind her.

Suddenly, the parrot squawked and Mother picked up her pencil and scribbled something on a note pad. "Yes, we'll buy a ton of cotton," she said.

"You mean to tell me that you buy every time that bird screeches?"

"And why not? He's made me the richest woman in Jackson Heights. I mean, the richest *honest* woman in Jackson Heights."

"But don't you realize that bird squawks every thirty seconds? It's just a nervous reflex!"

"The hell it is."

"Just watch," I said. "I'll time it and maybe this will convince you."

Both mother and the parrot stared at me as I held my watch inches from my nose. Thirty seconds passed, thirty-five, fifty, a minute went by and still the damned bird remained silent. I looked up—humiliated—and saw Mother's gloating smile.

"By the way, before I forget, Carmen Elvira asked me to ask you to read for the Christmas Benefit at the Colombian Civic Center. And I want you to know that Colombia's Beauty Queen has already accepted. They're trying to get the soccer team. Can you imagine, you on the stage, with all those luminaries? I'd be so proud of you. This is a moment of real effervescence in the Colombian community. That soccer team of ours has really unified Jackson Heights."

Just to spite her, I added, "Sure—was put together with the Cali cartel's money. Besides, I'm not giving readings these days."

"You can read from 'Christopher Columbus,'" she said, not willing to concede defeat. "You know, I've never been able to read the whole thing."

Her philistinism was more than I could bear. "I don't want to hear Christopher Columbus's name again for the rest of my life," I snapped back. "I'm sick of it."

"You wrote it, I didn't. Or you can read from your novel, if you have anything written, that is. But you cannot, I repeat can*not*, decline. This is a benefit for the Colombian Civic Center, Santiago. I have to think of the family's name. After all, I'm the one who lives here."

"The Civic Center indeed," I ranted. "It should be called the Cynic Center because it's full of people laundering drug money while they pretend to care about culture."

"Squawk," went Simón Bolívar.

"What? What?" said Mother, turning to face the screen. "Oh. Bananas. Of course we'll buy bananas, darling."

Walter Mosley

Pet Fly

From *The New Yorker*

I had been seeing Mona Donelli around the building since my first day working in interoffice mail. Mona laughing, Mona complaining about her stiff new shoes or the air-conditioning or her boyfriend refusing to take her where she wanted to go. She's very pretty. Mona wears short skirts and giggles a lot. She's not serious at all. When silly Mona comes in she says hello and asks how you are, but before you get a chance to answer she's busy talking about what she saw on TV last night or something funny that happened on the ferry from Staten Island that morning.

I would see Mona almost every day on my delivery route—at the coffee-break room on the fifth floor or in a hallway, never at a desk. So when I made a rare delivery to the third-floor mortgage department and saw her sitting there, wearing a conservative sweater buttoned all the way up to her throat, I was surprised. She was so subdued, not sad but peaceful, looking at the wall in front of her and holding a yellow pencil with the eraser against her chin.

"Air-conditioning too high again?" I asked, just so she'd know that I paid attention to the nonsense she babbled about.

She looked at me and I got a chill, because it didn't feel like the same person I saw flitting around the office. She gave me a silent and friendly smile, even though her eyes seemed to be wondering what my question meant.

I put down the big brown envelope addressed to her department and left without saying anything else.

Back in the basement, I asked my boss, Ernie, what was wrong with Mona.

"Nothing," he said. "I think she busted up with some guy or something. No, no, I'm a liar. She went out with her boyfriend's best friend without telling him. Now she doesn't get why the boyfriend's mad. That's what she said. Bitch. What she think?"

Ernie didn't suffer fools, as my mother would say. He was an older black man who had moved to New York from Georgia thirty-three years ago. He had come to work at Carter's Home Insurance three days after he arrived. "I would have been here on day one," he told me, "but my bus got in on Friday afternoon."

I'd only been there for three weeks. After I graduated from Hunter College, I didn't know what to do. I had a B.A. in poli sci, but I didn't really have any skills. Couldn't type or work a computer. I wrote all my papers in longhand and used a typing service. I didn't know what I wanted to do but I had to pay the rent. When I applied for a professional-trainee position that Carter's Home had advertised at Hunter, the personnel officer told me that there was nothing available but maybe if I took the mail-room position something might open up.

"They hired two white P.T.s the day after you came," Ernie told me at the end of the first week. I decided to ignore that. Maybe those people had applied before me, or maybe they had skills with computers or something.

I didn't mind my job. Big Linda Washington and Little Linda Brown worked with me. The Lindas had earphones and listened to music while they wheeled around their canvas mail carts. Big Linda liked rap and Little Linda liked R&B. Neither one talked to me much.

My only friend at work was Ernie. He was the interoffice mail-room director. He and I would sit in the basement and talk for hours sometimes. Ernie was proud of his years at Carter's Home. He liked the job and the company, but he had no patience for most of the bosses.

"Workin' for white people is always the same thing," Ernie would say.

"But Mr. Drew's black," I said the first time I heard his perennial complaint. Drew was the supervisor for all postal and interoffice communication. He was a small man with hard eyes and breath that smelled of vitamins.

"Used to be," Ernie said. "Used to be. But ever since he got promoted he forgot all about that. Used to be he'd come down here and we'd talk like you'n me doin'. But now he just stands at the door and grins and nods. Now he's so scared I'm gonna pull him down that he won't even sit for a minute."

"I don't get it," I once said to Ernie. "How can you like the job and the company if you don't like the people you work for?"

"It's a talent," he replied.

"Why'ont you tuck in your shirt?" Big Linda Washington said, sneering at me on the afternoon after I had seen Mona Donelli at her third-floor desk. "You look like some kinda fool, hangin' out all over the place."

Big Linda was taller than I, broader, too, and I'm pretty big. Her hair was straightened and frosted in gold. She wore dresses in primary colors, as a rule. Her skin was berry black. Her face, unless it was contorted from appraising me, was pretty.

We were in the service elevator, going up to the fifth floor. I tucked the white shirttails into my black jeans.

"At least you could make it even so the buttons go straight down," she remarked. "Just 'cause you light-skinned you can't go 'round lookin' like a mess."

I would have had to open up my pants to do it right, and I didn't want Big Linda to get any more upset than she already was.

She grunted and sucked a tooth.

The elevator opened, and she rolled out her cart. We had parallel routes, but I went in the opposite direction, deciding to take mail from the bottom of the stack rather than let her humiliate me.

The first person I ran into was Mona. Now she was wearing a one-piece deep-red dress held up by spaghetti straps. Her breasts were free under the thin fabric, and her legs were bare. Mona was short, with thick black hair and green eyes. Her skin had a hint of olive but not so deep as what you think of as a Sicilian complexion.

"I can see why you were wearing that sweater at your desk," I said.

"What?" she replied, in a very unfriendly tone.

"That white sweater you were wearing," I said.

"What's wrong with you? I don't even own a white sweater."

She turned abruptly and clicked away on her red high heels. I wondered what had happened. I kept thinking that it was because of my twisted-up shirt. Maybe that's what made people treat me badly, maybe it was my appearance.

I continued along my route, pulling files from the bottom and placing them in the right "in" boxes.

"If the boxes ain't side by side, just drop it anywhere and pick up whatever you want to," Ernie had told me on my first day. "That's what I do. Mr. Averill put down the rules thirteen years ago, just before they kicked him upstairs."

Bernard Averill was the vice-president in charge of all nonprofessional employees. He administered the cafeteria workers, the maintenance staff, secretarial services, and both the interoffice and postal mail departments. He was Ernie's hero because he was the only v.p. who had worked his way up from an entry-level position.

When I'd finished the route, I went through the exit door at the far end of the hall to get a drink of water. I planned to wait there long enough for Big Linda to have gone back down. While I was at the water fountain, a fly buzzed by my head. It caught my attention because not many flies made it into the air-conditioned buildings around Wall Street, even in summer.

The fly landed on my hand, then flew to the cold aluminum bowl of the water fountain. He didn't have enough time to drink before zooming up to the ceiling. From there he lit on the doorknob, then landed on the baby finger of my left hand. After that he buzzed down to the floor. He took no more than a second to enjoy each perch.

"You sure jumpy, Mr. Fly," I said, as I might have when I was a child. "But you might be a Miss Fly, huh?"

The idea that the neurotic fly could be a female brought Mona to mind. I hustled my cart toward the elevator, passing Big Linda on the way. She was standing in the hall, talking to another young black woman.

"I got to wait for a special delivery from, um, investigations," Big Linda explained.

"I got to go see a friend on three," I replied.

"Oh." Big Linda seemed relieved.

I realized that she was afraid I'd tell Ernie that she was idling with her friends. Somehow that stung more than her sneers.

She was still wearing the beaded sweater, but instead of the eraser she had a tiny whiteout brush in her hand, half an inch from a sheet of paper on her violet blotter.

"I bet that blotter used to be blue, huh?"

"What?" She frowned at me.

"That blotter—it looks violet, purple, but that's because it used to be blue but the sun shined on it, from the window."

She turned her upper torso to look out the window. I could see the soft contours of her small breasts against the white fabric.

"Oh," she said, turning back to me. "I guess."

"Yeah," I said. "I notice things like that. My mother says that's why I never finish anything. She says I get distracted all the time and don't keep my eye on the job."

"Do you have more mail for me?"

"No, uh-uh, I was just thinking."

She looked at the drying whiteout brush and then jammed it back into the small bottle that was in her other hand.

"I was thinking about when I saw you this morning," I continued. "About when I saw you and asked about the air-conditioning and your sweater and you looked at me like I was crazy."

"Yes," she said, "why did you ask that?"

"Because I thought you were Mona Donelli," I said triumphantly.

"Oh." She sounded disappointed. "Most people figure out that I'm not Mona because my nameplate says Lana Donelli."

"Oh," I said, suddenly crushed. I could notice a blotter turning violet but I couldn't read a nameplate.

Lana was amused.

"Don't look so sad," she said. "I mean, even when they see the name some people still call me Mona."

"They do?"

"Yeah. It's a problem having an identical twin. They see the name and think that Mona's a nickname or something. Isn't that dumb?"

"I didn't know you had a sister, but I saw Mona on the fifth floor in a red dress, and then I saw a fly that couldn't sit still, and then I knew that you had to be somebody else," I said.

"You're funny," Lana said, crinkling up her nose, as if she were trying to identify a scent. "What's your name?"

"Rufus Coombs."

"Hi, Rufus," she said.

"Hey," I said.

My apartment is on 168th Street, in Washington Heights. It's pretty much a Spanish-speaking neighborhood. I don't know many people there, but the rent is all I can afford. My apartment—living room with a kitchen cove, a small bedroom, and a toilet with a shower—is on the eighth floor and looks out over the Hudson. The four fifty-eight a month includes heat and gas, but I pay my own electric. I took it because of the view. There was a cheaper unit on the second floor, but it had windows that look out on a brick wall and I was afraid I'd be burglarized.

"Do you own a TV or a stereo?" my mother asked when I was trying to decide which apartment to take.

"You know I don't."

"Then you ain't got nuthin' to burgle," she said. I had called her in California, where she lives with my uncle.

"But they don't know that," I said. "I might have a color TV with VCR and a bad sound system."

"Lord," my mother prayed.

I didn't own much; she was right about that. Single mattress on the floor, an old oak chair that I found on the street, and kitchen shelving that I bought from a liquidator, for bookshelves, propped up in the corner. I also have a rice pot, a frying pan, and a kettle, with cutlery and enough plates for two.

I have Rachel, an ex-girlfriend living in the East Village, who will call me back at work if I don't call her too often. My two other friends are Eric Chen and Willy Jones. They both live in Brooklyn and still go to school.

That evening, I climbed the seven flights up to my apartment. The elevator had stopped working a month ago. I sat in my chair and looked at the water. It was peaceful and relaxing. A fly was buzzing against the glass, trying to get out.

I got up to kill him. But up close I hesitated. His coloring was unusual, a metallic green. The dull-red eyes seemed too large for the body, as though he were an intelligent mutant fly from some far-flung future on late-night television.

He buzzed against the pane, trying to get away from me. When I returned to my chair, he settled. The red sun was hovering above the cliffs of New Jersey. The green fly watched. I thought of the fly I'd seen at work. That bug had been black and fairly small by fly standards. Then I thought about Mona and then Lana. The smallest nudge of an erection stirred. I thought of calling Rachel, but I didn't have the heart to walk the three blocks to a phone booth. So I watched the sunset gleaming around the fly, who was now just a black spot on the window. I fell asleep in the chair.

At 3 A.M. I woke up and made macaroni and cheese from a mix. The fly came into the cooking cove, where I stood eating my meal. He lit on the big spoon I'd used to stir the dinner and joined me for supper.

Ernie told me that mortgaging didn't get much interoffice mail.

"Most of their correspondence comes by regular mail," he explained.

"Aren't they on the newsletter list?"

"She a white girl?"

"So?"

"Nuthin'. But I want you to tell me what it's like if you get it."

I didn't answer him.

I began delivering invitations to office parties, sales-force newsletters, and Productivity Tips penned by Mr. Averill to Lana Donelli. We made small talk for thirty seconds or so, then she'd pick up the phone to make a call. I always looked back as I rounded the corner to make sure she really had a call to make. She always did.

The following Monday, I bought a glass paperweight with the image of a smiling Buddha's face etched in the bottom. When I got to Lana's desk, she wasn't there. I waited around for a while but she didn't appear, so I wrote her a note that said "From Rufus to Lana" and put the leaded-glass weight on it.

I went away excited and half scared. What if she didn't see my note? What if she did and thought it was stupid? I was so nervous that I didn't go back to her desk that day.

"I really shouldn't have left it," I said that night to the green fly. He was perched peacefully on the rim of a small saucer. I had filled the inner depression with a honey-and-water solution. I was eating a triple cheeseburger with bacon and fries from Wendy's. My pet fly seemed happy with his honey water and only buzzed my sandwich a few times before settling down to drink.

"Maybe she doesn't like me," I said. "Maybe it's just that she was nice to me because she feels sorry for me. But how will I know if I don't try and see if she likes me?"

"Hi," I said to Lana the next morning. She was wearing a jean jacket over a white T-shirt. She smiled and nodded. I handed her Mr. Averill's Productivity Tips newsletter.

"Did you see the paperweight?"

"Oh, yeah," she said without looking me in the eye. "Thanks." Then she picked up the phone and began pressing buttons. "Hi, Tristan? Lana. I wanted to know if . . ." She put her hand over the receiver and looked at me. "Can I do something else for you?"

"Oh," I said. "No. No," and I wheeled away in a kind of euphoria.

It's only now, when I look back on that moment, that I can see the averted eyes, the quick call, and the rude dismissal for what they were. All I heard then was "Thanks." I even remember a smile. Maybe she did smile for a brief moment, maybe not.

On Tuesday and Wednesday, I left three presents for her. I left them when she was away from her desk. I got her a small box of four Godiva chocolates, a silk rose, and a jar of fancy rose-petal jelly. I didn't leave any more notes. I was sure that she'd know who it was.

On Thursday evening, I went to a nursery on the East Side, just south of Harlem proper. There I bought a bonsai, a crab-apple tree, for three hundred and forty-seven dollars and fifty-two cents. I figured I'd leave it

during Lana's Friday lunch break and then she'd be so happy that Monday she'd have to have lunch with me, no matter what.

I suspected that something was wrong when my pet fly went missing. He didn't even show up when I started eating a beef-burrito supreme from Taco Bell. I checked the big spider's web near the bathroom window, but there were no little bundles that I could see.

That evening I was on edge, thinking I saw flies flitting into every corner.

"What's that?" Ernie asked me the next morning when I came in with the tiny crab-apple tree.

"It's a tree."

"Tree for what?"

"My friend Willy wanted me to pick it up for him. He wants it for his new apartment, and the only place he could get it is up near me. I'm gonna meet him at lunch and give it to him."

"Uh-huh," Ernie said.

"You got my cart loaded?" I asked him.

Just then the Lindas came out of the service elevator. Big Linda looked at me and shook her head, managing to express contempt and pity at the same time.

"There's your carts," Ernie said to them.

They attached their earphones and rolled back to the service elevator. Little Linda was looking me in the eye as the slatted doors closed. She was still looking at me as the lift rose.

"What about me?"

"That's all I got right now. Why don't you sit here with me?"

"O.K." I sat down, expecting Ernie to bring up one of his regular topics, either something about Georgia, white bosses, or the horse races, which he followed but never wagered on. But instead of saying anything he just started reading the *Post*.

After a few minutes I was going to say something, but the big swinging door opened. Our boss, Mr. Drew, leaned in. He smiled and nodded at Ernie and then pointed at me.

"Rufus Coombs?"

"Yeah?"

"Come with me."

I followed the dapper little man through the messy service hall to the passenger elevator, which the couriers rarely took. It was a two-man elevator, so Drew and I had to stand very close to each other. He wore too much cologne, but otherwise he was perfect for his supervisory job, wearing a light-gray suit with a shirt that hinted at yellow. I knew that he must have been in his forties, but he could have passed for a graduate student. He was light-skinned like me, with what my mother called good hair. There were freckles around his eyes. I could see all of that because Mr. Drew avoided my gaze. He wouldn't engage me in any way.

We got out on the second floor and went to his office, which was at the far end of the mail-sorting room.

I looked around the room as Drew was entering his office. I saw Mona looking at me from the crevice of a doorway. I knew it was Mona because she was wearing a skimpy dress that could have been worn on a hot date. I only got a glimpse of her before she ducked away.

"Come on in, Coombs," Drew said.

The office was tiny. Drew actually had to stand on the tips of his toes and hug the wall to get behind his desk. There was a stool in front of the desk, not a chair.

By the time he said, "Sit down," I had lost my nervousness. I gauged the power of Mr. Leonard Drew by the size of his office.

"You're in trouble, Rufus," he said, looking as sombre as he could.

"I am?"

He lifted a pink sheet of paper and shook it at me.

"Do you recognize this?" he asked.

"No."

"This is a sexual-harassment complaint form."

"Yeah?"

"It names you on the complaint."

"I don't get it."

"Lana Donelli . . ." He went on to explain everything that I had been doing and feeling for the last week as if they were crimes. Going to Lana's desk, talking to her, leaving gifts. Even remarking on her clothes had been construed as if there was a sexual innuendo attached. By the time he was finished, I was worried that the police might be called in.

"Lana says that she's afraid to come in to work," Drew said, his freckles disappearing into angry lines around his eyes.

I wanted to say that I didn't mean to scare her, but I could see that my intentions didn't matter, that a small woman like Lana would be afraid of a big, sloppy mail clerk hovering over her and leaving notes and presents.

"I'm sorry," I said.

"Sorry doesn't mean much when it's got to this point," he said. "If it was up to me, I'd send you home right now. But Mr. Averill says he wants to talk to you."

"Aren't you supposed to give me a warning?" I asked.

Drew twisted up his lips, as if he had tasted something so foul that he just had to spit it out. "You haven't been here a month. You're on probation."

"Oh," I said.

"Well?" he asked after a few moments.

"What?"

"Go back to the mail room and stay down there. Tell Ernie that I don't want you in the halls. You're supposed to meet Mr. Averill at one-forty-five, in his office. I've given him my recommendation to let you go. After something like this, there's really no place for you here. But he can still refer the matter to the police. Lana might want a restraining order."

I wanted to tell him that a restraining order was ridiculous. I wanted to go to Lana and tell her the same thing. I wanted to tell her that I bought her a rose because she wore rose toilet water, that I bought her the tree because the sun on her blotter could support a plant. I really liked her. But, even while I was imagining what I could say, I knew that it didn't matter.

"Well?" Drew said. "Go."

Ernie made busywork for us that morning. He told me that he was upset about what had happened, that he'd told Drew to go easy.

"You know if you was white this wouldn't never have happened," Ernie said. "That girl just scared you some Mandingo gonna rape her. You know that's a shame."

I went up to the third floor a little before twelve. Lana was sitting at her desk, writing on a yellow legal pad. I walked right up to her and started talking so she couldn't ignore what I had to say.

"I just wanted to tell you that I'm sorry if you think I was harassing you. I didn't mean it, but I can see how you might have thought I was . . ."

Lana's face got hard.

". . . but I'm gonna get fired right after lunch and I just wanted to ask you one thing."

She didn't say anything, so I said, "Is it because I'm black that you're so scared'a me?"

"You're black?" she said. "I thought you were Puerto Rican or Spanish or something. I didn't know you were black. My boyfriend is black. You just give me the creeps. That's why I complained. I didn't think they were going to fire you."

She didn't care if I lived or died. She wasn't even scared, just disgusted. I thought I was in love, and I was about to be fired, and she'd never even looked close enough to see me.

I was so embarrassed that I went away without saying another word. I went down to the mail room and sorted rubber bands until one-thirty-five.

Vice-president Bernard Averill's office was on the forty-eighth floor of the Carter's Home Building. His secretary's office was larger by far than Mr. Drew's cubbyhole. The smiling blonde led me into Averill's airy room. Behind him was a giant window looking out over Battery Park, Ellis Island, and the Statue of Liberty. I would have been impressed if I wasn't empty inside.

Averill was on the phone.

"Sorry, Nick," he said into the receiver. "My one-forty-five is here."

He stood up, tall and thin. His gray suit looked expensive. His white shirt was crisp and bright under a rainbow tie. His gray hair was combed back, and his mustache was sharp enough to cut bread, as my mother is known to say.

"Sit down, Mr. Coombs."

He sat also. In front of him were two sheets of paper. At his left hand was the pink harassment form, at his right was a white form. Outside, the Budweiser blimp hovered next to Lady Liberty.

Averill brought his fingertips to just under his nose and gazed at a spot above my head.

"How's Ernie?" he asked.

"He's good," I said. "He's a great boss."

"He's a good man. He likes you."

I didn't know what to say to that.

Averill looked down at his desk. "This does not compute."

"What?"

He patted the white page. "This says that you're a college graduate, magna cum laude in political science, that you came here to be a professional trainee." He patted the pink sheet. "This says that you're an interoffice-mail courier who harasses secretaries in the mortgage department."

Averill reached into his vest pocket and came out with an open package of cigarettes. At orientation they'd told us that there was absolutely no smoking anywhere in the building, but he took one out anyway. He lit up and took a deep drag, holding the smoke in his lungs for a long time before exhaling.

"Is there something wrong with you?" he asked.

"I don't think so," I said, swallowing hard.

Averill examined me through the tobacco haze. He seemed disgusted.

Staring directly into my eyes, he said, "Do you see this desk?"

The question petrified me, but I couldn't say why. Maybe it was the intensity of his gaze.

"I could call five or six women into this office right now and have them right here on this desk. Right here." He jabbed the desk with his middle finger.

My heart was racing. I had to open my mouth to get enough air.

"They're not going to fill out any pink slips," he said. "Do you know why?"

I shook my head.

"Because I'm a man. I don't go running around leaving chocolates on empty desks like bait. I don't fake reasons to come skulking around with newsletters."

Averill seemed angry as well as offended. I wondered if he knew Lana, or maybe her family. Maybe he wanted to fight me. I wanted to quit right then, to stand up and walk out before anything else happened. I was already thinking of where I could apply for another job when Averill sat back and smiled.

"Why are you in the interoffice mail room?" he asked, suddenly much friendlier.

"No P.T. positions were open when I applied," I said.

"Nonsense. We don't have a limit on P.T.s."

"But Ms. Worth said—"

"Oh." Averill held up his hand. "Reena. You know, Ernie helped me out when I got here, twenty-three years ago. I was just a little older than you. They didn't have the P.T. program back then, just a few guys like Ernie. He never even finished high school, but he showed me the ropes."

Averill drummed the fingers of his free hand between the two forms that represented me.

"I know this Lana's sister," he said. "Always wearing those cocktail dresses in to work. Her boss is afraid to say anything, otherwise he might get a pink slip, too." He paused to ponder some more. "How would you like to be a P.T. floater?"

"What's that?" I asked.

"Bumps you up to a grade seven and lets you move around in the different departments until you find a fit."

I was a grade B1.

"I thought you were going to fire me."

"That's what Drew suggested, but Ernie says that it's just a mixup. What if I talked to Lana? What if I asked her to hold this back, to give you a second chance?"

"I'd like that," I said. "Thanks."

"Probably be better if I let Drew fire you, you know," he said, standing up. I stood, too. "I mean if you fuck up once you'll probably just do it again, right?"

He held out his hand.

Watching the forbidden smoke curl around his head, I imagined that Averill was some kind of devil. When I thanked him and shook his hand, something inside me wanted to scream.

I found six unused crack vials a block from the subway stop near my apartment. I knew they were unused because they still had the little plastic stoppers in them.

When I got upstairs, I spent hours searching my place. I looked under the mattress and behind the toilet, under the radiator, and even down under the burners on the stove. Finally, after midnight, I decided to open the windows.

The fly had crawled down into the crack between the window frame and the sill in my bedroom. His green body had dried out, which made his eyes even bigger. He'd gone down there to die, or maybe, I thought, he was trying to get away from me. Maybe I had killed him. Later, I found out that flies have a very short life span. He probably died of old age.

I took his small, dried-out corpse and put it in one of the crack vials. I stoppered him in the tiny glass coffin and buried him among the roots of the bonsai crab apple.

"So you finally bought something nice for your house," my mother said after I told her about the changes in my life. "Maybe next you'll get a real bed."

Chang-rae Lee

The Volunteers

From *The New Yorker*

When I was a young man, I didn't seek out the pleasure of women. At least not like my comrades in arms, who in their every spare moment seemed ravenous for any part of a woman, in any form, whether in photographs or songs or recounted stories, and, of course, whenever possible, in the flesh. Pictures were most favored, being easy. I remember a corporal who kept illicit photographs of disrobed maidens in his radio codebook, a sheaf of images he had salvaged from a bombed-out colonial mansion in Indonesia. Whenever I walked by the communications tent, he would call out in a most proper voice, "Lieutenant Kurohata, sir, may I receive an opinion from you, please?"

The women in his pictures were Western, I think French or Dutch, and had been caught by the camera in compromising positions—bending over to pick up a dropped book, for example, or being attended in the bath by another nude woman. Corporal Endo had perhaps a score of these, each featuring a different scene, and he shuffled through them with an unswerving awe and reverence that made me think he might be a Christian. Of course, I shouldn't have allowed him to address me so familiarly, as I was superior to him in rank, but we were from the same province and home town, and he was exuberantly innocent and youthful and he never called to me if others were within earshot. I knew that he had never been with a woman, but in going through his photos he seemed to have become privy to the secrets of lovemaking.

I myself, at that time, had been initiated only once, but, unlike the Corporal, I found little of interest in the hand-size tableaux. They held for me none of the drama that he clearly savored in them. Instead, they smacked of the excess and privilege of a sclerotic, purulent culture—the very forces that our nation's people were struggling against, from Papua New Guinea and Indonesia to the densely forested foothills of old Burma, where we were posted, approximately a hundred and twenty-five kilometres from the outskirts of Rangoon. The women in the photo cards were full figured, and no longer really young, though several of them were attractive in an exotic manner.

The image I preferred was the one of the bath, and although Corporal Endo offered several times to give me that particular card, I didn't want the worry of keeping it among my few personal things. Should I be killed, those items, along with my ashen remains, would be tendered to my family in Japan, as was customary. In most cases, the officer in charge of such transferrals checked the package to make sure that it contained only the most necessary (and honorable) effects, but one heard of embarrassing instances when grieving elders were forced to confront awkward last notions of their dead. I feared it would be especially shaming in my circumstance. When I was a young boy, I had left the narrow existence of my birth family and our ghetto of hide tanners and renderers—most of us were ethnic Koreans, though we spoke and lived as Japanese, if ones in twilight—to live with a Japanese couple, well-to-do and childless, who treated me as if I were their son. I believed that as adoptive parents they might shoulder the burden of my vices even more heavily than if I had been born to them, blood of their blood, as there would be no excuse but their raising of me. Indeed, I wanted to prove myself in the crucible of the battlefield, and to prove to anyone who might suspect otherwise the worthiness of raising me away from the lowly quarters of my kin. Still, being twenty-three years old and having been with only one woman, a prostitute, during my first posting, in Singapore, I was periodically given to the enticements of such base things, and unable to stop myself from stepping into the radio tent whenever the Corporal addressed me.

"Have I shown you this new series, sir?" he said one sweltering afternoon, reaching into the back flap of his codebook. His eyes seemed bright, almost feral. "I traded some of mine to a fellow in munitions. He had these. He said he was tired of them, sir."

There were several photographs pasted into a small journal which depicted women and men together, patently engaging in sexual intercourse. I had never seen such pictures before. The style of the photography was documentary, almost clinical, as though the overexposed frames were meant for a textbook on human coitus. To my mind, there was nothing remotely titillating in them, save perhaps the shocking idea that people had willingly performed the acts while someone else had photographed them.

The Corporal took more than a customary delight in these pictures. He seemed to be drawn into their stark realism, as if he desired to inhabit them somehow. In the week or two after he had first shown them to me, I encountered him several times in the camp, and in each instance I found him further dishevelled in appearance, wholly unwashed and reeking most awfully, even more than the camp norm, the private journal clutched in his hands. His face had erupted in a sudden rash of pimples. He was, as I have said, callow and youthful, and, at nineteen, without much developed musculature or much hair on his lip. He was the youngest boy of a fairly prominent family in our town, and he had been trained in coded field communications to take advantage of his obvious intelligence and to avoid the likely consequences of his physical immaturity if he became an infantry regular, which, long before an enemy confronted him, would mean certain injury and possibly death at the punitive hands of superiors.

I took pity on him, though I was afraid that lurking beneath his quick mind was an instability, a defect of character which I was certain would lead him to a troubling circumstance. As one of the brigade's medical personnel, I decided to write a memorandum to Captain Ono, the physician-in-charge, advising that the Corporal be evaluated and possibly even relieved of his duties and disarmed, but, like almost everything else in wartime, the memo was lost, or ignored.

This was in the early fall of 1944, when it seemed that our forces were being routed across the entire region. Admiral Yamamoto's transport plane had been ambushed and destroyed by American fighter planes more than a year before, and the general mood, if still hopeful, was certainly not as ebullient as it had been in the high, early times of the war, when the Burma Road fell, and then Mandalay. And now, under regular threat of attack from British and American bombers—though, as if we'd been forgotten, none ever seemed to come for us—the behavior of the brigade, and most notably that of Corporal Endo, grew increasingly more extreme.

Late one evening, he came to my tent, behind the medical quarters, and asked if he could come inside and speak to me. He had washed up, and he looked much like the Corporal of old. Although I was weary and about to retire, it was clear that the Corporal was troubled. There was a trenchant, focussed look in his eyes, as if an idea had taken a profound hold over him and he was useless before it.

He didn't speak right away, and I asked him if I might help him with something.

He replied, "Please forgive me, Lieutenant. I'm rude to request a moment from you and then waste your time." He paused for a few seconds, and then went on. "You've been most generous to me, and I feel that my conduct has been inappropriate. There is no excuse. I feel ashamed of myself, so much so that I sometimes wish I were no longer living."

"There's no need for such a sentiment, Corporal Endo," I said, concerned by his words. "If your shame comes from showing some of your pictures to me, you must obviously know that it was always my choice to look at them. You did not force them on me."

"Yes, of course, Lieutenant," he answered, bowing his head at a supplicant angle. "I'm sorry, sir, for the implication. But, if you'll excuse me, it wasn't only the pictures I was talking about. Please forgive my insolence, but it is another thing that makes me feel desperate."

He paused again, folding his arms across his belly as though he were suddenly cold. Then he said, "You see, sir, it's about the new arrivals everyone has been talking about. It's known around camp that they're scheduled to be here soon, and I've received messages for the quartermaster that the supply transport will likely arrive by tomorrow."

"What about it, Corporal?"

"Well, sir, I've looked around camp yesterday and today, and I haven't been able to see where they'll be housed, once they're here. I thought that, as one of the medical officers, you might know."

"The housing of the female volunteers will no doubt be quickly determined, but not by me. I'm not in charge of their status or medical care. That will be Captain Ono's area, as he's the chief medical officer. Anyway, I don't see why this is your concern, Corporal."

The Corporal bobbed repeatedly, his face still quite serious. "Yes, sir. Should I then speak to Captain Ono?"

I didn't answer, as I was certain that I would grow annoyed if our conversation went on any longer. But I also feared that the Corporal might provoke Captain Ono. The Captain was a controlled man, almost grimly so, wound up within himself like a dense, impassable thicket. A week earlier, he had beaten a private nearly to death for accidentally brushing him as he passed on a narrow footpath near the latrines. Ono had ordered the man to kneel, and, in plain view of onlookers, beat him with the butt of his revolver, until the private was bloody and unconscious. He treated the man soon thereafter in the infirmary, saving his life with some quick surgical work to relieve the building pressure of blood on his brain. In fairness, it was an isolated act of violence. Still, I was concerned for Corporal Endo, and so I said to him, "Will you tell me what your interest in all this is? You won't find the Captain very patient, if he agrees to speak to you at all."

The young Corporal nodded gravely. "Yes, sir. I'm grateful for your advice. You see, sir, I was hoping that I could be among the first of those who might meet the volunteers when they arrive. If there is to be a greeting in the camp, for example, I would be honored to take part."

"Corporal Endo," I said sternly. "There will be no public greeting or reception of any kind. You ought to strike any such notion from your thoughts. As to meeting the female volunteers, it is the officer corps that will first inspect them. I'm new to this myself, but enlisted men, I've been informed, will be issued their tickets shortly thereafter, and it will be up to you to hold a place for yourself on the queue. I see you are most anxious to meet the volunteers, as most of the men will be when they learn of their arrival, but I suggest that you remain as circumspect as possible. I am also ordering you not to spread further news of their arrival. There will be time enough for foment in the camp. We don't need any beforehand."

"Yes, Lieutenant."

"The other piece of advice I have is that you put away all the picture cards you've collected. Don't look at them for a while. I believe you've developed an unhealthy dependence upon them. Do you think this may be true, Corporal?"

"Yes, sir," he said regretfully.

"Then take my advice. Bundle them up and put them in the bottom of your footlocker. Or perhaps destroy them. There's an atmosphere of malaise in the camp, and I believe it's partly due to a host of anticipations, both good and bad."

The Corporal nodded. "It's assumed among the men that the British and Americans will soon mount another major offensive, in the northern and eastern territories," he said.

"No doubt they will. As the commander instructed the officers last week, we must ready ourselves for death and suffering. When the female volunteers do arrive, perhaps it would be good if you make your own visitation. This is most regular. But keep in mind, Corporal Endo, the reasons we are here. As the commander, Colonel Ishii, has told us, it is our way of life that we're fighting for, and so it behooves each one of us to carry ourselves with dignity, in whatever we do. Try to remember this. I won't always be around to give you counsel."

"Yes, sir. Thank you, sir."

"Is that all?"

"Yes, sir," he answered, rising to his feet. He bowed, but didn't lift his head immediately, and said, "Sir?"

"Corporal?"

"If I may ask, sir," he said weakly, almost as a boy would who already feared he knew the answer. "Will you be visiting the volunteers as well?"

"Naturally," I replied. "You may take your leave now, Corporal."

In truth, I hadn't yet thought of the question he'd posed, and for the rest of the night I wondered what I would do. I had wanted to assure the Corporal of the commonness of our procedures, and yet the imminent arrival of these "volunteers," as they were referred to, seemed quite removed from the ordinary. Certainly, I had heard of the mobilization of such a corps, in northern China and in the Philippines and on other islands, and, like everyone else, I appreciated the logic of deploying young women to maintain the morale of officers and foot soldiers in the field. And, like everyone else, I suppose, I assumed that it would be a familiar event, just one among the many thousands of details in a wartime camp. But when the day finally came, I realized that I had been mistaken.

The convoy arrived a week later. It had been delayed by an ambush of native insurgents and had suffered significant damage and loss of supplies. There were at least a dozen men with serious injuries, three of whom were beyond help. Two trucks had been abandoned en route, and I remember the men crowding around the remaining truck, which bore sacks of rice and quantities of other foods, like pickled radishes and dried fish. At the time, we were still in contact with the supply line, and there were modest but decent rations available to us. It was clear, however, that the supplies were steadily growing sparser with each transport. The ambush had left the truck riddled with bullet holes, and one of the sergeants ordered a few of his men to pick the truck bed clean of every last grain of rice, which had drizzled out of holes in the burlap. The soldiers looked as if they were searching for grubs. It was a pathetic sight, particularly when the sergeant lined up the men after they finished and had them pour their scavengings into his cap, which he in turn presented to the presiding officer-in-charge.

I believe we had nearly forgotten what else had been expected, when a lone transport drove slowly up the road. It turned before reaching us in the central yard, and headed to the house of the commander, a small hut of palm wood and bamboo and thatch, situated at the far end of an expansive clearing. I could see that the doctor, Captain Ono, had just emerged from the commander's quarters and was standing at attention on a makeshift veranda. The driver stopped and folded down the back gate of the truck bed. He called into the dark hold and helped to the ground an older woman wearing a paper hat. She then turned to bark raspily inside. There was no answer and the woman shouted again, louder this time. The girls then climbed down from the truck, one by one, holding their hands above their eyes, shading them from the high Burmese light.

They were dressed like peasants, in baggy, crumpled white trousers and loose shirts. One might have thought they were young boys, were it not for their braided hair. The older woman and the driver pulled each girl by the arms as she descended and stood them in a row before the steps of the veranda. That there were only five of them seems remarkable to me now, given that there were nearly two hundred men in the encampment, but at the time I hadn't thought clearly about what was awaiting them in the coming days and nights. Like the rest of the men, I was simply struck by their presence, by the white shock of their oversized pants, their dirty, unshod feet, the narrowness of their hands and their throats. And soon enough the comprehension of what lay beneath the crumpled cotton shook me, as if I'd just heard an air-raid siren, and probably had the same effect on every other man standing at attention in that dusty clay field.

Captain Ono ordered the woman to march the girls up the steps. They looked frightened, and all but one ascended quickly to the veranda landing. The last one hesitated, though just momentarily, and the Captain stepped forward and struck her in the face with the back of his hand, sending her down to one knee. He did not seem particularly enraged. He then struck her again, and she fell back limply. She did not cry out. The older woman waited until Captain Ono withdrew before helping the girl up. The Captain knocked on the door. It was opened by the house servant and the Captain entered, followed by the older woman and the five young girls.

That night there was an unusually festive air in the camp. Groups of soldiers squatted outside their tents singing songs and trading stories in the temperate night air. There had been no ration of sake in the supply shipment except for a few large bottles for the officers, but the men didn't seem to mind. Strangely enough, Corporal Endo seemed to be the only one in a dark mood, and he sought me out as I took an evening walk. As I made my way along the camp's perimeter, listening to the rhythmic din of birds and insects calling out from the jungle, I thought of the sorry line of girls entering the house. They had spent the better part of the afternoon inside with the commander, shielded from the intense heat of the day. The Captain had come to the infirmary that afternoon to inform me of my new duties. He told me that, from the next day on, I and not he would be responsible for maintaining the readiness of the girls. Very soon the fighting would resume, he said with a chilling surety, and his time and skills would be required elsewhere. Since I was the paramedical officer—field-trained but not formally educated—it would be more than appropriate for me to handle their care. They were quite valuable, after all, to the well-being and morale of the camp, and vigilance would be in order.

Corporal Endo found me just short of the southeast checkpoint, beyond which our squads were regularly patrolling. To the left, one could see the faintest glimmers of light from the commander's hut, some fifty metres away, filtering through the half-cleared vegetation of the perimeter. There was no sound, just weak electric light glowing through the slats of the hut's bamboo shutters.

"Lieutenant, sir," Endo said, addressing me gloomily, "I've been thinking all afternoon about what's to come in the next days."

"You mean about the expected offensive from the enemy?"

"I suppose, yes, that, too," he said, regarding the light from the hut. "There's been much radio traffic lately. Almost all concerning where they'll strike, and when."

"Near here, and soon," I replied, echoing what Captain Ono had told me.

"Yes, sir," Endo said, "that seems to be the conclusion. But what I was thinking of mostly was the volunteers."

"You'll have your due turn," I said, annoyed that he was still preoccupied with the issue. "It will be a day or two or three, whatever is determined. In the meanwhile, you should keep yourself busy. It's an unhealthy anticipation that you are developing, Corporal."

"But if I can make myself clear, sir, it's not that way at all. I'm not thinking about when I'll see one of them. In fact, sir, I'm almost sure of *not* visiting. I won't seek their company at all."

This surprised me. "Of course, you're not required to," I said. "No one is."

"Yes, sir, I know," he said softly, following me as I made my way along the path back toward the main encampment, which led directly past the commander's hut. We walked for some time before he spoke again. "The fellows in the communications and munitions areas drew lots this morning, to make things orderly, and by sheer chance I took first place among my rank. There was much gibing and joking about it, and some of the fellows offered me cigarettes and fruit if I would trade with them. I had to leave the tent then, and they probably thought I was being a bad winner."

We had reached the point on the path which was closest to the hut. The sentry noticed us and let us pass; he was a private I had recently treated for a mild case of dysentery. Again there was hardly a sound save the sharp, high songs of the nighttime fauna.

"So why did you leave?" I asked.

"You see, sir," he continued, "I've decided not to visit those girls. I don't really know why, because it's true that every day I've been in this miserable situation I've been thinking about being with a woman, any woman. But yesterday, after I saw them arrive in the camp, I suddenly stopped wanting that. I know I must be sick, Lieutenant. I do in fact feel sick, but I didn't come to ask for any treatment or advice. I don't want my lot anymore, but I don't want any of the others to have it, either. So I thought I could ask you to hold it for me, so none of the fellows can get to it."

He then showed me a torn-edged chit, a tiny, triangular bit of rice paper with a scribble on one side. It was nothing. His fellows would certainly just jostle for their places when the time came, chits or not. But the Corporal handed the scrap to me as if it were the last ashes of an ancestor. I thought for a moment that he had deceived me about his virginity and was suffering from an untreated syphilitic infection, but I saw only the straining earnestness of his narrow, boyish face.

I unbuttoned the chest pocket of my shirt and deposited the bit of paper. I said nothing to the Corporal. He was genuinely grateful and relieved, and he bowed almost wistfully before me, making me feel as though I had indeed come to his aid, that I had helped save him from whatever fate he imagined would befall him were he to visit the ones delivered for our final solace and pleasure. And I recall understanding this last notion. For although it was true that the talk throughout the camp was still of the glorious brightness of our ultimate victory, the surer truth, as yet unspoken, was that we were now facing our demise. Famous, of course, is the resolve of the Japanese soldier, the lore of his tenacity and courage and willingness to fight in the breach of certain death, but I will say, too, that for every man who showed no fear there were three or four or five others whose mettle was as unashamedly wan and mortal as yours or mine. As the defenders of the most far-flung sector of the occupied territory, we had little question about the terrible hours ahead of us. It was a startlingly real possibility that every man in the camp would soon be dead.

I guided Corporal Endo quickly past the commander's hut, his gaze almost rigidly locked upon the shuttered windows. We had gone some thirty paces when he grabbed me roughly by the shoulder.

I looked up and saw that the door had opened. A man stood on the open porch, his hands on his hips. He seemed to be surveying the darkened compound, and the Corporal and I both stopped in our tracks, trying not to make a sound. From the silhouette it was clearly the commander, Colonel Ishii, with his thick torso and bowlegs and the distinctly squared-off shape of his head. He was naked, and he was inhaling and exhaling deeply from his belly. These days people might call the commander a health nut, and some of his ministrations were quite peculiar. He would exercise vigorously in the early morning, an intense regimen of calisthenics and stretching which would challenge a seasoned drill sergeant. Then, sweating like a plow ox, he would deliberately allow himself to be bitten by swarms of mosquitoes, letting the ravenous insects feed freely on his belly and chest and back. It was a way of bleeding himself. One would assume he'd have suffered terribly from malaria, but he seemed perfectly fit.

The commander took a step down and I thought he must have seen us. I was ready to address him to avoid seeming as if we were trying to conceal ourselves in the darkness, but then he bent down to peer beneath the floorboards of the hut, which was set up off the ground on short posts. After a moment's inspection, he straightened and began speaking down into the crawl space, his tone eerily gentle, as if he were addressing a favorite niece who was misbehaving.

"There is little reason to hide anymore. It's all done now. It's silly to think otherwise. You will come out and join your companions."

There was no answer.

"You must come out sometime," he continued. "I suppose it's more comfortable under there than out in the jungle. I can understand that.

But you know there is food inside now. The cook has made some rice balls. The others are eating them as we speak."

"I want to be with my sister," a young voice replied miserably. She was speaking awkwardly, in Japanese, with some Korean words mixed in. I hadn't heard much of that language since my childhood, and I found myself suspended, anticipating the old tenor of the words. "I want to know where she is," the girl said. "I must know. I won't come out until I know."

"She's with the camp doctor," the commander said. "She's having her ear looked at. The doctor wanted to make sure she was all right."

I wondered whether the girl knew that the doctor was the same man who had struck her sister down. There was a pause, and the commander simply stood there in his blunt nakedness, the strangest picture of tolerance.

I heard the girl's weak reply. "I promised my mother we would always stay together," she said.

The commander said to her, "That should be so. You are good to try to keep such a promise. But how can you do so from down there? Your sister will be back with you tomorrow. For now, you must come out, right at this moment. Right at this moment. I won't wait any longer."

Something must have shifted in his voice, a different note that only she could hear, for she came out, scuttling forward on her hands and knees. When she reached the open air she didn't get up but stayed crumpled at his feet. She was naked, too. The clouds had scattered, and in the dim violet moonlight the sight of them, if you did not know the truth, was almost a thing of beauty, a painter's scene, conjured to address the subject of a difficult love. The commander offered his hand and the girl took it and pulled herself up, her posture bent and tentative as though she were ill. She was crying softly. He guided her to the step of the porch, and it was there that her legs lost their power and she collapsed. The commander grabbed her wrist and barked at her to get up, the sharp report of his voice sundering the air, but she didn't move. She was sobbing wearily for her sister, and I understood that she was calling her sister's name, "Kku-taeh," which, I knew, meant bottom, or last.

The Colonel made a low grunt and jerked the girl up by her wrist. It looked as if he were dragging a skinned calf. He got her inside and a peal of cries went up. He shouted for quiet with a sudden, terrible edge in his voice. Meanwhile, the sentry had heard the outburst and run around to the front, instinctively levelling his rifle on us as he came forward. As I raised my hands, the sentry yelled "Hey there!" and I realized that Corporal Endo, inexplicably, had begun to sprint back into the darkness of the jungle.

I shouted "Don't shoot!" but the sentry had already fired once in our direction. The shot flew past well above me, though I could feel it bore through the heavy air. There was little chance that it could have hit the Corporal, or anyone else. The sentry seemed shocked at his own reaction, however, and dropped his rifle. I was relieved, but the commander had already come out of the house, his robe hastily wrapped around his middle, a shiny pistol in his hands. Over the sentry's shoulder I could see the commander take aim from the veranda and fire twice. Then a questioning, half-bemused expression flitted across the sentry's face, and he fell to the ground.

The commander walked over and motioned to me with the gun to let down my hands. He had recognized me as the doctor's assistant. "Lieutenant Kurohata," he said almost kindly, not even looking down at the sentry's body. I knew the man was dead: one of the bullets had struck him in the neck and torn away a section of his carotid artery. The ground was slowly soaking up his blood. "You are a medical man, are you not?" the Colonel said. Up close he was more inebriated than I had surmised, his eyes sleepy and opaque. "You can help me then, I hope, with a small confusion I was having this evening."

He paused, as if trying to remember what he was saying, and in the background I could hear the chaotic shouts of orders and footfalls coming from the main camp. I replied, "However I am able, sir."

"What? Oh, yes. You can aid me with something. I was being entertained this evening, as you may know, and it occurred to me that there was a chance of ... a complication. You know what I'm talking about, Lieutenant?"

"Yes, sir," I said, though in fact I had no idea.

"They are young, after all, and likely fertile." He paused a moment, and said, as if in an aside, "And, of course, being virginal, that can't protect them, can it?"

"No, sir."

"Of course not," he concurred, as if I had asked him the question.

The commander's query surprised me. He was in his mid-thirties, which is not old in the world, but this late in the war he was practically ancient; I thought that he would have known—unlike Endo and myself—the many ways of women and amour, and yet he seemed to be even more ignorant of them than we were. He crossed his arms in an almost casual pose, though he kept a tight hold on the pistol, which poked out beneath one folded arm. "One grows up with all kinds of apocrypha and lore, yes? I mean us men. A young woman naturally receives guidance about such matters, estimable information, while it seems we are left on our own, each by each and one by one. To our own devices."

At that moment a squad of armed men came running up to us. The commander raised his free hand and waved them forward. The squad leader, a corporal, seemed shocked to find the lifeless body of the sentry lying in awkward repose by our feet.

"Remove him," the commander said. Two of the men lifted up the corpse by his armpits and calves. Someone gathered the dropped rifle and the bloody cap. As they left, I realized that neither the commander nor I had spoken a word of explanation to the men, nor had any of them even whispered a question.

"You'll look after this," the commander said to me matter-of-factly, referring, I understood immediately, to the death report, which was filled out whenever time and circumstances allowed. The next day I would note in the necessary form that the sentry, a Private Ozaki, had been shot dead by a forward sniper who was sought out by our patrols but never found.

I bowed curtly and the commander acknowledged me with a grunt. I waited while he ascended the low porch and went inside. As I started back for my own tent, I could hear him speaking again, in a calm, unagitated tone. "Look at my girls," I heard him saying, repeating himself slowly, with a sort of wonder, like a father who has been away much too long. "Look here at my girls."

By midmorning the day was already muggy and bright. I hadn't gone in search of Corporal Endo the night before, nor did I have any interest in doing so amid the early bustle of the day. No one knew that he had inadvertently instigated the shooting, or that he had even been present. When it was announced that patrols would be increased to prevent further sniping, I hoped he would keep quiet and let the event pass. The commander, whom I saw during his morning exercise, seemed fresh and fit.

That afternoon, the commander relinquished the girls to my care. I ordered that they be housed temporarily in one of the barracks, displacing a handful of men. A receiving house was being built by a crew of native tradesmen, who were following specifications provided by Captain Ono. I was to oversee this as well, but there was little left to be done.

The comfort house, which is how it was known, was a narrow structure with five doorways, each with a rod across the top for a sheet that would be hung as a privacy screen. The whole thing was perhaps as long as a large transport truck, ten metres or so. There were five compartments, of course, one for each of the girls; these were tiny, windowless rooms, no more than the space of one and a half tatami mats. In the middle of each space was a wide plank of wood meant for lying down on. The plank was widest where the shoulders would be, and then it narrowed again for the head, so that its shape was like the lid of an extra-broad coffin. This is where the girls would receive the men. After their duties were over, they would sleep where they could in the compartment. They would take their meals with the older Japanese woman, who was already living in her own small tent, behind the comfort house. She would prepare their food and keep hold of their visitors' tickets and make sure they had enough of the things a young woman might need, to keep herself in a minimally respectable way.

I alone was responsible for their health. The girls' well-being aside, I was to make certain they could perform their duties for the men in the camp. The greatest challenge, of course, would be preventing them from contracting venereal disease. It was well known what an intractable problem this was in the first years of fighting, particularly in Manchuria, when it might happen that two out of every three men were stricken and rendered useless for battle. In those initial years there had been comfort houses set up with former prostitutes shipped in from Japan by Armysanctioned merchants, and the infection rate was naturally high. Now that the comfort stations were run under military ordinances and the women were not professionals but, rather, those who had unwittingly enlisted or had been forcibly conscripted into the wartime women's volunteer corps, the expectation was that disease would be kept in check. Most of the volunteers were not Japanese, of course, just normal girls from Korea and China and wherever else they could be found. Now it was the men who were problematic, and there was a stiff penalty for anyone known to be infected who did not seek treatment beforehand. I had one of the sergeants announce final call for the camp in this regard, as I hoped to quarantine anyone who might infect a girl. Only two men came forward complaining of symptoms, both of whom were in the ward already.

I was to examine the girls and state their fitness for their duties. I had put on a doctor's coat and was waiting for the women to be brought to the infirmary. The intense heat of the day seemed to treble inside the room, and my stiff white coat was another layer over my regular uniform. I hadn't eaten anything yet that day, because of the sticking temperature and a crabbed feeling of an incipient illness.

The older woman, Mrs. Matsui, poked her head in the open doorway and bowed several times. She was pale and pock-faced and dressed in the tawdry, overly shiny garb of a woman who had obviously once been in the trade. She was clearly, too, a full Japanese, and the fact of this bothered me now, to have to see her cheapness against the line of modest girls who trailed her.

They were all fairly young, ranging from sixteen to twenty-one. At the head was a tallish girl with a dark mole on her cheek. The two beside her were more retiring in their appearance, their eyes averted from me; they seemed to be clinging to one another, though they weren't touching at all. The next girl, I realized, was the one who had hidden beneath the commander's hut. She had a firm hold of the hand of the girl behind her, whom I realized must be her sister, the one she called Kku-taeh.

She was the only one who gazed directly at me. She met my eyes as someone might on any public bus or trolley car, though her regard was instantly fixing and cool. She had a wide, oval-shaped face, and there was some bruising along the side of her jaw and upper neck. She had been housed with Captain Ono while the rest of them had gone on to entertain the commander; the doctor had reserved her, implying to the commander that she was not a virgin like the others, who would offer him the ineffable effects of their maidenhood, which to a soldier is like an amulet of life and rebirth.

I told Mrs. Matsui to ready the girls for examination and she ordered them to remove their clothing. They were slow to do so and she went up to the girl with the mole and tore at her hair. The girl complied and the rest of them began to disrobe. I did not watch them. I stood at the table with a writing board and the sheets of paper for recording their medical histories and periodic examinations. There was special paperwork for everything, and it was no different for the young women of the comfort house. The girl with the mole came to me first. I nodded to the table and she lifted herself up gingerly. She was naked and in the bright afternoon light coming from the slatted window her youthful skin was practically luminous, as though she were somehow lit from inside. For a moment I was transfixed by the strangeness of it all, the sheer exposed figure of the girl and then the four others who stood covering themselves with their hands, their half-real, half-phantom nearness, which I thought must be like the allure of pornography for Corporal Endo. But then Mrs. Matsui came around the front of the girl on the exam table and without any prompting from me spread her knees apart.

"You'll probably see they're all a bit raw today," she said hoarsely, like a monger with her morning's call. "Nothing like the first time, right? But you'll believe me when I say they'll be used to it by tomorrow."

Her cloying tone and familiarity put me off, but she was right. The girl's privates were terribly swollen and bruised, and there were dried smears of crimson-tinged discharge on her thighs and underside. Mrs. Matsui had just delivered the four of them from the commander's hut, and the faint, sour odors of dried sweat and spilled rice wine and blood and sexual relations emanated from the girl. When I reached to examine her more closely, she curled her hips away and began whimpering. Mrs. Matsui held her steady, but I didn't touch her then. I inspected the others; I didn't touch them, either, and the condition was more or less the same. I was just beginning to examine the last one, Kku-taeh, when the door swung open. It was the doctor, in his fatigues, entering the room.

"What do you think you are doing?" Ono said sharply, staring at Kku-taeh.

I answered, "The required examinations, Captain. I've nearly completed them, and I'll have the records for you shortly."

"I don't need *records* from you," he said, not hiding his irritation. He pushed Mrs. Matsui aside, then took hold of the girl by the back of her neck. Her shoulders tightened at his touch. He was applying subtle pressure, enough that she was wincing slightly, though not letting herself cry out.

"I need order from you, Lieutenant. Order and adherence to our code. What appears to elude you is the application of principle. The true officer understands this. You examined them, yes. But in doing so you abandoned far more important principles. This examination room, for example, is a disgrace and besmirchment upon our practice." He nodded at the clothes in piles on the floor. "You follow your duties but your conduct is so often middling. In truth, I remain unconvinced of you. Now you'll get them out of here and ready for receiving the officer corps tonight. The comfort house is done?"

"Yes, sir."

"Then you can leave the examination room, Lieutenant."

"Captain, sir," I said, glancing at the girl beside him. She was stony-faced and grimly silent. "I have not yet completed the examinations."

The doctor was still staring at Kku-taeh, not acknowledging my statement. Already he seemed to consider us gone. I had known from the first moment I met him that he was a man of singular resolve, and even hardness, particularly when it came to the care of his patients, and I had always admired him for this. He had a wife and a young child back in Japan, whose attractive portraits he kept on his desk. Those portraits had been steady witness to numerous bloody surgical procedures, and I thought that anyone else would surely have retired them to a private cabinet. And now he had a girl unclothed on the table, and he was pushing her to lie down on her back, his drawn, unhumored face hovering above her shallow belly.

Mrs. Matsui gathered the rest of the girls, trying to quiet Kku-taeh's sister, who refused to leave the room, with a quick slap. The three other girls had to work together to drag her out. On the table, Kku-taeh remained oddly unmoved, almost dead to her and everything else. I removed my white coat, and left it folded on the desk chair. When I shut the door I did not look back into the room.

I was relieved to be outside. I stopped at the enlisted mess tent, and the steward there offered to prepare me a cup of tea. I sat on an upended crate and waited, welcoming the small kindness. In the corner of my vision Mrs. Matsui and the others were half carrying the hysterical girl toward the comfort house, which seemed, being so newly built, a lone clean island in the growing fetor of the camp. With dusk, I knew, the officers would recommence their visitations.

I also noticed what I thought to be the slight figure of Corporal Endo, crouched at the far end of the central yard, where it gave way to dense jungle. He was sitting back on his haunches, his canvas radioman's cap pinched down over his brow to shade his eyes from the fierce daylight. He must have seen me, but he did not wave or make a gesture; he appeared to be surveying the goings on, particularly the troop of girls making their way to Mrs. Matsui's tent behind the comfort house. Perhaps he had been waiting for them to come out from the medical hut, or perhaps he had just then crouched to rest. Whatever the case, he would never tell me or anyone else. Even now, more than fifty years afterward, I wonder what might have come of Endo had the following events not occurred. Would he have married? Would he have had children? Or would he have lived a solitary life, as I have, and known only the scantest taste of a woman's love? And even now what he did next remains a mystery to me, and I remain useless before the memory, inert with fascination and dread. I keep revisiting the scene, turning it over, again and again, like one of Endo's tattered picture cards.

He rose from his crouch and began to trot toward Mrs. Matsui and the girls. The distance between them was not great, perhaps sixty or seventy metres, and I was able to see the whole event, from start to end. The Corporal was not a natural runner, and he appeared to be awkwardly exercising, though hardly a soul was exerting himself any more than was necessary those days. Some small part of me probably fathomed what he intended, and yet I simply watched like a disinterested spectator, whose sudden glint of prescience is somehow self-fulfilling.

The Corporal approached and ordered the women to halt. I could barely hear what was said, though I could gather that Mrs. Matsui was objecting to what Endo seemed to want, which was an immediate private audience with one of the girls. Mrs. Matsui was pointing toward the medical hut, but he pushed her aside. The three girls who had been supporting Kku-taeh's sister backed away, and she fell weakly to her knees; it was Endo who raised her up with a stiff pull. She was not fighting him; in fact, her movement seemed to lighten, as if he were an old acquaintance and she were pleased to see him. Some men had noticed the commotion and were calling to him, asking what he was up to, what he was doing, shouting it in a hearty, knowing way. He ignored them and dragged the girl along, quickly arriving at his original position at the edge of the bush. After the two of them disappeared into the dense foliage and had not returned for several minutes, the corporals and privates working near the trucks began to jog over, and it was then that I knew something irregular had occurred. I slipped beneath the netting of the mess tent and slowly made my way across the dusty red clay of the yard, past the officers' quarters and latrines, then past the narrow comfort house, its walls rough-hewn and smelling of fresh-cut wood, to where the canopy rose up again and the shade cooled the air. My legs felt unbearably heavy. The half-dozen or so men were gathered there, in the trodden entrance of a patrol trail, the couple in their midst, Endo sitting on the ground with the girl lying beside him.

Her throat was slashed, deeply, very near the bone. She had probably died in less than a minute. There was much blood, naturally, but it was almost wholly pooled in a broad blot beneath her, the dry red earth turned a rich hue of brown. There was little blood on her person, hardly a spatter or speck anywhere save on her collar and on the tops of her shoulders. It was as though she had gently lain down for him and calmly waited for the cut. The oddity was that he was unsoiled as well, completely untouched. There was nothing even on his hands, with which he was rubbing his close-shaven head. I asked him what had happened, but he did not seem to hear me. He sat there, his knees splayed out, his cap fallen off, an errant expression on his face, like that of a man who has seen his other self.

Finally, someone asked me what they ought to do, and, as I held rank,

I told the men to take Corporal Endo under arms to the officer-in-charge. I recall, now, having remained at the trail after Endo had been escorted away. I ordered the rest of the men to fetch a stretcher for the girl's body, and for a few moments I was left alone with her. In the sudden quiet of the glade I felt I should kneel down. Her eyes were open, coal-dark but still bright. She did not look fearful or sad. And, for the first time, I appreciated what she truly looked like, the delicate cast of her young girl's face.

Endo was kept under close watch that night, and after a brief interrogation by Captain Ono he confessed to the deed. The following morning, just after dawn, in front of the entire garrison, he was executed. Mrs. Matsui was present, as was Kku-taeh, who looked upon the proceedings coldly. She stood aside from the other girls. The officer-in-charge announced that Endo had been charged not with murder but with treasonous action against the corps. He should be considered as guilty as any saboteur who had stolen or despoiled the camp's armament or rations. Endo looked small and frail; he was so frightened he could hardly walk. He had to be helped to the spot where he would kneel. By custom he was then offered a blade, but he dropped it before he could pierce his belly, retching instead. The swordsman standing beside him did not hesitate and struck him cleanly. Endo's headless body pitched lightly forward, his delicate hands outstretched, as if to break his fall.

Lois-Ann Yamanaka

Ten Thousand in the Round

From *Conjunctions*

My madda always saying she the lucky one. She got ten thousand wishes for her whole life. Thass plenny enough wishes, if you ask me. Far as wishes go, no mo' too much going around far as I can see.

She use her first one when I was born. She wish me dead.

Kill um, God. Kill this fuckin' thing.

She saying this soft up until the time the doctor yelling at her to "Oosh, girlie, oosh." Then yelling at the nurse to "Strap this girl's arms down."

Thass when my madda started swinging and yelling at him to "Kill this fuckin' piggie" she get stuck up her Japanee trap.

Far as she concern, they all sugar plantation pigs except the Japs and haoles. And she don't give a horse's ass if she less one mo' fuckup from the get-go child.

Wish.

My madda yelling the most filthiest words at the plantation doctor who take out one appendix for every so-wa stomach he treat. So he tell her, "Shaddap, small girl," and shove the forceps up her chocho, clamp um on my head and pull me out from deep inside her.

Ten thousand.

Ten thousand.

Nine thousand nine hundred ninety-nine 'cause a wish is thin, thin as a pheasant's eyelid.

We living in Aunty Momo's old plantation house down the Mill Camp with black-eye susan and scraggly lawa'e down the crack sidewalk. We there only a little while and my madda in the bedroom with Ernie Agliam.

My madda make one more wish. This time she wish for a boy from Ernie. But we neva get no baby.

We got a empty crib, and Carnie and me being push around in a baby carriage built for twinnies.

She pushing C and me through the Mill Camp and up to the Shopping Centre. The days real hot and long. No mo' baby in her 'cause it died, but her stomach still flabs.

Ernie neva come around no mo' in his bust-up yellow truck yelling for his ole lady come outside chew the fat little while.

C, she four. I three. I wish I was dead.

I seen death in my face in the pictures I found in the mildew box, way, way back in the moss and termite nest under the house.

And my teacher says like Jimminy says and wez suppose to believe them:

If you wish upon a star
doesn't matter who you are.

Does.

My madda stirring her coffee slow and telling Aunty Nancy about something while she pulling the little petals offa the African daisies from the Suyat's backyard I picked for the table. Something call The-Pill.

"I wish I wen' get um from the clinic and take um every day like that fuckin' doctor said," she tell. "I wish. I wish." She hitting her forehead with hand and wasting all her wishes.

"Shut yo' mouth, Iris," Aunty Nancy tell.

"Acting like he fuckin' Supa-man with the goddam riddem method like he can pull out before he come. Yeah, right," my madda tell and she throw the bolohead flower stem at me.

"You so fuckin' dumb," Aunty Nancy says to my madda. "Yeah, maybe she just sitting there, but she listening to every word you saying. And one day, one of these days, Iris, you mark my words, yo' very own evil mouth going come back fo' get your rotten ass."

She glare down at me. I one small girl but I undastand everything, every word. "What? What?" she yell at me. "What the fuck you like, hah? What you staring fo', hah? You get eye problems?"

I no say nothing. I pick up the broken flowers but I don't dare move from the spot.

"Look her," my madda says to Aunty Nancy. "All kinky her hair and she get chocho lips just like her fadda, that man-hoa loser, welfare, good-fo'-nothing."

Wish.

Wish.

Ma, no put no extra candles on my bertday cake.

No tell me when the day turn light purple, "There the first star, Lucy."

No make me fold the thousand-one gold cranes for Roxy's wedding.

No baby teeth in a jar.

No rabbit feet.

Or wishing well.

Or touch blue, yo' dream come true.

No falling stars over Wood Valley.

I neva use my wishes like that once a night, every second, minute or hour of passing time.

'Cause it's every day I glad I made it through another one.

It's every minute I glad I still here.

Ten thousand wishes, gasp for rain.

Ten thousand wishes, fall like a sigh.

Ten thousand wishes in the round:

I am the girl with the kinky hair.

The Jap with the green eyes.

The hurtful one.

The stupid one.

The sullen one.

The hateful one.

The one full of evil whose madda cannot take and she force to wish for a joint, a 'lude, a line.

Nine thousand nine hundred ninety-eight.

She lucky. She can get stoned and fall asleep.

Ma, I sleeping back here in this man's back seat.

Wish my eyes to close.

One.

Wish my heart to stop.

Two.

Wish my tongue he swallow.

Three.

His hand stop, his mouth no laugh.

Four. Five.

Ma, you know him. He take me home all the time 'cause you tell me call him Uncle. He take me look for puka shells down the cove. He take me to the ponds.

Wish my body outta here quick.

Ma, before he want this too much.

I have her eye in my pocket. Thass only a marble so I put um in my mouth, all spit, and ha-rack um out in the mud puddle by Yoshimura Store.

And every crack I see, I step on um hard.

Step a crack. Step a crack.

I put her teeth in my fist, though it's only puka shells I shake in a baby jar, glinting and clinking mother-of-pearl fangs.

I have hair from her brush, a horsehair braid I will use to paint a mural with one day, "The Story of My Life."

I get her heart with my shoe. Thass only a stone.

And I step a crack, hard.

I tell my friends that it ain't no wasted wish to ask my madda make me canned peach halves with mayonnaise and grated Velveeta on leafs of romaine lettuce all cold and slippery.

And every morning, my madda make me scramble eggs and bacon and toast, every morning like their maddas with pancakes and syrup. But I leave the pancakes part out. Might make the story mo' real.

Ask Carnie,

How come your sista so quiet and moon face? She stand around the whole recess kicking the dirt or dangling her arms and legs on the tire swing, legs spread and spinning 'til her hair fly in a blur.

And Carnie says, she no even flinch, " 'Cause she's a so-sho and emo-sho mal-adjust, thass why. And no spread um around that she my sista."

Ma, this Uncle, he age thirty, and I just a little girlie. He kissing my thighs and making um all slippery. You always say he leading me to dark corners. I one fuckin' little ho-a.

You watching me.

Yeah, thass right, you watching every move I make.

Then how come you no can see?

The man you call my Uncle, watching me.

Ma, spend your wishes quick and fast. He kissing me higher and higher and taking deep breaths and moaning.

We coming home from the beach with a Baggie full of puka shells and a panty full of sand, the sea inside me.

"Bye, Baby," Uncle tell when I get out the truck.

"Say bye, stupid," my madda says as she shove me hard. "What's your problem, hah kid?"

"Eh, Iris," Uncle yell. "Come up the gym tonight. Fil-Am league night. You and Nancy drink with me, Ernie, WillyJoe, all the boiz. All-nighta, Babe. Leave the kids home. They only fuckin' troubles."

I look away from him. I dunno why she make me go with him. She tell me in the house, "Uncle said you guys get nuff brown shells fo' make me one opera length lei."

She looking hard at me. " 'Til you get nuff fo' three brown strands, Lucy, you go with Uncle. And I not asking, I telling."

I look at the shells in my hands. We got plenny purples and pinks. Thass when I look up in the lavendar sky.

Star light, star bright, first star I see tonight:

I wish I may, I wish I might—

nine thousand nine hundred sixty-nine.

One wish for light.

One for twinnies.

One for the red umbrella I take over the bridge to Coconut Island.

Two wishes for brown shells.

Two for rain that fall like a sigh.

Three wishes for Jimminy.

Three for extra candles.

Three for the faces in those pictures under the house, give um light.

I going sing from my skin, Ma, 'til every pore open, 'til every hair stand for you 'cause it's all in the breathing, the right way of this song.

I just a little girlie and all your ten thousand almost gone.

Ask God, Ma, ask God for just a couple mo'.

Ask God give you just five mo' so you can say five times, but might take six:

I wish I could love her.

I wish I could love her.

Four more times now.

I wish I could love her.

I wish I could.

I wish I could.

I wish I could.

Love her, my Lucy.

Most Japs go to the Buddhist Church except us. We go the plantation Methodist Church. Nobody go for God:

Roxy go 'cause Ernie go.

Who go 'cause his madda Lizzy Agliam force him go.

Who go 'cause her sista Gramma Mary go and Lizzy no like her sista Mary be mo' religious than her.

Mary who is WillyJoe gramma and Ezra hanai madda.

Mary and Lizzy who make their bachelor bradda Uncle Primo, short for Primavero, get up from his hangover so he no go Church of the Holy Mattress, Father Pillow, Amen.

My madda go 'cause Roxy go, and nobody but nobody, take her man from under her nose even if she keeping Uncle on the side.

Who make C and me go. But C no care 'cause they serve Kool-Aid and Rice Crispie cookies in Sunday School and she can check out all the 39 and Under league mens.

I go 'cause of God.

I pray hard every day for God remember me.

No forget me.

I ask the Holy Spirit:

Put a star next to my name in God's Book: I wuz hea'.

I sitting in this church, third pew, for early morning choir practice while the Preacher's wife teaching us some new hymns. Me and my sista singing to help our English be better, so we can sound less ignerant, so we pronounce correct for once, so we can sing, *God. How great thou art.* Great *thou* art? What *thou* mean?

I ask my madda when she show up for the service, but she no answer except to say that she know the Preacher's wife helping us be good girls who talk good and act good, not like her, when all the Preacher's wife doing in that early morning choir practice is correcting our talk and telling us how to say those big ass church words, not what they mean.

The Preacher think he there for God. I no think so. He all white in those yellow and red robes, up high on that pulpit yelling words at us every Sunday morning.

I swear he nuts 'cause half of the congregation only talk Filipino. And they looking at him like where the hell the guy who use to preach to us in Filipino before the real service?

Us had our own service before and now no mo'. Us had Mr. Llamas playing *How Great Thou Art* on his fiddle for the Filipino service before this preacher came.

Mr. Llamas would tell me what *thou* mean.

My sista sitting next to me in a white dress from Western Store and she acting floozy with the white gloves she got last Easter.

I love how she fold her hands together like a little lady and bow her head when the Preacher say, "Let us pray—dear heavenly Father"; the way she whisper at the end, "Amen," when she stepping on my shiny black shoes 'cause I whistling. The part:

let me take you down
'cause I going to
twoo-berry fields
nothing is real.

And Ma eyeing Roxy who eyeing Ernie who smiling at his madda who cussing out her youngest brother Uncle Primo who giving the elbow to WillyJoe to sign to Ezra, "We go drink Cuervos afta church pau. I get all the limes pre-cut already, and no let Gramma Mary see."

Ezra same age with WillyJoe and Ezra deaf and dumb, but he so handsome, he turn heads, so long as he in one slow cruising car and nobody ask him one question.

During Responsive Reading time, when the Preacher read some lines of scripture and us respond our lines from the back of the hymn book, I watch Lizzy Agliam fanning herself with a lacy white fan; she pretending like she can read, and all the other old ladies, they acting too, while the Preacher stare down at them with those blue ice eyes like they spoiling the whole thing.

I reading loud as I can; I the only one reading loud and clear. Everybody else mumbling the words, even the ones who know how to read. Nobody like make shame with no *funny kind pidgin talk* like the Preacher call um.

Black bold letters mean Preacher. "A thousand thousands that kept ministering to him," he read with Bible thumping feeling.

Red mean congregation: "And ten thousand times ten thousand that kept standing right before him."

"Who, C, who the ten thousand?" I ask my sista.

She no give a shit. She watching WillyJoe. She elbow my chest.

Let me take you down.

Then she refold her white-gloved hands.

"Who?" I ask her.

"Like I give a flying fuck," she tell when all her staring at WillyJoe end up in nothing.

They reading on without me, black, red, black, red.

The ten thousand.

I panicking. Who the ten thousand?

I see WillyJoe signing to Ezra. "The Shining Ones," he tell him.

No ask me how I know their secret sign language, I just know. Then he look at me. "Who shine on you, through you and around you." Ezra smiling.

And now I know.

"The Shining Ones," I tell C.

"Who?" she tell. "What shining one? Like me butane your knees again? You like shine, hah, Lucy?"

"I seen WillyJoe tell Ezra," I tell her.

"How can? Ezra deaf, stupid." Then she pause to catch his eye. "WillyJoe?" She still looking his way and when he finally turn, she lick her lips. WillyJoe no look our way for the rest of the service.

Gramma Mary humming the tune of the hymn the Preacher chose. Last preacher we had let Mr. Llamas play his fiddle while all the old ladies sing real joyous hymns, smiling and singing like they mean it.

"Hymns, dey prayers in song," Mr. Llamas tell us every Sunday. But not anymore. Us no even know some of the words. Force to mumble or hum, like what is tri-bu-la-shun?

I use to think about the meaning of the songs like Mr. Llamas use to tell us, sing like we singing on God's bertday. Now, I thinking about words like tri-bu-la-shun. And my mind start singing *(let me take you down)*, the way one song stick to your head from the time you wake up to the time you sleep. And your head cannot unshake um.

At morning sermon time, the Preacher says, "God, He so great. He bein' so great to this church that He bless us richly. God, He give me a callin' when I was prayin' on ma knees at semi-nary school to come to this town and spread the news of the gospel to ya'll sinners.

"For it is your sin that will cause your down-fall, fall into the WORLD. The world of porno-graphy, false theo-logy, wrongful bio-logy and worse of all, worse of all, FOR-ni-CAAA-shun.

"You are the for-ni-cator. I've seen it with my own two eyes. You girl and that man. You girl and that man. You sister and that brother. All God's chillun, making all kinds of hell-ish trouble for yourselves.

"You going burn, burn, I tell you. All your people burning now. That's why God called me here to be HIS servant. Called me to SAVE you, to baptize you in the name of the Father (amen), the Son (praise be), and the Holy Spirit (almighty).

"For the sin of ADULT-ery must be confessed. Must be given to God. Must be for-given by Him and HIM alone. Yes, sister, you are an ADULT-eress causing the fall of that brother, like Eve to Adam. Baring your skin to him in the darkness of motel rooms. A-whoring and causing the fall of that brother.

"He is my brother. He is holy onto me. And you, my sister, child of sin, for-ni-caaa-shun, and adult-ery, turn, I say to you, TURN ye to Grace."

He looking straight at all the ho-as. At least he got that right. I picking one scab off of my knee while the Preacher yell on.

There Roxy. She seen me staring. She give me one upward head jerk like hi, how you doing, and why you staring at me, you saying I one ho-a, hah, Lucy?

She the very sinner the Preacher talking about, stealing her best friend's ex-old man and coming to church again only to dress up in lacy red prom dress for Ernie who bringing his madda, the brown teeth stain Lizzy.

Roxy sitting right behind him all obvious, and him, he stretch both his arms across the back of the pew, turn his head to her little bit and give her one upward head jerk, like howzit baby.

Then he pull his black comb out of his shirt pocket to give his pomade head one swift comb or two. Ernie's big fingers tapping on the pew back, and I wish, I really wish he could see Roxy all holy, bowing her head and praying, praying real hard as she can that Ernie ask her if she need a long ride home after church.

I singing the final hymn, the way the Preacher's wife want me to, singing loud and trying so hard, but the words ain't clear. Ain't my language.

Singing, *Just as I am wit'out one plea, but da-at dye blood was shed fo' me.*

And I like hide from God, run, and no let Him see my stupid face and all these stupid people around me fuckin' everything up, they all a bunch of fuckin' holy phonies gone a-whoring 'til I hear:

Shine, Lucy. Shine.
On you.
Through you.
Around you.

No ask me how I hear this. First, I think thass WillyJoe talking to Ezra. But Ezra deaf. Where that voice coming from? Only nuts hear things. I looking around all panic, but everybody else carrying on with the final verse of the last hymn. Then come to me:

They not words, they lights. They blue and green lights. And the whole like church smell like sandalwood from the forest above the town.

Everybody singing on. The Preacher move to the front of the pulpit to call all the sinners forward in the benediction.

I dunno what fo' do.

The whole church filling with light. WillyJoe look up through the stain glass window behind the pulpit. He raise his face to the light.

Ezra standing up and raising his hands to the lights that connecting in blue and green strands to his fingers.

Hah, what? Only us three see this? Me, one deaf and dumb man, and one handsome weirdo who talk strange things?

And then I think, So what, Preacher, you can see or what? So how come we see the lights and you cannot?

He go on praying about sin, praying that some sinners come forward and confess themself to him.

Don't spend another day in the darkness of your sin.

Ma madda nodding her head, amen, brother, amen. "What she acting fo'?" Roxy whispering in Ernie ear.

And then I think, So what, Preacher, how come you cannot see, yet we the one sound stupid to you? And ignerant. But you no see the blue green lights of the Shining Ones right here in your plantation Methodist Church.

Telling us more about tri-bu-la-shun. Come forward you sinners. Any Sunday without one lost sheep walking forward to the slaughter is one black mark in God's Book.

Uncle Primo try to make Ezra sit down and Gramma Mary close her eyes to the bright lights. Then WillyJoe stand up next to Ezra. And Lizzy Agliam shoving Ernie to make his fuckin' cousins sit down. Crazy fuckas.

Still the service go on. Like nothing happening. So the blue green lights turn off.

And they both sit down.

They holding each other.

Everybody else buzzing and laughing like they just witness two nuts crack up, and of all places, in church. Damn drug addicts, alcoholics.

Then WillyJoe turn to me. He no say nothing but my eyes no can lie.

I seen the blue green lights. Put a star next to my name, God, in your Book. WillyJoe and Ezra too. Gramma Mary even if she shut her eye. Thass four stars, God, no forget.

I hate the way the Preacher pat me on my back on the way outta the church saying, "God loves you, sister." He no even know my name. And how he shake my sista's white-gloved hand all lightly and treat her like one lady—he no even know *what* she did with that hand.

I barely squeeze by the fat Preacher before I tell him, "This Word mine, no matters how I—" He put his hand on the back of my head and oosh me out the door.

I watch my sista trying to catch ride with WillyJoe and Ezra. Roxy climbing in the truck between Lizzy Agliam and Ernie. My madda calling Uncle from the phone in the church office. Uncle Primo waiting for Gramma Mary who walking toward me.

"Ten thousand times ten thousand that kept standing right before him," she whisper to me. "No close yo' eyes to the lights. No be like me. No make the beam come weak. Shine, Lucy. Shine."

Robert Antoni

My Grandmother's Tale of How Crab-o Lost His Head

From *The Paris Review*

Papa-yo! So you want to hear this nasty story? In truth, it is a story you own daddy used to beg me to tell him all the time when *he* was a youngboy too. You daddy, and he wicked brothers, and all they badjohn-boyfriends just the same. The whole gang of them sitting around me in the big circle—still wearing they schoolboy-shortpants and they scruffy-up washykongs—all with the big smiles on they faces and they bony knees crossed before them like if I was born yesterday, and I haven't raised up nine of them myself, and they think they can hide anything from *me*. Because of course, the youngboys can't hardly contemplate nothing more than they *own* little crab-os poking out between they legs, that they can't keep they hands out they pockets five minutes together without squeezing, and stretching, and playing with it—particularly when I start to give them *this* story—and in truth, that is a nastiness they never *do* grow out of no matter how long they live, *papa-yo!*

Well then, it happened in the old, old-time time, this story, and it happened in a village up on the north coast of this same island of Corpus Christi. It is a little village that you know good enough yourself, because you have passed through many times going on excursions with the scoutboys, just there beyond the rickety bamboo bridge, on that same trace following the coast beneath the foots of the mountains. The village is settled there on the banks of a river the Spanish explorers named *Madamas* when they drew out the first maps, even though the Caribs had long called she *Yarra* in they own tongue—that is to say, "the river of women's tears"—winding she way down from the forest of rain, and golden parrots, and green monkeys in the mountains, to empty sheself below in the blue Caribbean Sea. The village, as you have already discerned, is called *Blanchisseuse.* It means, in the local French patois, *washerwoman,* because that was the name the people gave to this woman living on top the mountain up above the village. Of course, they all knew that that was not she *real* name in truth. Because to this day nobody had ever found the courage to approach the woman sheself and ask her she name. It was the only name they knew her by, and so many long years that after a time the little village and the people theyselves came to be called by the same name too, that is to say, the village of Blanchisseuse.

She wasn't an oldwoman. Still, even the oldest oldmen in the village could never remember a time when she didn't live in the big estate house, perched high on top the mountain looking down over the village. Just how she came to own the house and all the many lands of the big estate nobody knew for sure. Some used to say how that estate was purchased by a wealthy Portugee planter from the King of Spain, because that was long before the English pirates arrived with they long blue beards, and they ships shooting off all the cannons. And so it happened that many years later—after Spain and England *both* began to lose interest in all these islands sinking down in the sea—when the price of sugar and cocoa beans fell, and the tradings away in Europe were already finished, that they say this Portugee planter abandoned he estate and picked up heself to go back home. Some used to say the woman was the mistress of this rich Portugee—she was very very beautiful in truth—and that is why he left the estate to her. They said she was waiting there in the big house for him to return to her from across the sea. But most people said she wasn't the mistress of the Portugee planter a-tall. She was he own outside child by a Yoruba slavewoman, and that is where she got the color of she skin, deep and rich liked burned saffron. Most said the Portugee planter did not *abandon* he estate, but that one day the woman decided to take it for sheself. They said that on the same morning of she thirteenth birthday—the very same morning the woman saw she first menses—

she murdered both she Portugee father and she Yoruba mother with two clean swipes of she cutlass across they throats.

She was a very tall woman. Some said as much as seven feet, but it was difficult to tell, because she always wore she hair piled in the tall jackspaniard-nest up on top she head. She was very particular about she clothes, always dressed head to foot only in white. A white kerchief tied up around she beehive-nest of hair, a white lace shawl draped over she shoulders. With she long white dress dragging behind in the Martinique style—layers upon layers of white frills rippling down she long neck, down over she ripe tot-tots, and down round she smooth, shapely bamsee—rippling from beneath she chin all the way down to she toes. On she feet she always wore white alpagats. And beneath the dress one confusion of starched white undergarments—camisoles, and corsets, and garters and such—and so many starched crinoline petticoats, that they said she dress would have stood up in the corner without her inside. So many starched white petticoats that on still mornings you could hear the soft rustlings of she footsteps all the way down below in the village, rustling louder and louder until at last the *swoosh!* sucking the air behind her like a tall seawave, one by one as she walked past each of the little board houses of the village. Nobody never saw her dressed in any other way, and nobody never saw her without she cutlass neither. She used to wear it tucked beneath the hair, shoved front to back at the base of the tall jackspaniard-nest, with the handle of purpleheart wood protruding out in front above she forehead, and the long silver blade poking out behind.

Early every morning she would descend from the house up on top the hill, the big bundle of laundry tied up in a white sheet toting on top she head. Back and forth and back and forth along the trace cut out from the side of the mountain, sometimes passing for a second behind a huge immortelle tree covered in blossoms of bright orange, or a tall poui bursting out only in pink. Sometimes disappearing for a moment inside a cottonwool cloud that had drifted in off the sea to lie lazy against the flanks of the mountain—then all in a sudden appearing from out the cloud with a *woosh!* on the other side—back and forth and back and forth until after long last, she arrived at the banks of the river down below.

And the first thing she would do there was to take off all she clothes. She would put down the big bundle of she laundry balanced on top she head, the thatch picnic basket hanging from the bend of she arm, packed full with fruits that she would eat for she lunch. Now, very slow and careful, garment by garment by garment, she would strip sheself down to nothing but the skin of she birth. First the white bodice, one by one unfastening the bright mother-of-pearl buttons following along she spine before she would unclasp the long frilly skirt. Next, one by one, she would pull the thin lace camisoles up over she ripe tot-tots—the breeze could blow fresh and cool cool up at the top of that mountain, you know?—up over she beehive-nest of hair. Then, after long last—the moment they had all been waiting patiently to arrive—she would twist she slender arms behind she back, and she would unclasp the delicate lace brassiere. Sweet heart of Jesus! One by one, very slow and careful, she would expose to the morning air giggling before them, the perfection of she burned saffron tot-tots. First she would take out the right one and then, very careful, the left. And Johnny, those tot-tots were so exquisite—so smooth, and soft, and delicate giggling before them in the bright morning sun—they all knew that after that first, dizzying moment, never in they lives would the air taste so sweet again!

Now, one by one, she would step from out the crispy crinoline petticoats. She would unclasp the corsets, the garters, untie the white ribbons of she alpagats bowtied around she ankles. Now she would roll the fine silk stockings down along the smooth slender thighs. Very slow and careful, every twist, every stretch, until after long last—with one last suffocating gasp of air—she would slip down along she long legs the whisper of she little lace panties. *Everything!* Every last ruffling, and lace, and silky white garment, leaving nothing a-tall but the cutlass tucked beneath she hair. Until at last she stood before them naked naked. Dressed in nothing but the splendor of she burned saffron skin.

Because of course, just as you have already surmised, every manjack and womanjill too had gathered there by the river secretly to watch her. All hiding behind the bushes and the boulderstones, all hanging like monkeys peering from out the tops of all the trees—all there assembled like a band of bobolees with they eyes opened wide wide and they long red tongues dripping down—only to watch at this woman undressing sheself. And Johnny, by the time she reached to the last crinoline petticoat, by the time she finished with the last white gasp of she little lace panties, by then she had them all *bassodee.* Every oldman and oldwoman, every google-eye little schoolboy and schoolgirl just the same. In truth, the spectacle of watching this woman strip sheself down was so strenuous—so exciting, and exhausting, and so *painful*—many of those villagers realized that they would never satisfy that itch prickling beneath they skins never again. The vision of so much excruciating beauty had ruined they lives forever, and after that first delightful, terrible experience, they vowed never again to return to the banks of that river.

But just as you would suppose too, the majority of those wajanks went running crab-o-in-hand every morning of life. They just couldn't hold theyselves back. Just couldn't keep away. And no matter *how* many times they swore that the next morning they were *not* going back to that river—only putting goatmouth loud on theyselves each time they said it like poor Hax the butcher—of course, soon as the next morning arrived, it was always just the same. Because next morning, first thing, soon as they jumped out the bed—before they crab-os could even go down a little bit to give them a chance to make they first wee-wee—they were already hurrying behind it. Following it like the divining rod poking out trembling before them, *straight* for the banks of that river. All dodging behind a rockcliff or a treetrunk, ducking beneath the banyans of a mangrove bush—and again, just as you have already discerned—no sooner could this woman arrive to begin taking off all she clothes, when they had already started up doing on theyselves every *thinkable* kind of nastiness behind them bushes.

Because the truth, if you want to know about all these wajanks strutting around the place each one like the cock-of-the-walk heself, the truth is that not a one of these men had ever even found the courage to approach her. Most of them were too weak in they knees anyway—by the time this woman was already to take she bath—to manage nothing more than to scrub up theyselves to the final fistful of froth. But Johnny, the main reason wasn't they lack of intentions, trembling up the lengths of they stiff limbs. It wasn't they lack of enthusiasm, ready to burst at the tips of they busy fingers. Not so a-tall! They main reason was *fear.* They all believed that this Blanchisseuse was an obeahwoman—or worse still a sukuyant, a lagahoo, or a diabless—and no man in he right head would tangle heself up with none of that! They all knew good enough that the smoothness of she ripe bamsee—the intoxication of each little nip of she jiggling, burnished gold tot-tots—was only the inkling as to what she evil powers could do. But even more than *any* of that, the thing those wa-janks feared most of all, was nothing more than the cutlass tucked beneath she jackspaniard-nest of hair.

From the time each of them was a little boy, they mummies had warned them all with the story of Hax the butcher. Poor Hax, who got heself in that terrible practice of hurrying back from the river to he shop every morning, only to relieve heself on a defenseless bettygoat, or a soft woolly sheep, or the unsuspecting she-calf tethered quiet in the corner. And of course, soon as he could manage to satisfy heself—in the great frustration mounting beneath he leather apron since early morning—he would grab for the big butcher knife waiting there on the counter, and he would slit the throat of the poor animal to carve her merciless up.

One morning Hax lost control of he senses, even before the woman reached to she first alpagat. He jumped out from behind the oleander bush, he face as pink as those same flowers behind his back, crab-o standing up stiff like a standpipe before him. But poor Hax never even had a chance to stumble a second step. The woman slipped she cutlass out from beneath the beehive-nest of hair, and with little more than a flick of she slender wrist, she swiped he standpipe off clean at the base!

Hax let loose a bugle-eye bawl to wake the dead. He took off running in a bolt, blood spraying out in every direction. With all he worthless companions in crime doing nothing more of course than jumping out bush after bush as he staggered past, only to escape the shower from poor Hax's amputation. But even before Hax could reach to the safety of he shop, he fell down face-first in the middle of the trace, dead in the pool of he own terrible misfortune. That night, beneath the torchlight of a midnight vigil, the villagers buried him there on the banks of the same river. And early some mornings, even before the first of the villagers arrive at the banks of that river, you can see him still. To this very day. Still crawling around like a newborn babe on he hands and knees—but with the same sad, oldman's sigh dragging down he face—still searching in the weeds beneath he oleander bush, two hairy huevos and a cornstarch-plaster stuck up between he legs.

First thing, once she had stripped down naked, the woman would bathe sheself. She would enter the tranquil water up to she knees, and using half of a calabash shell she would dip the water out to pour it over she shoulders. With a block of soap that she had made from coconutoil and sandalwood fragrance, she would soap sheself down very careful, rinsing after with the calabash. Now she would move out deeper into the water until it reached to the middle of she thighs. She would slip the cutlass out from beneath the jackspaniard-nest, put it to hold between she teeth clenched tight together, and she would let loose all she nest of hair to wash it out. Sweet heart of Jesus! Johnny, every time she bent over graceful to rinse out she hair, every time she raised up those two perfect half-moons of she bamsee tall in the air—with she *pussy* of course half-exposed too, winking out from between she burned saffron cheeks at all those youngboys, all with they chickenbone-necks stretching farther and farther only in hopes of catching a single *glimpse*—every morning, without fail, one or two of those youngboys would drop down *ploops!* to the ground in a dead faint.

When she finished rinsing she hair good and proper, she would wring it out and tie it up again in the nest on top. She would slip the cutlass back in its place beneath. Now she would climb out the river and begin all the washing. But she wouldn't dress sheself back straight away. Because those same clothes she had just finished taking off, were just the ones she would take up to wash out first. She would soap them all down with the coconut-sandalwood soap, every garment very careful, and she would leave the soapy-up clothes to soak in a pool cut out from the rocks. Now she would untie the bundle of laundry, and she would soap down the sheets and towels and all the linens, everything a pure white just like she clothes. Now she would begin the labor of beating out all the washing against the rocks, piece by piece, raising up a petticoat or a camisole or a frilly lace bodice above she head, and she would bring it down with a hard *tha-wack* against the rocks. And since everything was pure white, it would require plenty *tha-wacking* and soaking and rinsing and *tha-wacking* against the rocks again, before it was clean enough to satisfy this woman.

By now of course most of the oldmen and youngboys had satisfied theyselves too—the women and girls had wandered off long before—and now, slow but sure, most of them had left the river to go about they business. Home to they breakfast or off to school, the men to they fishing boats or out to the canefields, or whatever else it was they did for they livelihood. Even the local borachos had stolen off by now, gone to the parlor to fire-back they first chupitos of rum. Then again there was always a handful who still couldn't find the conviction of they stiff limbs to carry theyselves away. The sight of this woman beating out she clothes, the vision of she beautiful tot-tots—yellow-gold dangling before them like two ripe zabuca-pears, only the plucking of they arm's reach away—was still too tantalizing for them to turn they backs. They could only remain there crouching behind a stinging-suzie tree, or peering out from between the branches of a simple-simon bush, the pacing of they breaths and the poundings in they chests, the scrubbings up and down of they thin wrists synchronized by the rise and fall of a soapy white camisole against the rocks.

By the time she had soaped and scrubbed and beaten out all the washing, by the time she had spread everything in the sun to dry—each garment arranged careful on the grass, spread over a bush, or hanging from the limbs of a tree—by then even the last of those youngboys and oldmen had stolen theyselves reluctant away. Now the woman would take up she picnic-basket with all the fruits, she would wade up the river, and she would climb out on the big white boulderstone shaped like the egg of an ostrich. Above the boulderstone was the leafy bois-cano to provide a cool shade, and there the woman would sit to eat she lunch: a pawpaw, or a ripe mammy-sapote fruit. A hand of sweet-plantains, or little sicreyea-bananas, or soft silk-figs. A few portugals, dillies, julie-mangoes or eden or doudou. Sugarapples, guavas, caimets, or whatever else was in season and bearing on the trees of she estate up at the top of the mountain. And after she had finished she lunch she would lie back quiet awhile, beneath the cool shade of the bois-cano, reclining on she big ostrich egg. Then, every afternoon, after she had finished she nap, she would sit up slow to stretch sheself awake, and she would begin to sing. Very soft and gentle, a melody sweet as those same little sicreyeas of she lunch. And every day too, soon as she would begin to sing, Crab-o would crawl out slow from he hole beneath the rock. He would sit there with he head raised up tall, because of course in those days Crab-o—no different from all the other animals, the reptiles and fishes and crustaceans and so on—Crab-o still had he head sure enough. So with a dreamy smile on he face, he would sit there on the rock to listen the woman sing:

Yan-killi-ma
Kutti-gu-ma
Yan-killi-ma
Nag-wa-kitti

Of course by now it was early afternoon, and all the villagers had left the banks of the river to go back home. So there was no one but Crab-o to hear the woman sing. Even so no one of the village could have said what was the meaning of those words of she song. Because in truth, that song was passed down to the woman from she mummy when she was only a child. Those words came from the old Yoruba tongue, and not even the oldest grandmothers of the village could remember that language scarce a-tall. Blanchisseuse didn't even understand the precise meaning of those words of she song *sheself.* In truth, it was only Crab-o, who would crawl out from he hole every afternoon without fail to watch the woman and listen, who had at last come to decipher the meaning of she words. But fortunate enough for Crab-o, the melody of the woman's song was so beautiful—so much like a sweet, restful dream—he could sit and listen again and again without tiring. Even though the meaning of the words—which only Crab-o had come to understand—the meaning was not so beautiful a-tall:

You will kill me
My love
You will kill me
My beautiful one

So Crab-o knew, not only what the words of she song meant, but also that he must never come too close to this woman. Never must he come within range of she quick-slicing cutlass. Yet the melody of she song was too beautiful for Crab-o to remain hidden inside he hole. So every afternoon when the woman would carry she picnic-basket to the big egg-shaped boulderstone beneath the bois-cano, Crab-o would crawl out from he hole to watch her and listen. But only close enough that he could hear the words of she beautiful, horrible song.

By the time she waded back down the river to the place where she had left the washing it would all be dry on the one side. Now, very careful, she would turn all the garments, the sheets and towels and all the linens. And in truth there was such a quantity of laundry that by the time she could finish turning them over, the first ones would be crispy and dry on the other side too. Now she would fold up all the washing very careful. The white linen tablecloths, the white crocheted mantles for all the side-boards, the coverlets, and blankets, and pillowcases for all the many beds of the big house. And she would tie up everything together in a huge bundle in the white sheet. Now she would dress sheself back in all the clean white garments, the camisoles, the petticoats, the long Martinique dress dragging behind with all the frills. Until at last she had rolled up and clipped into place again in the garters she soft silk stockings, and she had bowtied again the ribbons on both she white alpagats. Now she would hoist the big bundle up on top she head, take up the empty picnic-basket hanging from the bend of she elbow, and she could begin she long, slow journey back and forth and back and forth along the path cut out in the side of the hill. Until at long last, with the sun just disappearing behind the back of the mountain, the woman would reach she estate at the very top.

And so time passed. Year after year it was just the same, until one day a tragedy befell the little Hindu girl of the village. She name was Moyen. And of all the many little girls of the village, Moyen was the most pure, and innocent, and the most beautiful of all the rest. She was tall and thin with big dark eyes, and rich masala skin, and she long black hair reaching in a single thick braid all the way down below she waist. This Moyen had only reached to she thirteenth year—no older than *you* sitting there in you schoolboy-shortpants—when one fateful day she lost both she mummy and she daddy in a distressing accident. Moyen's daddy was up high in a tall coconut palm picking the nuts and throwing them down to she mummy collecting them below. All in a sudden the belt made from lianas that passed around he waist and the trunk of the palm burst, and poor Moyen's daddy fell to the hard ground below. He was dead the same instant. But Johnny, this was only the first half of this terrible tragedy. Because Moyen's mummy was so distressed now by the death of she husband, that she took away he sharp cutlass still clutching tight in the grip of he hand, and she passed the blade in a single quick slice across she throat!

So now the people of the village had to look after this little orphan-child Moyen. They gave her all the care and devotion that they could afford, even sharing with her what little food they had for theyselves and they own children. Because Johnny, this little village hidden away behind Papa God's back—despite all the beauty of those green mountains, and the river, and the blue Caribbean Sea—this Blanchisseuse wasn't no different from all the other little villages of the island. Just like all the rest the people of Blanchisseuse suffered from poverty too, and plenty hardship, struggling they best only to survive. Soon Moyen came to realize that in a village of so many hungry children, there was no room for an orphan-child like her. Moyen decided that she must find *some* way to care for sheself and provide for she own food and shelter. That is when she thought up the idea to go and speak with the woman living in she big estate up at the top of the mountain. Because of course, this woman is all alone in the huge house, and she had all those trees laden with fruits of every kind that you could ever dream, with only her to eat them. Moyen made up she mind that despite the consequences of that cutlass tucked beneath she jackspaniard-nest, she must go and speak with her, and beg the woman to teach her to do the washing. In this way Moyen could exchange she labors for a place to live, and of course, some of those fruits only waiting on the trees to eat.

But just like all the people of the village Moyen was terrified to confront this tall woman with she legendary cutlass. No one had ever dared to approach her before. Not in all the long history of the village—with only the one exception—and of course, everybody knew what happened to him. In truth, no one before had even mounted up the courage sufficient to mumble a quick "bon-dia" to this woman, and no one could say what might be she response. But after only a few weeks Moyen had grown so hungry, so miserable, and sad, and so distressed—that Moyen realized she didn't have no choice a-tall. And that same evening, with she belly grumbling after several days with scarce anything to eat—as soon as Moyen saw the woman begin to climb the trace leading up to she house, the big bundle of laundry toting as always up on top she head—Moyen went following behind her. She didn't even know if the woman was aware that she was following behind. Not until they reached to the very top of the mountain, just there at the entrance to the tall iron gates. All in a sudden the woman turned around, so quick that Moyen almost bounced her up! She stood there staring down at the child from beneath she big bundle, she hands poised on she hips and a vex look on she face, with little Moyen only cowering below in the cold dark shadow of this woman.

"Eh-eh!" she said. "What is it you following behind me for, child?"

Moyen could only look down at the ground at she dusty feet. She could only take in a deep breath, and mumble what it was she wanted.

The woman didn't answer for a long time. And the longer she waited, of course, the more terrified Moyen began to feel. She skinny arms and legs were trembling, when at last the woman took the bundle down from off she head. She let it drop to the ground with a loud *poof!* and a giant exhale of dust at little Moyen's feet.

"Take it up!" she said in a harsh voice. "I going to teach you to wash the clothes, and I going to give you a place to sleep."

Now the woman paused again. She slipped the bright cutlass out from beneath she jackspaniard-nest of hair, the empty picnic-basket dangling still from the bend of she other arm. Little Moyen could only take a step backward—she was ready to turn around quick and pelt back down the hill as fast as she could run—but the woman only raised she cutlass slowly up in the air. She pointed it up at the top of the big mango tree above they heads, the very limbs of the tree straining and ready to break for the quantity of fat eden-mangoes dangling from each of the branches.

"You can eat all the mangoes you want from this tree," the woman told her. "But you can't eat the fruit of *any* other tree on this estate!" The woman paused again. "That is," she said, "until you can guess my name. Every evening, when we reach to the entrance of this gate, I will give you three chances."

A smile burst out quick quick on little Moyen's face, stretching one ear all the way to the next! Now she could dare to raise she head and look into the eyes of this woman.

"*Blanchisseuse!*" she said in a loud voice.

Now it was the woman who smiled for the first time. "That is the name of the village," she said. "It is what the people call me. But it ain't *my* name!"

Moyen looked down at she feet again. And after a few deep breaths, she ventured a next guess.

"Miss April?"

"No!"

"Miss Betty-Lou?"

"No!" she said, smiling still, and she slipped the cutlass again beneath she jackspaniard-nest of hair. The woman turned around, the empty picnic-basket hanging from one elbow with she arms cocked and resting against she hips, the ruffles of she Martinique dress dragging in the dust behind, and she walked down the long entrance to the house. Leaving Moyen there to struggle and strain with all she strength, only to hoist this bundle of washing up on top she head. At first Moyen took three dangerous steps backward—almost tumbling down over the side of the cliff behind her—before she could steady sheself, and she went stumbling after the woman.

Now Moyen put away all the folded-up linens inside the tall cedar presses, she made back the big bed of this woman with the fresh-laundered sheets, the white wool blanket and a fresh white coverlet, and then all the many other beds of the big house, before she began to cover the side tables with they white crocheted mantles. And only after she had set the diningroom table with the clean white tablecloth, positioned all the porcelains, the crystal glasses and all the silvers—each setting with a clean white serviette—after all that, the woman at last led Moyen to the back of the house to show the child she room. Only a tiny bedroom no bigger than one of the closets of the big house, without even a window to look out from, a little iron cot in the corner covered over with a prickly coconut-fiber mattress. That room had belonged to one of the slaves of the old estate, long long before in the time of great prosperity. But Moyen didn't even pause to contemplate the wretchedness of she little room.

She didn't even waste time to sit on the cot a moment to rest sheself. As soon as the woman turned to leave, Moyen took off hurrying out the back door of the kitchen, hurrying around the house in the direction of that mango tree in the front yard. Poor little Moyen was famished in truth! And of all the many fruits on the big estate—all those sour-sweet king-oranges, and portugals, all the sweet pawpaws and all the rest—mangoes were the fruit Moyen loved to eat the most! Even if she could have had she choice of whatever of the fruits she wanted, Moyen knew good enough that those juicy eden-mangoes were just the fruit that she would have chosen. In addition, that mango tree seemed to have more fruits hanging from each of its branches than all the other trees of the estate together.

First thing Moyen grabbed up two rockstones, and she pelted them one after the next up at the tree. And Johnny, that tree was so laden with fruits that in two seconds she was holding in she hands two of the fattest, prettiest mangoes you have ever dreamed of in all you life! Moyen bit into one straight away, ripping off the rosy skin in a long strip between she teeth. Now she bit and bit and bit into the smooth orange flesh—not even stopping to worry about the juice dribbling down she throat, and neck, and soaking up in all she coarse crocusssack-dress—with she budding little tot-tots poking out beneath. On the contrary, Moyen took the greatest of pleasures in all that sweet sticky juice, bathing sheself down with it, biting and chewing and swallowing in such a great haste she scarce even gave sheself a chance to breathe. And after she devoured the flesh of those two mangoes, she sucked and sucked on the two oval-shaped seeds until they were nothing but a hairy kneecap-bone, tucked beneath each of she puffed-up cheeks. Moyen didn't waste no time to pelt more rockstones. Now she climbed up quick to the top of that mango tree, and she began to shake and shake with all she strength. And Johnny, little Moyen didn't pause from she shaking before the ground beneath the tree was covered over with twenty or thirty big juicy mangoes!

Moyen hurried back inside the house, she took up the small paring knife from the top drawer inside the kitchen, and she returned to the tree. After collecting up all those rosy mangoes in a neat pile like the vendors in Victoria market, all they fruits on display, Moyen sat sheself comfortable beneath the tree, leaning she back against the smooth trunk. Now little Moyen began to suck mangoes in truth! Now Moyen began, one by one, to cut off the fat mango cheeks at each side of the flat seeds. She would hold one of a cheeks like a small bowl in the palm of she hand, and she would slice a neat checkerboard pattern in the smooth, orange flesh. Now she would push up the cheek inside-out, with a star of perfect mango cubes protruding from the curl of skin. Now Moyen started to bite them off one by one—each perfect cube as sweet as a cube of sugar—swallowing them down and taking the greatest of pleasures in every juicy bite. And when she finished with each pair of cheeks, Moyen sucked the oval seeds until she had sucked them dry.

After five or six of those big eden-mangoes Moyen had reached she limit. Still, she continued slicing off more cheeks. She continued criss-crossing the orange flesh, turning the rosy cheeks inside-out and biting off the cubes of flesh, until she had consumed the entire pale of mangoes. Sweet heart of Jesus! It had been so long since Moyen had eaten anything a-tall—so many days that she stomach had remained empty empty—in no time a-tall that first pile of mangoes was reduced to nothing more than a heap of rosy curls of mango skins, and a little graveyard of hairy kneecap-bones. And even though Moyen was plenty satisfied by now, she climbed up in the tree to shake down twenty or thirty more mangoes.

All in a sudden Moyen realized she wasn't feeling too good *a-tall.* The poor child's stomach was so full—so bloat-o with all those big lovely mangoes—that Moyen began to fear she belly might burst in truth. It was all she could manage to pull sheself up to she feet and stumble to the side of the cliff, just beyond the entrance to the tall gates. Not until she began to vomit over the side of the cliff, could the child feel any relief a-tall. And poor Moyen continued to vomit and vomit until she emptied out she stomach of every one of those mangoes she had just taken such a great pleasure in filling it up. Moyen felt so weak after all that vomiting, she only had the strength remaining to drag sheself back to she little coconut-fiber mattress—the woman didn't even give her one of the clean white sheets to cover it over—and little Moyen drifted off slowly to sleep, mumbling a curse that *never* again would she eat another mango in all she life!

Next morning, even before the sun could rise, the woman was there at she bedside shaking Moyen awake. The child was still very sick—so weak and dizzy she could scarcely stand on she trembling toothpick-legs to lift she crocusssack-dress up above she head—but the woman made Moyen strip the beds of all the sheets and coverlets and blankets just the same. She made Moyen strip the diningroom table of the big white cloth and all the serviettes, the white crocheted mantles on each of the presses and sideboards, and Moyen tied up everything in the huge white bundle. The woman watched as little Moyen struggled to hoist it up on top she head—not even offering the child a hand to assist her—with Moyen following as best she could toting the bundle behind. Back and forth and back and forth along the trace cut out in the side of the mountain, until at last they arrived at the banks of the river.

Like a little acolyte attending the Dame Lorraine Bishop heself, little Moyen assisted the woman to strip off all she clothes. Standing on the tips of she toes to unbutton each of the shiny mother-of-pearl buttons, Moyen helped her off with the frilly Martinique dress, all the stiff crinoline petticoats one by one, the lace camisoles. She unclasped the corset, unclipped the garters, and she knelt in the grass at the feet of this woman to untie the silk ribbons of she alpagats, one slender ankle and then the next. And Johnny, when at last she stood before Moyen stripped down naked, even she was overwhelmed by the beauty of this woman. Now Moyen sat in the cool grass to watch the woman bathe sheself. Because in truth, even though she was all sticky-up from that mango juice on she skin, she crocusssack-dress stiff and scratchy and so uncomfortable, she was too tired to bathe sheself beside the woman. Too weak from all that vomiting of the previous evening, and too exhausted after that long walk down the mountain toting all that laundry. Moyen could only rest sheself a quiet moment while she had the chance. Because in no time a-tall the woman was climbing out the river again, and now she began the lessons of how to wash the clothes.

The woman instructed Moyen how to soap-down everything with the coconut-sandalwood soap, very careful and patient, garment by garment by garment. How to soak the clothes in the pool cut from the rocks, how to rinse them out. The woman instructed Moyen how to beat all the laundry, *tha-wack tha-wack tha-wack* against the rocks, before she showed Moyen how to spread everything on the bushes to dry.

Now the woman took up she picnic-basket, she selected two ripe eden-mangoes to give Moyen, and she left her there with all the laundry to turn them over as soon as the top side was dry. By this time of course Moyen was so tired that all she wanted in the world was to close she eyes a second and rest sheself. And she *would* have too if only she'd been able, because those two eden-mangoes were calling out to her so loud and boisterous, she could never even close she eyes for the stretch of a minute. Just the thought of that sticky, too-sweet orange flesh made she stomach turn inside-out nauseous again. But poor little Moyen was so hungry she could think of nothing else. She could only sit there in the grass staring at these two juicy mangoes holding in each of she hands, and after a time Moyen began to feel so sad and so desperate that she began to cry. At last she decided to take just one little bite—just *one*—and she ripped off a strip of the rosy skin, swallowing down a mouthful of the dripping flesh.

Of course, after that first taste Moyen could never hold sheself back. She began to chew and suck and swallow as fast as she could manage, the juice dripping down she neck over she budding tot-tots, one fat mango and then the next. And of course, no sooner had all that too-sweet mango flesh filled up Moyen's little stomach, when she began to feel sick again, and it was all she could managed to crawl on she hands and knees to the side of the river, and vomit it all straight back up. Fortunate for Moyen the egg-shaped boulderstone of this woman was up river from where she vomited the mangoes instead of down—because there was no way to know how the woman would reprimand her if she saw all that nastiness floating past—and Moyen lay on she back on the cool grass beside the river. Dizzy and weak and so miserable, and at last she closed she eyes to cry sheself asleep.

But the woman appeared in no time a-tall to reprimand her anyway, not for all the vomit, because she gave Moyen a proper cursing when she found all the laundry already dry on the one side. Now Moyen hurried to turn all the clothes, and when everything was crispy and dry, she helped the woman to fold it up. All the pillowcases and sheets and coverlets, the big white tablecloth and all the serviettes, and Moyen tied it all together in the big bundle. Now Moyen attended the woman to dress sheself, garment by garment, and she hurried to hoist the bundle up on top she head, stumbling behind the woman. Only when they reached to the very top of the mountain, there before the tall iron gates at the entrance to that estate, did the woman turn around to address her again.

"Well Moyen," she said, "you are getting thinner! Tell me what is my name?"

Moyen could only stare down at the ground at she dusty feet. "Miss Clementina?" she questioned.

"No!"

"Miss Dorothy?"

"No!"

"Miss Elizabeth-May?"

"No!"

The woman smiled again, she two hands poised on she hips, and she turned around again to walk in the direction of the big house.

Every evening it was the very same thing, the moment they reached to the tall rusty gates:

"What is my name, Moyen? You are getting *thinner!*"

"Miss Josephine?"

"No!"

"Miss Mary?"

"No!"

"Miss Rosita?"

"No!"

And Moyen would look up at all those lovely, sickening eden-mangoes dangling from the tree just behind the gates. She would shake she head, and she would go to she bed hungry again.

Soon Moyen had learned to wash the clothes every bit as well as the woman. She was just as careful, and she took the same pains with all the soaping and rinsing and the beating against the rocks. Now the woman had nothing to do a-tall, once she had bathed sheself and rubbed she skin to glistening with the coconutoil, nothing but sit beneath the yellow poui beside the river and observe Moyen going about she labors. Soon the woman became so bored with sheself in truth—sitting there only waiting for lunch to come so she could wade up the river to she egg-shaped boulderstone—she decided to take the first of she lovers.

She pondered about it the whole night long, and the next morning, as Moyen followed behind her toting the bundle of laundry—just as they were passing the last little board house of the village—the woman paused for a moment, and she entered into the shop of Mr Chan the Chinee grocer. She slipped she cutlass out from beneath the jackspaniard-nest of hair, and she pointed it down at Mr Chan, sitting there on he little cedar-wood stool behind the counter. Mr Chan was at that very moment handing over a package of saltprunes he had just finished ringing on the register for Mistress Myrtle, but he jumped up straight away just the same. Mr Chan didn't even pause to lock the door of he grocery behind him! He took off hurrying before Moyen and the woman along the trace—with a little assistance from the sharp cutlass poking every few steps in he skinny yellow bamsee—*straight* to the banks of the river. Only when they arrived did Mr Chan realize he was still clutching the cellophane package of saltprunes in he trembling hands. These he began now to eat—one after the next in a great hurry—because that was the only way he could think to calm he nerves, while Moyen assisted the woman to take off she clothes. And Mr Chan was still sucking the last of those saltprunes when the woman ascended the bank of the river again after she bath. Now, while Moyen busied sheself with all the washing, the woman directed Mr Chan to a private place beneath the huge banyan tree. There in a gully of moist leafy ferns, in the privacy beneath that banyan tree, the woman exercised Mr Chan until it was time for lunch, and there wasn't a *single* jook remaining in he hard yellow bamsee! Of course, those three or four wajanks fortunate enough to find theyselves hiding up at the top of that same banyan, were so distracted by this bird's-eye view of all the pumping, and thumping, and boisterous harumping going on below in the gully of soft ferns, that it was all they could manage to hang on tight with they left hand—while still taking good advantage of they right—and not tumble out the tree *bo-doops* flat on top them!

The following morning, a Tuesday, the woman stopped at the house of Pierre the French tobacco-planter. Wednesday morning was Ram-sol the Hindu roti-man. And Thursday morning was Orinoco, the Amerindian hunter from the rain-forests of Venezuela. Every day the woman chose a different race and ancestry, a different color of skin and texture of hair and scent beneath he arms, so as never to become bored with sheself again, waiting beside the river for Moyen to finish the washing. And of course, just as you have already supposed, at the end of the week, early on that Sunday morning, the woman didn't have *no* choice remaining but to slip she cutlass out from beneath she jackspaniard-nest of hair, and point it down at Ernesto, the Yankee tourist from the windy plains of Illinois. This Ernesto was an adventurer, a collector of all kinds of wild specimens from the tropical forest. So he had brought with him he net, he tin of mosquito-spray and he tall rubber boots—he big magnifying glass and he bottle full to the brim with sugarcubes—only in hopes of capturing for heself the very rare blue-murmerer mariposa, and so to complete he collection. At least, that was he *intentions.* Until that fateful Sunday morning, when the woman waylaid Ernesto from he bright mariposas.

Of course, what the woman appreciated most about all she vast variety of lovers wasn't only the range and shape and size of they crab-os—that would be obvious enough—but in addition, she took a very keen interest in the particular *verbal* response each of them made at the moment of he greatest excitement. Because besides being what is sometimes referred to in the islands as a "backyard-scientist," this woman was also a little bit of an apprentice *linguist* on top. So with all the dedication and control of a careful scientific investigation, she set sheself to discover the precise correlation between the two.

For example, Mr Chan the Chinese grocer. He had, just as you would expect, a corkscrew crab-o. And at the moment of he profound excitement he would bawl out a cry like a kung-fu fighter letting loose a series of chops:

ha-chong! ha-chong! ha-chong!

Felix the African fisherman, by contrast, had the most healthy specimen of them all. He crab-o would stand up tall and thick and very proud, and at the moment of he climax, he would let loose a series of deep solemn drumbeats. Just like he is back at home beating out a message on he conga:

bom! bom! bom! bom!

Clifton the English merchant, on the other hand, had a crab-o that curved hard to the right, and at the precise moment of *he* orgasm, he would begin to giggle uncontrollable. Whereas Pierre the Frenchman curved radical to the left, and of course, at the moment of he supreme passion he would begin very sentimental to weep. Ram-sol the Hindu roti-man had a long thin crab-o reaching down between he knees, unless of course it was standing up almost to touch he nose, and he would let loose a deep

ommmmm!

just at the appropriate moment. Salman the Muslim of course had a crab-o much the same—except not so extreme in the length nor meager in circumference—and just as you would expect, he would always offer up he prayer of thanksgiving:

ah-lah! ah-lah! ah-lah!

Orinoco the Amerindian hunter had a short thick crab-o with a wide girth like the ones you see in the paintings of Las Casas and the Spanish Captains, and at the height of he profound passion, he would let loose a bawl like a Warrahoon spying a quenk:

ay-ay-ay-ay-ay!

But the Yankee tourist from the windy plains of Illinois, this Ernesto, he had the saddest little crab-o of them all. Neither was it corkscrew, nor curving, nor short-and-thick nor tall-and-long. Neither was it pudgy, nor pickle-shaped, nor with a pointy head nor even a flat. On the contrary, the crab-o of this Ernesto was short and squat and very *scrawny*-looking, and to tell the truth, it put you very much in mind of the eraser end of a pencil. But this wasn't even the most peculiar trait of Ernesto the mariposa-collector. The funniest thing—and just the opposite of anything that you would expect—was that when *he* reached to the moment of he extreme excitement, instead of keeping he mouth shut considering especially the proportions of he little business, he would make more noise than all the rest together. And in the midst of a restful, peaceful Sunday morning! So much noise and confusion that the first time she heard it, the woman was afraid he had burst the little purple vein at the side of the pencil-eraser. Just at the profound instant, just when you would expect him to hold he tongue, Ernesto would start up singing at the top of he voice—even to drown out all the hallelujahs of Jehovah the Almighty Conquerer just up the road—singing loud and patriotic for all the world to hear:

God bless A-mer-i-ca!
Land that I love!
Stand beside her!
And guide her!

and so on and so forth until the woman had no choice a-tall but to quick scrape off a handful of moss from the bottom of the boulderstone beside her, and to stuff it inside he mouth!

Meantime poor little Moyen had scarce any chance to listen to all this singing. All this dramatic conga-beating, and praise-giving, and all the rest that was the pleasures of this woman, and she scientific-linguistic investigations. Moyen was much too busy beside the river struggling with all the clothes. And even if she *could* have listened with half-an-ear to all this confusion, she was far too distracted by the loud grumbling inside she own belly. All the time that Moyen was busy washing and *tha-wacking* and fussing over all the laundry, she could think of nothing more than all those fruits on the estate that the woman wouldn't permit her to eat. All those pom-see-tays and pomeracs and barbadines. All the grape-fruits and caimets and pinefruits, and on and on until she could no longer bear the pain in she belly, and she would begin again to cry. And it was late one afternoon, when she had finished scrubbing the clothes and spreading them all out on the grass—and she was waiting for them to dry with the woman and Mr Chan making every kind of obscene kung-fu chop in the gully with all the ferns—that Moyen became so sad and distressed, she began to wade up the river to escape all that terrible *ha-chung! ha-chung! ha-chung!*

Moyen climbed up to rest sheself on the big white boulderstone in the shape of an ostrich-egg, cool beneath the shade of the bois-cano. Of course, no sooner had she sat sheself down when Crab-o appeared, side-stepping from out the hole beneath the rock. He sat there watching up at Moyen, and after a time he realized that this poor little girl was weeping. And of course, being as sensitive and tender of feelings as Crab-o was, in no time a-tall *he* started up weeping just the same. So there the two of them sat, tears rolling down they cheeks, until at last Crab-o raised he voice.

"Why are you crying little girl?" he asked her.

Moyen, of course, paid him no mind a-tall, knowing good enough—even in all she innocence—that crab-os can do plenty plenty things, but they can *never* talk.

"Tell me what is the matter," he said again. And this time Moyen realized that it *was* Crab-o, in truth, who had spoken.

"Oh Crab-o," Moyen sighed, "you know the woman living in the big house up on top the mountain?" And Crab-o nodded he head. "Well, she won't give me none of the fruits of the estate unless I can guess she name, and I don't know she name, Crab-o. *Nobody* knows she name! I have asked in the village, I have asked all around, and nobody knows!"

Crab-o had already spied those two lovely eden-mangoes beside Moyen on the rock, because of course, that was *he* favorite fruit too. "So what about those mangoes?" he asked her.

"Oh," Moyen sighed again, "I can't eat no more mangoes! That is the only fruit the woman would let me eat, and I have eaten *so* many mangoes I feel to die!"

"Well," Crab-o said, sniffing still. "You can dry you tears little girl. Because *I* will tell you the woman's name. But you can *never* tell her where you heard it from," Crab-o warned. "And you must be very careful, you mustn't guess it straight away!"

Now it was Moyen who nodded she head, and she offered Crab-o the two rosy mangoes.

"She name," Crab-o said, raising he head up tall and smiling, "is *Yan-killi-ma, Kutti-gu-ma, Yan-killi-ma, Nag-wa-kitti.*"

So Moyen, smiling sheself now for the first time in weeks and weeks, jumped down from the rock and hurried sheself back down the river. And that evening, when they reached to the top of the mountain at the end of the day, just before the tall iron gates, the woman turned around to face her again:

"You are getting *thinner,* Moyen! Tell me what is my name?"

This time Moyen put down the bundle of clothes she was toting on top she head. She paused a long minute, and she scrunched up she pretty little face like if she was concentrating good and hard. Then at last she answered:

"Miss Ruthy?"

"No!"

Moyen paused again. "Miss Xena?"

"No!"

This time Moyen paused even longer. She shook she head again and again. At last she raised she big dark eyes to look up at the woman. "I know what it is," she said. "It's *Yan-killi-ma, Kutti-gu-ma, Yan-killi-ma, Nag-wa-kitti!*"

All in a sudden the smile disappeared from the woman's face. The burned saffron skin of she cheeks turned to a crimson brighter than those mangoes dangling from the tree above she head. All in a sudden the woman went vie-kee-vie in truth! She could never *believe* this child had guessed she name.

"I know who told you," she bawled. "I know who told you. *Crab-o* told you my name! *Crab-o* told you my name!"

And with that the woman pulled out the shiny cutlass from beneath she jackspaniard-nest—with Moyen thinking of course she was coming after *her,* ready to turn around quick and run for all she life—but the woman only passed her straight, continuing in a hurry on down the hill. Leaving Moyen there, of course, to eat any kind of fruit that she heart desired.

The woman walked all the way down to the banks of the river again. By this time twilight was just beginning to fall, turning the green river to a sheet of rippling gold. Crab-o had just finished consuming the very last morsel of sweet mango flesh. Because just like little Moyen, the first time *she* tasted those ripe juicy mangoes, Crab-o could never stop eating until he had eaten them both, he belly ready to burst. Now he heard the woman singing again, as she came wading up the river toward the egg-shaped stone:

Crab-o, Crab-o
Se-set-ou dit-ou
Ma-qua-nom!

This, of course, was the local patois that Crab-o could understand as good as any of us. The woman was saying that she knew perfectly well who had given away the name. So Crab-o was thinking to escape inside he hole first thing. But in truth he was feeling so full and lazy after eating those two huge mangoes, that he paused a moment to take a deep breath and gather up he strength. By the time Crab-o saw the flash of the woman's cutlass it was too late. Crab-o entered heself backwards inside he hole like he always did, but he was so big and bloated after eating so much mango, so fat and chuff-chuff, that no matter *how* hard he pushed and shoved and strained, he could never fit heself back inside he hole. Still, he pushed and he shoved and he strained, struggling with all he strength to squeeze heself back inside. And in truth Crab-o managed—all except for he head—protruding out from the top of the hole.

With one quick slice of she cutlass the woman chopped it off! It was too late for Crab-o, there wasn't nothing he could do, and he had lost he head forever.

So the story goes
Everyone knows
Headless Crab-o stayed
With only a back
Crick-crack!

But this story is not yet finished as you might believe. Because even that revenge on Crab-o could never satisfy the anger of this woman. She remained sitting up in she bed the whole night stewing, beating she fist against the pillow and cursing, and the next morning, a Monday morning, she was still in a terrible rage. Still vex and hot-up with sheself when Mr Chan appeared unsuspecting from behind he gru-gru bush, finishing off the last of he cellophane package of salt-prunes—he crab-o standing up tall in the air with a big smile on he face—ready for he day of adventures. But Johnny, there wasn't no smile on the face of this woman a-tall. She took only *one* look—and without even pausing to consider the consequences—she slipped she cutlass out from beneath she jackspaniard-nest. In one clean swipe the woman decapitated the head of *he* crab-o too! All that remained of poor Mr Chan's crab-o was the wrinkled skin at the end like a turtle-neck jersey, with no head remaining to poke out from the neck a-tall!

Of course, the anger of this woman still had not subsided by the following morning, a Tuesday, and she performed the same unsuspecting decapitation on Felix the African fisherman. The next day was Wednesday, and it was the beheading of the Englishman Clifton. Thursday morning was Pierre the Frenchman, Friday Ram-sol the Hindu roti-man, and Saturday of course was Orinoco the Amerindian hunter.

Even when Sunday morning arrived at the end of the week, the woman was still too vex to relax sheself. Ernesto the Yankee tourist appeared from behind he loveluck bush, wearing nothing a-tall but he tall rubber boots and a big smile on he face, he mariposa net and bottle of sugarcubes in each of he hands. The woman reached straight away for she cutlass, ready to perform the final beheading like all the rest. And she *would* have too—for a moment she even considered asking to borrow he magnifying glass so as to perform the operation proper—but the truth was that when she bent over to inspect he little pencil-eraser, poking out so sad between he two fuzzy quail eggs, something touched the heart of this woman. She realized, of course, that if she performed this final decapitation, poor Ernesto the mariposa-collector wouldn't have hardly nothing remaining of he little crab-o a-tall. It would be the same old story all over again of Hax the butcher, and in truth the woman could never live with that one on she conscience again.

Meantime Ernesto took only *one* glance at the face of this woman—not to mention she long silver cutlass raised high in the air, ready to swipe off its final decapitation—and he dropped he net and he glassbottle of sugarcubes, he knapsack and all he mariposa-catching equipment the same instant. Instead, he grabbed on with both hands clutching tight to the *real* prize—which was nothing other than he scrawny little crab-o—and he took off running to catch the first American Airlines flight, straight back to the windy plains of Illinois.

That, of course, was a fortunate thing for us too. Even though of *all* the crab-os in all the world, the Yankee one is the only crab-o with a head still poking out from its turtle-neck jersey. Because despite that Ernesto didn't return to Illinois with he prize blue-murmerer mariposa as was he intentions, he brought back with him something of far greater importance. In addition to he little pencil-eraser: it is the very same tale that you have just finished hearing.

Johnny, you can finish the ending of this story just as easy as me. Because everybody knows that this Ernesto isn't only a great adventurer, a collector of wild specimens from out the tropical forest, but he is also a very famous American author too. And in time Ernesto wrote out this story of how he had survived he adventure in the jungles of the savage Caribbean, without losing he head like all the rest. Of course, Ernesto could only relate he tale with all those same careful, real-life newspaper details that have become the trademark of all the famous Yankee writers. Including not only the precise proportions of he *own* little crab-o, but also the crab-os of Mr Chan the Chinee grocer. Of Orinoco the Amerindian hunter. He told them about Clifton the English merchant, and Pierre the French tobacco-planter. He painted out for them faithful word-pictures of the crab-os of Salman the Muslim, and Ram-sol the Hindu roti-man. And of course, he could never leave out the dangerous dimensions of Felix the African fisherman! To finish things off Ernesto gave he story a title with lots of intrigue and drama to make sure it would be a best-seller, even though he title, just like all he others, was exactly the *opposite* of what the tale was telling: *The Sad Story of the Savage American Practice of Circumcision.*

The result, Johnny, was everything that you would expect. And it has brought the biggest boom ever to we tourist industry. Because in no time a-tall the *whole* of America was telling this story too, even despite its confusing backwards title. In no time a-tall even the travel brochures began to include—just beside the pictures of golden parrots, and green monkeys, and sparkling white beaches—precise descriptions of what, today, has become the most cherished of *all* we national treasures. Johnny, it is none other than you own decapitated Caribbean crab-o.

Diane Thiel

Family Album

From *The Dark Horse*

I like old photographs of relatives
in black and white, and staring straight ahead.
They knew this was serious business.
My favorite album is the one that's filled
with people none of us can even name.

I find the recent ones more difficult.
I wonder, now, if anyone remembers
how fiercely I refused even to stand
beside him for this picture—how I shrank
back from his hand and found the other side.

Forever now, for future family
we will be framed like this, although no one
will wonder at the way we are arranged.
No one will ever wonder, since we'll be
forever smiling there—our mouths all teeth.

Fred D'Aguiar

A Son in Shadow

From *Harper's*

I know nothing about how they meet. She is a schoolgirl. He is at work, probably a government clerk in a building near her school. At the hour when school and office are out for lunch their lives intersect at sandwich counters, soft-drink stands, traffic lights, market squares. Their eyes meet or their bodies collide at one of these food queues. He says something suggestive, complimentary. She suppresses a smile or traps one beneath her hands. He takes this as encouragement (as if any reaction of hers would have been read as anything else) and keeps on talking and following her and probably misses lunch that day. All the while she walks and eats and drinks and soaks up his praise, his sweet body-talk, his erotic chatter and sexy pitter-patter, his idle boasts and ample toasts to his life, his dreams about their future, the world their oyster together.

Am I going too fast on my father's behalf? Should there have been an immediate and cutting rebuttal from her and several days before another meeting? Does he leave work early to catch her at the end of the school day and follow her home just to see where she lives and to extend the boundaries of their courtship? Throwing it from day to night, from school to home, from childhood play to serious adult intent? Georgetown's two-lane streets with trenches on either side mean a mostly single-file walk, she in front probably looking over her shoulder when he says something worthy of a glance, or a cut-eye look if his suggestions about her body or what he will do with it if given half a chance exceed the decorum of the day—which is what, in mid-Fifties Guyana? From my grandmother it's, "Don't talk to a man unless you think you're a big woman. Man will bring you trouble. Man want just one thing from you. Don't listen to he. Don't get ruined for he. A young lady must cork her ears and keep her eye straight in front of she when these men start to flock around. The gentleman among them will find his way to her front door. The gentleman will make contact with the parents first. Woo them first before muttering one thing to the young lady. Man who go directly to young ladies only want to ruin them. Don't want to make them into respectable young women—just whores. Mark my words." My grandfather simply thinks that his little girl is not ready for the attentions of any man, that none of them is good enough for his little girl, and so the man who comes to his front door had better have a good pretext for disturbing his reverie. He had better know something about merchant seamen and the character of the sea, and about silence—how to keep it so that it signifies authority and dignity, so when you speak you are heard and your words, every one of them, are rivets. That man would have to be a genius to get past my grandfather, a genius or a gentleman. And since my father is neither, it's out of the question that he'll even use the front door of worship. His route will have to be the yard and the street of ruination.

So he stands in full view of her house at dusk. It takes a few nights before her parents realize he is there for their daughter. Then one day her father comes out and tells him to take his dog behavior to someone else's front door, and the young man quickly turns on his heel and walks away. Another time her mother opens the upstairs window and curses him, and he laughs and saunters off as if her words were a broom gently ushering him out of her yard. But he returns the next night and the next, and the daughter can't believe his determination. She is embarrassed that her body has been a magnet for trouble, that she is the cause of the uproar, then angry with him for his keen regard of her at the expense of her dignity, not to mention his. Neighbors tease her about him. They take pity on the boy, offer him drinks, some ice-cold mauby, a bite to eat, a dhalpouri, all of which he declines at first, then dutifully accepts. One neighbor even offers him a chair, and on one night of pestilential showers an umbrella, since he does not budge from his spot while all around him people dash for shelter, abandoning a night of liming (loitering) and gaffing (talking) to the persistence and chatter of the rain. Not my father. He stands his ground with only the back of his right hand up to his brow to shelter his eyes zeroed in on her house. She steals a glance at him after days of seeming to ignore the idea of him, though his presence burns brightly inside her heart. She can't believe his vigilance is for her. She stops to stare in the mirror and for the first time sees her full lips, long straight nose, shoulder-length brunette hair, and dark green eyes with their slight oval shape. Her high cheekbones. Her ears close to her skull. She runs her fingers lightly over these places as if to touch is to believe. Her lips tingle. Her hair shines. Her eyes smile. And she knows from this young man's perseverance that she is beautiful, desirable. She abandons herself to chores, and suppresses a smile and a song. She walks past windows as much as possible to feed the young man's hungry eyes with a morsel of that which he has venerated to the point of indignity. She rewards his eyes by doing unnecessary half-turns at the upstairs window. A flash of clavicle, a hand slowly putting her hair off her face and setting it down behind her ears, and then a smile, a demure glance, her head inclined a little, her eyes raised, her eyelids batted a few times—she performs for him though she feels silly and self-conscious. What else is there for a girl to do? Things befitting a lady that she picked up from the cinema. Not the sauciness of a tramp.

Her mother pulls her by one of those beautiful close-skulled ears from the window and curses her as if she were a ten-cent whore, then throws open the window and hurtles a long list of insults at this tall, silent, rude, good-for-nothing streak of impertinence darkening her street. The father folds his paper and gets up, but by the time he gets to the window the young man is gone.

My mother cries into the basin of dishes. She rubs a saucer so hard that it comes apart in her hands. She is lucky not to cut herself. She will have to answer to her mother for that breakage. In the past it meant at least a few slaps and many minutes of curses for bringing only trouble into her mother's house. Tonight her mother is even angrier. Her father has turned his fury against her for rearing a daughter who is a fool for men. Her mother finds her in the kitchen holding the two pieces of the saucer together and then apart—as if her dread and sheer desire for reparation would magically weld them whole. Her tears fall like drops of solder on that divided saucer. Her mother grabs her hands and strikes her and curses her into her face so that my mother may as well have been standing over a steaming, spluttering pot on the stove. She drops the two pieces of saucer and they become six pieces. Her mother looks down and strides over the mess with threats about what will happen if her feet find a splinter. She cries but finds every piece, and to be sure to get the splinters too she runs her palms along the floor, this way and that, and with her nails she prizes out whatever her hand picks up. She cries herself to sleep.

The next night he is back at his station, and her mother and father, their voices, their words, their blows sound a little farther off, fall a little lighter. His presence, the bare-faced courage of it, becomes a suit of armor for her to don against her mother's and father's attacks. She flies through her chores. She manages under her mother's watchful eye to show both sides of her clavicle, even a little of the definition down the middle of her chest—that small trench her inflated chest digs, which catches the light and takes the breath away, that line drawn from the throat to the uppermost rib exuding warmth and tension, drawing the eyes twenty-five yards away with its radiance in the half-light of dusk, promising more than it can possibly contain, than the eye can hold, and triggering a normal heart into palpitations, a normal breath into shallowness and rapidity.

"Miss Isiah, howdy! How come you house so clean on the west side and not so clean on the east? It lopsided! Dirt have a preference in your house? Or is that saga boy hanging around the west side of your house a dirt repellent?" The gossip must have been rampant in the surrounding yards, yards seemingly designed deliberately so people could see into one another's homes and catch anything spilling out of them—quarrels, courtships, cooking pots, music—and sometimes a clash of houses, a reaction against the claustrophobia of the yard, but not enough yards, not enough room to procure a necessary privacy in order to maintain a badly sought-after dignity—clean, well dressed, head high in the air on Sundays—impossible if the night before there is a fight and everyone hears you beg not to be hit anymore, or else such a stream of obscenities gushes from your mouth that the sealed red lips of Sunday morning just don't cut it.

My father maintains his vigil. Granny threatens to save the contents of her chamber pot from the night before and empty it on his head. Could she have thrown it from her living room window to his shaded spot by the street? Luckily she never tries. She may well be telling him that he doesn't deserve even that amount of attention. If there is any creature lower than a gutter rat—one too low to merit even her worst display of disdain—then he is it. How does my father take that? As a qualification he can do without? How much of that kind of water is he able to let run off his back? Poor man. He has to be in love. He has to be wearing his own suit of armor. Lashed to his mast like Odysseus, he hears the most taunting, terrible things, but what saves him, what restores him, are the ropes, the armor of his love for my mother. Others without this charm would have withered away, but my father smiles and shrugs at the barrage of looks, insults, gestures, silence, loneliness.

Watch his body there under that breadfruit or sapodilla tree; the shine of his status as sentry and his conviction are twin headlights that blind her parents. They redouble their efforts to get rid of his particular glare, then are divided by the sense of his inevitability in their daughter's life. My grandmother stops shouting at him while my grandfather still raises his cane and causes the young man to walk away briskly. My grandmother then opens the windows on the west side, ostensibly to let in the sea breeze but really to exhibit in all those window frames a new and friendly demeanor. My grandfather shouts at her that he can smell the rank intent of that black boy, rotten as a fish market, blowing into his living room and spoiling his thoughts.

But the windows stay open. And my mother at them. With the love Morse of her clavicles and her cleavage as she grows bolder. Smiling, then waving. And no hand in sight to box her or grip her by the ear and draw her away from there. Until one night she boldly leaves the house and goes to him and they talk for five minutes rapidly as if words are about to run out in the Southern Hemisphere.

My father's parents wonder what has become of their Gordon.

"The boy only intend to visit town."

"Town swallow him up."

"No, one woman turn he head, stick it in a butter churn and swill it."

"He lost to us now."

"True."

They say this to each other but hardly speak to him except to make pronouncements on the size of foreign lands.

"Guyana small?"

"What's the boy talking about?"

"Why, England and Scotland combined are the size of Guyana."

"How much room does a man need?"

"That woman take he common sense in a mortar and pound it with a pestle."

The two voices are one voice.

Opportunity is here now. The English are letting go of the reins, a whole new land is about to be fashioned. And he is planning to leave! What kind of woman has done this to our boy? The boy is lost. Talking to him is like harnessing a stubborn donkey. This isn't love but voodoo, obeah, juju, some concoction in a drink, some spell thrown in his locus. A little salt over the shoulder, an iodine shower, a rabbit foot on a string, a duck's bill or snake head dried and deposited into the left trouser pocket, a precious stone, lapis lazuli, amethyst, or anything on the middle finger, a good old reliable crucifix around the neck, made of silver, not gold, and at least one ounce in weight and two inches in diameter. A psalm in papyrus folded in a shirt pocket next to the heart. A blessing from a priest, a breathing of nothing but incense with a towel over the head. A bout of fasting, one night without sleep, a dreamless night, and a dreamless, sleepless, youngest son restored to them. He wants to stay around the house, he shows them why he loves his mummy and poppy and the bounteous land. There is no plan to flee. There is no city woman with his heart in her hand. And his brain is not ablaze in his pants. His head is not an empty, airless room.

They have one cardboard suitcase each, apart from her purse and his envelope tied with a string that contains their passports and tickets, birth certificates, and, for him, a document that he is indeed a clerk with X amount of experience at such-and-such a government office, signed "supervisor"—a worthless piece of shit, of course, in the eyes of any British employer. But for the time being, these little things are emblematic of the towering, staggering optimism that propels them out of Georgetown, Guyana, over the sea to London, England.

So what do they do? My mother is a shy woman. My father, in the two photos I've seen of him, is equally reserved. Not liable to experimentation. The big risk has been taken—that of leaving everything they know for all that is alien to them. My mother knows next to nothing about sex, except perhaps a bit about kissing. My father may have experimented a little, as boys tend to do, but he, too, when faced with the female body, confronts unfamiliar territory. Each burns for the other, enough to pull up roots and take off into the unknown. Yet I want to believe that they improvise around the idea of her purity and respect it until their marriage night. That they keep intact some of the moral system they come from even as they dismantle and ignore every other stricture placed on them by Guyanese society: honor your father and mother; fear a just and loving God; pledge allegiance to the flag; lust is the devil's oxygen. All that circles in their veins.

Over the twelve days at sea they examine what they have left and what they are heading toward. At sea they are in between lives: one life is over but the other has not yet begun. The talking they do on that ship without any duties to perform at all! My mother tells how her father, despite his routine as a merchant seaman, finds time to memorize whole poems by the Victorians: Tennyson, Longfellow, Browning, Jean Ingelow, Arnold, and Hopkins. The sea is his workplace, yet he makes time to do this marvelous thing. She tells how when he comes back to land he gathers them all in the living room and performs "The Charge of the Light Brigade" or "Maud" or "My Last Duchess" or "Fra Lippo Lippi" or "The High Tide on the Coast of Lincolnshire" or "Dover Beach" or "The Kingfisher" or "The Wreck of the Deutschland." He recites these poems to his creole-thinking children, who sit there and marvel at the English they are hearing, not that of the policeman or the teacher or the priest, but even more difficult to decipher, full of twists and impossible turns that throw you off the bicycle of your creole reasoning into the sand. If any of them interrupts my grandfather he stops in midflow, tells them off in creole, and resumes his poem where he left off. When particularly miffed by the disturbance he starts the poem from the beginning again. Does my grandfather recite these verses before or after he gets drunk, swears at the top of his voice, and chases my grandmother around the house with his broad leather belt?

But when my parents are out at sea, they have only the King James Bible in their possession. What they plan and rehearse is every aspect of their new life.

"Children. I want children."

"Me too. Plenty of them."

"I can work between births."

"Yes, both of us. Until we have enough money for a house. Then you can stay home with the kids."

"A nanny. Someone to watch the kids while we work. What kind of house?"

"Three bedrooms. A garden at the front, small, and back, large. A car—a Morris Minor. With all that room in the back for the children and real indicators and a wood finish." Neither has a notebook or dreamed of keeping one. They do not write their thoughts, they utter them. If something is committed to memory, there has to be a quotidian reason for it, apart from bits of the Bible and a few calypsos. My grandfather's labor of love, his settling down with a copy of Palgrave's *Golden Treasury* and memorizing lines that bear no practical relationship to his life, must seem bizarre to his children. Yet by doing so he demonstrates his love of words, their music, the sense of their sound, their approximation to the heartbeat and breath, their holding out of an alternative world to the one surrounding him, their confirmation of a past and another's life and thoughts, their luxury of composition, deliberation, their balancing and rebalancing of a skewered life. I imagine my mother benefits from this exposure in some oblique way—that the Victorians stick to her mental makeup whether she cares for them or not, that a little of them comes off on me in the wash of my gestation in her.

There is an old black-and-white photo (isn't there always?) and fragments of stories about his comings and goings, his carryings-on, as the West Indian speak goes, his mischief. "Look pan that smooth face, them two big, dark eye them, don't they win trust quick-time? Is hard to tie the man with them eye in him head to any woman and she pickney them. He face clean-shaven like he never shave. He curly black hair, dougla-look, but trim neat-neat. The man got topside." His hair, thick and wavy because of the "dougla" mix of East Indian and black, exaggerates an already high forehead. Automatically we credit such an appearance, in the Caribbean and elsewhere, with intelligence—"topside." And a European nose, not broad, with a high bridge (good breeding, though the nostrils flare a bit—sign of a quick temper!). And lips that invite kisses. "They full-full and pout like a kiss with the sound of a kiss way behind, long after that kiss come and gone." He is six feet tall and thin but not skinny, that brand of thin that women refer to as elegant, since the result is long fingers and economic gestures. Notice I say economic and not cheap. A man of few words. A watcher. "But when he relax in company he know and trust, then he the center of wit and idle philosophizing. He shoot back a few rums, neat no chaser, with anyone, and hold his own with men more inclined to gin and tonic. He know when to mind he Ps and Qs and when to gaff in the most lewd Georgetown, rumshop talk with the boys. What chance a sixteen-year-old closeted lady got against such a man, I ask you?"

But most of the puzzle is missing. So I start to draw links from one fragment to the next. He begins to belong—fleetingly, at first—in my life. As a man in poor light seen crossing a road mercifully free of traffic, its tar-macadam steamy with a recent downpour. As a tall, lank body glimpsed ducking under the awning of a shop front and disappearing inside and never emerging no matter how long I wait across the street, watching the door with its reflecting plate glass and listening for the little jingle of the bell that announces the arrival and departure of customers.

Or I cross Blackheath Hill entranced by the urgent belief that my father is in one of the cars speeding up and down it. Blackheath Hill curves a little with a steep gradient—less than one in six in places. It's more of a ski slope than a hill. Cars and trucks, motorbikes and cyclists all come down the road as if in a race for a finish line. Going up it is no different. Vehicles race to the top as if with the fear that their engines might cut off and they will slide back down. I want to be seen by my father. I have to be close to his car so that he does not miss me. I measure the traffic and watch myself get halfway, then, after a pause to allow a couple of cars to pass on their way up, a brisk walk, if I time it right, to allow the rest of the traffic to catch up with me, to see the kid who seems to be in no particular hurry to get out of their way looking at them. I step onto the sidewalk and cherish the breeze of the nearest vehicle at my back—Father, this is your son you have just missed. Isn't he big? Pull over and call his name. Take him in your arms. Admonish him. Remind him that cars can kill and his little body would not survive a hit at these high speeds. Tell him to look for his father under less dangerous circumstances.

I am searching the only way I know how, by rumination, contemplation, conjecture, supposition. I try to fill the gaps, try to piece together the father I never knew. I imagine everything where there is little or nothing to go on. And yet, in going back, in raking up bits and pieces of a shattered and erased existence, I know that I am courting rejection from a source hitherto silent and beyond me. I am conjuring up a father safely out of reach and taking the risk that the lips I help to move, the lungs I force to breathe, will simply say "No." No to everything I ask of them, even the merest crumb of recognition.

"Father." The noun rings hollowly when I say it, my head is empty of any meaning the word might have. I shout it in a dark cave but none of the expected bats come flapping out. Just weaker and weaker divisions of my call. "Father." It is my incantation to bring him back from the grave to the responsibility of his name. But how, when I only know his wife, my mother, and her sudden, moody silence whenever he crops up in conversation?

You ever have anyone sweet-talk you? Fill your ears with their kind of wax, rub that wax with their tongue all over your body with more promises than the promised land itself contains, fill your head with their sweet drone, their buzz that shuts out your parents, friends, your own mind from its own house? That's your father, the bumblebee, paying attention to me.

My sixteenth birthday was a month behind. He was nearly twenty. A big man in my eyes. What did he want with me? A smooth tongue in my ears. Mostly, though, he watched me, my house, my backside when he followed me home from school. His eyes gleamed in the early evening, the whites of his eyes. He stood so still by the side of the road outside my house that he might have been a lamppost, planted there, shining just for me.

My father cursed him, my mother joined in, my sisters laughed at his silence, his stillness. They all said he had to be the most stupid man in Georgetown, a dunce, a bat in need of a perch, out in the sun too long, sun fry his brain, cat take his tongue, his head empty like a calabash, his tongue cut out, he look like a beggar. They felt sorry for him standing there like a paling, his face a yard long, his tongue a slab of useless plywood in his mouth. "Look what Ingrid gone and bring to the house, shame, dumbness, blackness follow she here to we house to paint shame all over it and us. Go away, black boy, take your dumb misery somewhere else, crawl back to your pen in the country, leave we sister alone, she got more beauty than sense to listen to a fool like you, to let you follow her, to encourage you by not cursing the day you was born and the two people who got together to born you and your people and the whole sorry village you crawl out of to come and plant yourself here in front of we house on William Street, a decent street, in Kitty, in we capital."

I should have thanked my sisters; instead I begged them to leave him alone. Ignore him and he'll go away. My father left the house to get hold of the boy by the scruff of his neck and boot his backside out of Kitty, but he ran off when my father appeared in the door frame. With the light of the house behind him and casting a long, dark shadow, he must have looked twice his size and in no mood to bargain. Your father sprinted away, melting into the darkness. I watched for his return by checking that the windows I'd bolted earlier really were bolted, convincing myself that I had overlooked one of them, using my hands to feel the latch as I searched the street for him. But he was gone for the night. My knight. Shining eyes for armor.

My mother cursed him from the living room window, flung it open and pointed at him and with her tongue reduced him to a pile of rubble and scattered that rubble over a wide area then picked her way through the strewn wreckage to make sure her destruction was complete: "Country boy, what you want with my daughter? What make you think you man enough for her? What you got between your legs that give you the right to plant yourself in front of my house? What kind of blight you is? You fungus!"

As she cursed him and he retreated from the house sheepishly, she watched her husband for approval. These were mild curses for her, dutiful curses, a warm-up. When she really got going her face reddened and her left arm carved up the air in front of her as if it were the meat of her opponent being dissected into bite-size bits. That's how I knew she was searching for a way to help me but hadn't yet found it. Not as long as my father was at home. Soon he would be at sea, away for weeks, and things would be different.

That is, if my onlooker, my remote watcher, my far-off admirer wasn't scared off forever. And what if he was? Then he didn't deserve me in the first place. If he couldn't take a few curses he wasn't good for anything. If I wasn't worth taking a few curses for ... well, I didn't want a man who didn't think I was worth taking a few curses for! I loved him for coming back night after night when all he got from me was a glance at the window. Sometimes less than a glance. Just me passing across the window frame as I dashed from chore to chore under four baleful eyes.

It seemed like he was saving all his breath and words for when he could be alone with me. Then he turned on the bumblebee of himself and I was the hapless flower of his attentions. He told me about my skin that it was silk, that all the colors of the rainbow put together still didn't come close to my beautiful skin. That my face, my eyes, my mouth, my nose, the tip of my nose, my ears, my fingertips, each was a precious jewel, precious stone. He likened the rest of me to things I had read about but had never seen, had dreamed about but had never dreamed I would see: dandelions, apples, snow, spring in England's shires, the white cliffs of Dover. In his eyes my body, me, was everything I dreamed of becoming.

That was your father before any of you were a twinkle in his eye. More accurately, that was my lover and then my husband. Your father was a different man altogether. Suddenly a stranger occupied my bed. His tongue now turned to wood. All the laughter of my sisters, the half-hearted curses of my mother, my father's promise of blue misery, all came true in this strange man, this father, this latter-day husband and lover.

I saw the change in him. My hands were full with you children. He went out of reach. He cradled you as if he didn't know which side was up, which down. He held you at arm's length to avoid the tar and feathers of you babies. Soon I earned the same treatment, but if you children were tar and feathers I was refuse. His face creased when he came near me. What had become of my silk skin? My precious features disappeared into my face, earning neither praise nor blame—just his silence, his wooden tongue, and that bad-smell look of his. I kept quiet for as long as I could. I watched him retreat from all of us, hoping he'd reel himself back in since the line between us was strong and I thought unbreakable; but no. I had to shout to get him to hear me. I shouted like my mother standing at the upstairs window to some rude stranger in the street twenty-five yards away. I sounded like my father filling the door frame. My jeering sisters insinuated their way into my voice. And your father simply kept walking away.

Believe me, I pulled my hair and beat the ground with my hands and feet to get at him in my head and in the ground he walked on that I worshiped. Hadn't he delivered England to me and all the seasons of England, all England's shires and the fog he'd left out of his serenades, no doubt just to keep some surprise in store for me? The first morning I opened the door that autumn and shouted, "Fire!" when I saw all that smoke, thinking the whole street on fire, all the streets, London burning, and slammed the door and ran into his arms and his laughter, and he took me out into it in my nightdress, he in his pajamas, and all the time I followed him, not ashamed to be seen outside in my thin, flimsy nylon (if anyone could see through that blanket) because he was in his pajamas, the blue, striped ones, and his voice, his sweet drone, told me it was fine, this smoke without fire was fine, "This is fog."

He walked away and everything started to be erased by that fog. That smoke without fire crossed the ocean into my past and obliterated Kitty, Georgetown, the house on William Street, everything he had touched, every place I had known him in. I swallowed that fog. It poured into my ears, nose, eyes, mouth. He was gone. I got a chest pain and breathlessness that made me panic. There wasn't just me. There were you children. I had to breathe for you children. The pain in my chest that was your father had to be plucked out, otherwise I too would be lost to you all, and to myself.

*

The first time I see him is the last time I see him. I can't wait to get to the front of the queue to have him all to myself. When I get there my eyes travel up and down his body. From those few gray hairs that decorate his temples and his forehead and his nose to the cuffs at his ankles and sparkling black shoes. He wears a black suit, a double-breasted number with three brass buttons on the cuff of each sleeve. He lies on his back with his hands clasped over his flat stomach. There is too much powder on his face. Let's get out of this mournful place, Dad. We have a lot of catching up to do. He has the rare look—of holding his breath, of not breathing, in between inhaling and exhaling—that exquisitely beautiful corpses capture. For a moment after I invite him to leave with me, I expect his chest to inflate, his lids to open, and those clasped hands to unfold and pull him upright into a sitting position as if he really were just napping because he has dressed way too early for the ball.

There are myths about this sort of thing. Father enslaves son. Son hates father, bides his time, waits for the strong father to weaken. Son pounces one day, pounces hard and definite, and the father is overwhelmed, broken, destroyed with hardly any resistance, except that of surprise and then resignation. Son washes his hands but finds he is washing hands that are not bloodstained, not marked or blemished in any way. He is simply scrubbing hands that no longer belong to him—they are his father's hands, attached to his arms, his shoulders, his body. He has removed a shadow all the more to see unencumbered the father in himself. There is the widow he has made of his mother. He cannot love her as his father might. While his father lived he thought he could. The moment his father expired he knew his mother would remain unloved.

I alight too soon from a number 53 bus on Blackheath Hill, disembark while the bus is moving, and stumble, trip from two legs onto all fours, hands like feet, transforming, sprouting more limbs, becoming a spider and breaking my fall. That same fall is now a tumble, a dozen somersaults that end with me standing upright and quite still on two legs with the other limbs dangling. Onlookers, who fully expected disaster, applaud. I walk back up the hill to the block of council flats as a man might, upright, on two legs. My other limbs dangle, swing as if they are two hands. Some days I will be out of breath, I will gasp and exhale, and the cloud before me will not be my winter's breath but the silken strands of a web, or worse, fire. Other days I might look at a bed of geraniums planted on the council estate and turn all their numberless petals into stone. A diamond held between my thumb and index finger crumbles in this mood, in this light, like the powdery wings of a butterfly.

I stare out of an apartment on the twenty-fourth floor of a tower block overlooking the nut-brown Thames. That wasp on the windowpane nibbling up and down the glass for a pore to exit through, back into the air and heat, tries to sting what it can feel but cannot see. My father is the window. I am the wasp. Sometimes a helping hand comes along and lifts the window, and the wasp slides out. Other times a shadow descends, there is a displacement of air, and it is the last thing the wasp knows. Which of those times is this? I want to know. I don't want to know. I am not nibbling nor trying to sting. I am kissing, repeatedly, rapidly, the featureless face of my father. It feels like summer light. It reflects a garden. Whose is that interfering hand? Why that interrupting shadow? My child's hand. My child's shadow. My son or my father? My son and my father. Two sons, two fathers. Yet three people. We walk behind a father's name, shoulder a father's memory. Wear another's walk, another's gait. Wait for what has happened to their bodies, the same scars, maladies, aches, to surface in ours.

I want to shed my skin. Walk away from my shadow. Leave my name in a place I cannot return to. To be nameless, bodiless. To swim to Wallace Stevens's Key West, which is shoreless, horizonless. Blackheath Hill becomes Auden's Bristol Street, an occasion for wonder and lament. Blackheath at 5:45 A.M. on a foggy winter morning becomes Peckham Rye. There are no trees on Blackheath, but angels hang in the air if only Blake were there to see them. On the twenty-fourth floor towering above the Thames, water, not land, surrounds me. Everything seems to rise out of that water. Look up at ambling clouds and the tower betrays its drift out to sea.

Ai

Charisma: *A Fiction*

From *Poets & Writers*

I didn't just read the Bible, I lived it.
I told my people, this is revolution.
I said, I interpret this attack
on my constitutional rights
with a gun and a guitar
to mean we are in trouble.
I held up a hand grenade, pulled the pin
and told them, "this one's for Jesus."
I prayed, "Lord, take me to heaven, take
me today
and I won't falter on the way."
Did my people desert me,
did they say this man is crazy?
No, they didn't.
They prayed with me.
They lay face down in Waco, Texas
to await death and resurrection,
as it came from all directions, all in
flames.

I never claimed to be the Jesus, who
    cured the sick
and caused the lame to walk.
I knew the sins of the flesh, I knew the
    shame
and I confessed my weakness.
I let my people be witness to it
and through it came my power
and the empty talk of changing sinful
    ways
that haunt a man,
until he betrays himself no longer
and gives in to the stronger urge
to fornicate and multiply dissolved.
I absolved myself between a woman's
    thighs
and I arose like Lazarus,
raised up from the dead
on the tip of his penis.
We had no life and death between us
    anymore,
we had rounds of ammunition
and all of you to listen to us burn
and in that burning learn
how to give your life for freedom
in Christian hunting season.
The ATF used child abuse as the excuse
to assault us in our home.
They had no proof
and if we had been left alone,
we might have shown the world
that God is like desire you cannot satisfy.
You must give in to Him, or die.

The Apocalypse cometh like a firestorm,
leaving some of us reborn,
others to smolder in the ruins
of New Jerusalem,
which will not come again,
until the war against the innocent is over.

Ifeona Fulani

Precious and Her Hair

From *Black Renaissance/Renaissance Noire*

All Precious really wanted was a boy to go with to the beach on Saturdays. She dreamed of strolling on the sand with a sweet-looking boy, arm in arm and affectionate, the envy of all the boy-less girls out there. She dreamed of water fights, of splashing with her boy in the sea foam, she in her bikini, laughing, sea-water sparkling on her face; and then watching the sun set at Ras Peter's restaurant, eating fish and festival, like tourists.

See Precious at seventeen: slender as a cane stalk, with skin like caramel, and a full, star-apple mouth. At night she tossed in her bed, the sheets hot against her skin, fingers tracing first the shape of her lips, then traveling across her breasts, and down to her thighs to touch the custard-apple flesh between them. Each morning she peered into the speckled wardrobe mirror, seeing long legs, a narrow waist, a slender shapely body. Yet all of this beauty was nullified in her eyes by a head of short, peppercorn hair that refused to grow.

The boy she really wanted was Neville Campbell, neighbor, sixth-former, and school Romeo. Precious lived only for glimpses of him. There were mornings when, dressed for school, she would wait behind the hibiscus bush at the entrance to her mother's yard until Neville came swaggering by. Blushing, and trembling like a periwinkle in the wind, she would fall in step beside him, he so crisp and lithe in his khaki uniform. Sometimes he smiled and said, *morning.* But usually he nodded and kept on walking, gazing at the road ahead. Afternoons after school, Precious would loiter on the dusty road, praying he would pass and notice her. Sometimes he did walk by, surrounded by a cohort of raucous, jostling boys, while Precious hovered by the roadside, hesitant as a lingering streak of mist.

Precious lived with her mother Lucille in a house by the main road, just before it curved downhill towards the coast. Precious resembled Lucille, who was slender and handsome with a neat head of low-cropped hair which she covered with a turban of pristine white cloth. Precious had many of Lucille's features, but she lacked her mother's practicality and common sense. The two of them lived alone, her father having migrated to America ten years back. (They should have joined him long before: he had filed for their papers, but such matters take a long time, or so he wrote in the letters sent with his monthly remittances back home.) Lucille fussed over Precious, her only child, her eyeball, but she was stern, not wanting to spoil her. She had ambitions for her daughter of a practical kind: sixth form, then college, followed by a respectable, well-paying job. Each night after reading her Bible, Lucille would pray softly, on her knees by the bed:

Maasa God, please bless my daughter, let her have ambition and sense. And I beg you, Lord, please let her turn out good.

But at seventeen, Precious's one ambition was to be Neville's girl.

When Precious began to pine for Neville, Lucille took in the dreaminess, the moping over schoolwork, the mooning by the garden gate. Trouble! she thought, pursing her lips. Boy trouble, it had to be, for as far as she knew Precious had had no chance to get into baby trouble—yet.

One evening after dinner, Lucille sat her daughter down for a cautionary word.

What wrong with you these days, Precious?

Nothing, Mama.

Is that boy Neville you making cow-eye after?

N-no, Mama, said Precious, biting back a giggle.

Can't you see he's not paying you one bit of mind? A sweet-boy like him, only have time for fool-fool, flighty-flighty girls. Not a decent child like you.

Y-yes, Mama. I know.

Hanging out at the beach with her best friend Lindy the following Saturday, Precious had a chance to see the truth of Lucille's words, for further along the beach, Christine Chang and Selina Brown paraded on the sand in scanty thong bikinis, swarmed by boys, Neville Campbell among them.

Precious's friend Lindy stared at Selina Brown's swivel hips. She breathed from deep in her chest like her granny did when she was vexed, and sucked air through her teeth.

You see those girls? she said, pointing at Selina. *They're good for nothing decent. They're just fly-bait for the sweet-boys.*

How do they do it? Precious wondered, entranced. Christine had no behind to speak of, and Selina's legs, thinner than green bamboo twigs, bowed gently at the knees. But they both had plentiful hair: hair that lifted in the wind and fanned around their shoulders, hair that caressed their cheeks, tempting boys to touch it.

At that moment, Precious resolved to get herself more hair.

She went first to Pauline, the buxom village postmistress who was also the village hairdresser. Pauline's salon was no more than a shack behind her house, but it was crammed full with women waiting to get their heads done on the day Precious stopped by.

You have to help me, Pauline, said Precious. *I want long hair and I need it fast!*

Pauline paused in the middle of a coloring job to run a hand over Precious's head.

Hmmm, she said, shaking her crop of bouncy bronze curls. *Not much here to work with . . . it'll have to be braids or African twists, or a weave . . . ?*

Precious decided on braids, the least expensive option. She saved lunch money for three weeks to pay for them, substituting anticipation for food, feeding on visions of herself transformed into a beauty with a head of luxuriant albeit false hair. On the appointed Saturday, she sweated for hours in a plastic chair in Pauline's stifling shack. The small room was hot, the atmosphere thick with fumes from straighteners and dyes blended with body odors, and the scent of fresh perspiration from Pauline's underarms. Sweat trickled down Precious's face, yet she sat patient and still while Pauline wove every strand of hair into an artificially extended plait. While Pauline pulled and tugged at her hair, Precious took delicious refuge in a dream of herself and Neville strolling arm in arm along the sand under the jealous nose of skinny, bandy-legged Selina Brown.

Precious was lightheaded with exhilaration when she stepped out of Pauline's den into the twilight, despite a prickling sensation on the surface of her scalp. She rushed home to dance before the mirror, laughing and swinging her new braids. Then she ran to wake up her mother, who was dozing on the verandah, to show off her new look.

Hmm..., said Lucille, who did not approve of extensions. Extensions were a vanity and therefore sinful, she believed, no matter how pretty. *More trouble coming*, she sighed. She pursed her lips together and frowned, then promptly fell asleep again.

That night Precious dreamed of Neville. He was swimming with long, supple strokes, swimming through waves of hair. The next morning she awoke with a smile on her lips and light shining in her eyes. She stretched, tossing back her braids, and then noticed a thin black thing on her pillow, coiled like a delicately patterned snake. She shrieked and ran to the mirror, frantically feeling along her hairline. *Oh my God! Oh my God!* Precious wailed as more braids came away, leaving a patch the size of a ten-cent piece above her right temple. The bald patch on her head or the braids in her hand—she was not sure which was worse.

Oh Mama, look what happened! She ran into Lucille's room, weeping like a child whose favorite doll had broken. Lucille sat by her dresser, her Bible open on her lap. She took in the situation with one glance.

You see where vanity lead you? Lucille muttered. She sat Precious down and started undoing the remaining braids before they too fell out. But the braids came away in Lucille's hands like dandelion fluff from its stem, exposing the smooth, reddened expanse of her daughter's entire scalp. Precious watched in the mirror, tears welling, chest heaving, wishing she were dead.

That day Precious stayed home from school. She tossed on her bed the entire day, now clutching her head in passionate regret, now imagining the snickering and whispering awaiting her next day at school. She spent a sleepless night trying hard not to visualize Neville's response to her baldness, though a small voice in her thoughts kept reminding her that he probably wouldn't notice.

The next morning Lucille pulled Precious out of bed and stood over her while she dressed. Then, taking a length of white fabric, Lucille wrapped a neat turban around her daughter's head.

I can't go to school like this! Precious wailed.

Is either this or your bald head exposed to the entire school! Lucille said, and pushed her out the door.

Laughter rippled through the classroom as Precious entered. *Precious born again!* Voices whispered and giggled and smirked. *Precious got the spirit like her mother!* Precious paused in the doorway, the focus of all eyes. A spirit did rise up in her at that moment: a spirit straightened up her spine, lifted up her head and lit a fire in her eyes. She scanned the room and the whispering ceased. Then, wide-eyed, smiling as though in a happy trance, she glided through the silence and sat at her desk, ready for class to begin.

Sister Homelia lived in a tumble-down house in a hollow at the bottom of the hill. She was hardly ever seen in the village, as she was too old and feeble to make the steep uphill climb. Yet everyone in the village knew of her skill with plants and herbs, and at some time in their life, each person found their way through the bush to Sister Homelia's house.

The day after the braids fell out, Precious called on Sister Homelia. After school let out, she headed downhill through the woods, climbing over fallen branches, dodging hungry mosquitos and flies the size of bees. There was no fence around Sister Homelia's garden, no gate or garden path, only a trail of hardened earth leading up to a listing front door.

*

The door opened before Precious even raised her hand to knock. *Come in, girl, come in.* Sister Homelia stood in the doorway leaning heavily on a walking stick, beckoning with her free hand. She appeared younger than Precious imagined she would be, her dark skin smooth and glossy, her figure slim as a girl's. But her neck crooked slightly, and her head drooped, wobbling from side to side like a ripe jackfruit about to fall. Her faded eyes peered at Precious, neither friendly nor hostile.

Precious stepped out of the sun into a sparsely furnished room musty with the smell of drying leaves, fresh earth, and recently boiled bananas.

S-sorry to trouble you, Sister Homelia, Precious began, but the woman interrupted.

Tell me, girl, what you want? She pointed to two chairs by a table under a small, curtained window.

It's my hair . . . Precious sat down, and Sister Homelia hobbled to her side, extending a crusty hand to touch her head.

Is that chemical foolishness you put on your head? As if to indicate the folly of such things, Sister Homelia raised a hand to her own braided gray hair,

N-no . . . it was extensions . . .

Aahmmmph! The old lady made a rattling noise deep down in her throat. *And now you want something to help it grow again?*

Y-yes, Sister. And I want it to grow long . . . long down my back like Christine Chang . . .

God gave you the hair you have for a reason, don' you know that, girl!

No boy wants a girl with picky hair like mine . . . was! Precious protested.

Aahmmp! Well. If you want that kind of hair, you'll have to do exactly as I tell you.

I'll do anything! Anything!

Ahmmmph!

So saying, Sister Homelia hobbled into an adjacent room, returning in a few moments with a brown paper bag.

Put a spoonful of this in a dish, mix it with some oil. Then . . . She bent towards Precious and whispered in her ear.

You not serious, Sister? said Precious, sweat beading her forehead.

The old woman nodded.

Start when the moon is dark, and put it on every night until the moon is bright.

Every night!

Yes, every night. Then when the hair begin to grow, you mustn't let water come near it. Not bath water, nor rain water, nor sea water. You hear me?

But it going to stink terrible! Precious wailed.

Aahmmph! Do you want hair, or don't you?

Sister Homelia hobbled over to the door, the tap-tap of her stick sending loud, lonely echoes through the room. She opened the door wide and stood in the doorway, her head gently bobbing from side to side.

Can nothing else help me? pleaded Precious, plaintive now, standing on the doorstep.

Nothing I know of.

So saying, Sister Homelia pushed the door shut.

As she scrambled through the thicket, Precious's mind was a tangle of thoughts. Could the mash of dried stuff in the brown paper bag really help her hair to grow? Would it be worth the awful smell, the inconvenience? A nightly application of stinky mess and then a shampoo every morning for two whole weeks! And without her mother finding out? Who had time for all that, and household chores and schoolwork besides?

But as Precious raised her hand to throw the paper bag in the bushes, a vision of Neville arose before her. Neville smiling, so tall, and so alluring her breath caught in her chest, her pulse picked up speed. *Choh, you too lazy, girl, and too coward!* said an admonishing voice in her head that reminded her of Lucille. *Nothing worth having come easy!* Precious sighed, and sighed again, acknowledging the voice's wisdom. Then she stuffed the paper bag in her backpack and resumed the trek home.

On the night of the new moon, Precious crept out to the bathhouse after Lucille had gone to sleep, the bag of herbs in one hand, a kerosene lamp in the other. By the weak, flickering lamplight, she scanned the ground for the final, unmentionable ingredient, and was relieved to find a fresh pile lying not far from the bathhouse door. Squatting on the bathhouse step, she mixed the slop in a worn enamel mug normally used to scoop up rainwater from the tank. She used a matted old paintbrush to apply the slop, which trickled down her neck in thick brown streams, soiling her nightdress, so that when the operation was over, she had to bathe again and wash out the nightdress, all by the failing kerosene light.

Back in her room, she was unable to lay down her messy head lest she leave stains on the pillow for Lucille to find. She sat crosslegged on the bed and leaned her back against the wall, sleeping fitfully until dawn. She woke at first cock-crow with a crick in her neck, but leaped up and ran to the bathhouse to shampoo her head before Lucille awoke.

The night after, she used a plastic bag as a headwrap to contain the latrine smell of the potion and to keep the mess off her pillow. During the day, she wore a turban with such nonchalance that younger girls at school began to emulate her, establishing a trend known forever after as *Precious's style.*

After the two weeks of nightly applications were over, Precious's hair began to grow. It grew so fast, one week later a thick fuzz had sprouted all over her head. Two weeks later, a fluffy cap of tight, glossy curls covered her scalp, and four weeks later, the hair touched her ears. The hair continued to grow, and each night she stood before the speckled mirror and unwound the turban, face rapt, blood fizzing, heart dancing in her chest. She had more hair than she'd ever had before. She scrutinized it in the mirror, turning this way and that as though uncertain it was really there.

The nightly unwrapping turned into a game of surprise, for as it grew the hair seemed to change. Fuzzy at first, then curly, it eventually grew as straight and heavy as Christine Chang's. But even as she rejoiced at its length, Precious wished the hair were curly: its straightness made her face look flat, made her eyes appear too small. And she was tempted to disobey Sister Homelia's warning and wash it, for her scalp flaked and itched so ferociously, she woke up at night to find relief in raking her fingernails hard over the scaling skin of her head.

When the hair hung past her shoulder blades, Precious decided the time had come to show it. She planned its first appearance for the day of Ras Peter's fish fry, an annual event that drew crowds from nearby villages and resorts along the coast. Neville and his posse would be there along with all the local youths, loitering by the sound system, ogling tourist girls, and quaffing chilled beer from the can.

The night before the fish fry, Precious braided the hair so it would wave by morning. She took a warm-water bath, pumiced her feet, and rubbed her skin smooth with cornmeal. She painted her nails with an orange glaze sneaked from Lucille's dressing table, and before falling into bed, she ironed her favorite shorts-suit of orange linen and hung it on the wardrobe in readiness, like a soldier preparing for battle.

She lay awake that night, hearing harmonies in the chirrups of night creatures and heartbeats in the deep rustlings of leaves. She rose before daybreak and padded softly to the kitchen. She made peppermint tea, taking care not to rattle the kettle or make a noise that would wake Lucille. She felt unusual that morning, tender and full of promise, like a hibiscus bud about to unfurl its petals and reveal its velvet heart. She took her tea out to the back of the house and sat outside on the doorstep. The tree-covered hillside and the plain below were still covered with soft swirls of mist. Rosy glimmerings of sunrise crept over the horizon, and in the distance, the protracted crowing of a raucous cockerel signaled daybreak.

Let the day be fine, Precious whispered. Then she laughed, for it was August, the month rain never fell.

Please let Neville be there, she prayed, though her heart knew for certain that only serious illness or injury would keep Neville away.

What if something goes wrong? she whispered, giving voice to her fear. It was hard to imagine what could go wrong, other than rain or Neville not showing, but fear of the unimaginable swooped like gas in the bottom of her belly. What if something did go awry? What if all her effort failed, all the longing failed, all the potions and the headwraps of the past three months proved to be effort wasted?

Set your mind on the best! As she shouted one of Lucille's favorite affirmations, she felt a power in the words she'd never felt before. She held on to the feeling, savoring its glow in her chest, drawing strength from it as she would from a dish of hot cow-heel soup. She felt ready. She straightened her spine like a trooper, and shook out the copious raven hair that was both her weapon and her charm.

*

When Precious emerged from her room dressed for the fish fry, Lucille thought she was seeing a vision in orange, swathed in waving black hair.

Oh my Lord! Where did that hair come from? she shrieked, then clapped her hand over her mouth, ashamed of her outburst.

It's all mine, Mama, come feel it, said proud Precious, offering her head for her mother's touch.

Precious, is it a wig?

It's mine, Mama, for real! Sister Homelia helped me grow it, sang Precious, who then waltzed out of the house, leaving her mother collapsed on a lounger, wailing and clutching her head.

Precious leaned against the front gate waiting for Lindy, hair blowing in the light breeze, model-like. Coming up the hill, Lindy froze in her tracks at the first sight of Precious; then she exploded into laughter.

Precious, you mad or something? Lindy stepped to left and to right surveying Precious's hair, as if she hoped her first impression were mistaken and would improve on closer inspection. *You mean you waste your mother's good money on a weave?*

Precious stared at Lindy in amazement. She had expected admiration, even envy, but not disbelief, and no, not laughter!

It's all mine, come, feel it. She offered her head to Lindy's skeptical tugs.

So how you get it to grow so long, so fast?

I got some herbal tonic from Sister Homelia, said Precious. *It worked good, eh? Don't you like it?* She felt uncertain suddenly, her confidence wavering, disturbed by Lindy's reaction.

Jesus, breathed Lindy, wide-eyed. *Now I know you really mad!*

The walk to the beach was not the triumphal approach Precious had anticipated, though by the time she and Lindy arrived at the spot where the fish fry was in full swing, her spirits had begun to rally. *She's just jealous!* Precious told herself, touching the hair as if drawing reassurance from it. *She wishes she had hair long like this.* She tossed her head and swung the hair and pressed on towards the excitement up ahead, leaving Lindy to follow her lead.

There were cars choking up the beach road, their stereos and radios blaring. Louder still, the bass throb of Ras Peter's sound system hovered in the atmosphere, a visceral wall of sound. As she moved across the sand toward the the music, Precious inhaled the salty wind, which carried the aroma of frying fish and the heady scent of punch made with strong rum and fragrant limes. Precious scanned the faces on the beach with a pounding heart. Local people were outnumbered by folks from neighboring villages, and there were tourists strewn lengthways and oblivious everywhere along the stretch of hot sand. *Let's get some fish,* Lindy was saying, but Precious was not hungry. She was too close to her quarry to rest for food, and she was perspiring under all that hair. She needed to find Neville while the hair was still wavy, before she dissolved in sweat.

She saw a huddle of young people by the mountain of speakers some fifty yards along the beach. Shading her eyes from the sun with her hand, she made out the tall silhouette of Neville. Without a word to Lindy, Precious set off towards the crowd, her pulse beating in her ears louder than the sound system's bass. As she drew close to the group, she saw two people break away, holding hands. They strolled in her direction, and as they came into view, Precious froze. The couple gazed into each other's faces, smiling. The boy was tall with a swagger in his walk, the girl clearly foreign, pale and blonde-haired, in a tourist's uniform of bikini briefs and a tight tank top.

Despite the heat of the sun, Precious began to tremble. She clutched her throat as though to stop the wail that rose from her belly and took flight on the sea breeze. *Neville with a white girl!* Tears spiked with anger welled in Precious's eyes, and the bitter taste of failure settled on her tongue. Not even Sister Homelia could help her now.

What was she to do, with Neville and the girl advancing across the sand? Should she keep walking, meet them face to face, ignore the smirk in Neville's eye? Or should she take her shame back to Lindy, who without a doubt was waiting to laugh her to scorn. Her face was burning in the acid yellow heat of the sun, and her scalp itched with such intensity that she craved the cooling touch of salt water on her head. Precious gazed longingly toward the sea.

Neville and the girl were approaching, and she could hear their laughter rising on the wind, blending with the seabirds' mocking cries. Precious turned on her heel, almost running towards the water. Not stopping to take off the linen outfit, she plunged into the sea, cleaving through its gentle waves like a large orange fish. She swam until she felt light-headed, then paused to catch her breath. Treading water, she looked back towards the beach, expecting to see Neville and the girl, diminished by distance. Instead her eye fell on a floating black mass that glistened like spilled oil on the aquamarine surface of the sea. Legs pedaling frantically, Precious reached quivering hands out of the water and explored her head. Her scalp felt clean, satin-smooth to the touch. She bobbed gently up and down, clutching her head and gasping deep breaths until her mind became calm and her body felt light, as though relieved of a weighty burden.

The merciless sun was burning, hot as a naked flame, and to cool off, Precious dove underwater, surfaced, and dove again, repeatedly, like a fish escaped from a net, enjoying its freedom.

Pico Iyer

The End of Empire

From *Harper's*

When I was five years old and (as it seemed to me) the only little Indian boy in Oxford, England, I had my first stage role ever, as the changeling in Shakespeare's *Midsummer Night's Dream*, passed back and forth between fairy king and queen amidst the dreamy lakes and illuminated, spirit-haunted trees of Worcester College. The Oxford University Drama Society must have been delighted to find a "real" Indian boy to play the half-real, motherless child, "stolen from an Indian king," in the play, and so, richly bribed with Rowntree's Fruit Pastilles and Corgi cars every day for two weeks, I got up each evening in turban and jeweled brooch and allowed myself to be fought over by rival worlds.

I knew far less about the "spicèd Indian air" than many of the English students around me, I'm sure, and probably had less interest in a place that was neither home to me nor exotic; many years would pass before I could see the aptness of the part. (At school, I would learn that it was rumored, incredibly, that I was the son of a maharajah; while for years, kindly Englishwomen would tell me, "You speak such good English, dear.") Certainly, I could never see how people of my parents' generation could have such a fondness for Oxford, the grimy, everyday industrial town in which I'd been born. England for them was Fabians and Romantic poets and high- and public-minded civil servants—it was Mountbatten, perhaps, and Jowett and Plato; for me it was union strikes and fish-and-chips and the sound of broken glass when the pubs closed down at 11:00 P.M. I couldn't really share their admiration for an England I knew too well or for an India I didn't know at all. England—where they were fifty times as likely to be beaten up on the streets as a white (even in 1990), I remembered reading—was as familiar as yesterday's breakfast.

Growing up, I'd heard, over and over, the classic stories of passage, nearly always of bright young boys from the colonies—tropical Dick Whittingtons—coming over to England to make their fortunes: of Mohandas Gandhi, dreaming of becoming an upstanding English barrister, and schooling himself in French and dancing lessons long after he left the Victoria Hotel in London; of Lee Kuan Yew—later to say he'd always felt indebted to his British school principal for caning him—coming over on the *Britannic* (shocked at the people copulating freely on the lifeboat deck) before returning to Singapore, with the only starred First in law at Cambridge; of Nelson Mandela, named after Admiral Nelson, they said, combining in his person, those close to him had told me, "the perfect English gentleman and the tribal chieftain." In the stories, the pattern was always the same: the young foreigner masters the ways of Britain so fully that he is perfectly equipped to undo them, armed, as Michael Manley, the prime minister of Jamaica (and a Marxist anti-imperialist), would say, with "nothing more than the finest tradition of self-criticism taught in British schools."

Much later, though, as I sat overlooking the backs of the Cambridge colleges on an outstretched English summer evening—the light as lingering and golden as in any tropical boy's imaginings—I began to hear a different second act. "The thing is, I admire the idea of England, but I can't stand the reality." My old Indian friend (of my parents' generation) was talking to me in a voice as plummy and rich as a major general's, the kind they don't seem to make anymore. "I don't know, call me sentimental, if you like—I suppose it's the weak, Indian, wishy-washy part of me—but I always thought that England meant fairness and free choice and all that kind of thing, that this was the center of decency. And now, of course, I find I'm much more English than the English.

"I mean, at least before, there used to be some sense of compassion. I know a colonial master-slave relationship isn't ideal, but if you're a slave it's the best thing you've got. I suppose some people would say those were all myths, of decency or whatever, but still it's better to have those positive myths than what we have now."

I looked at him in his New and Lingwood sweater, with the Coutts checkbook he'd made sure that I would notice; he lived in a thatched Elizabethan country cottage of the kind he must have dreamed of once, its address all bushes and thorns, "nr. Newmarket," and I felt as if I were watching someone play Othello after the theater had emptied and the lights were all turned off.

"I mean, if you're an Indian, they're happy to accept you so long as you speak like Peter Sellers and smell of curry and all that, because then you know your place. But if you don't, you might as well forget it. Because the typical Englishman doesn't understand that there is such a thing as class anywhere outside England, and that you and I are different from the Bangladeshi waiter at the local. The right wing want you to be nice smiling colonials, and the left wing want you to assert your solidarity and oppressedness by being 'ethnic,' and they refuse to allow you to be what you want to be. In many ways, the extreme right almost enjoy the extreme left—the Vanessa Redgraves—because they can see them as a good enemy. But if you're sort of middle-of-the-road, you get run over by both sides."

I looked at him and didn't know what to think. The punts were drifting past the shortbread-colored towers, and the late summer light was gilding the fields and distant spires as in the kind of watercolors the Empire used to send around the globe. My friend had a big heart, I knew, and a quick mind, but both were so lost inside the character he'd chosen to play that all I could hear, sometimes, was the sound of a lover disappointed, a boy who'd left everything he knew to pursue some ideal, unattainable woman, arriving at her doorstep only to find that she'd given herself over to some mobster from Las Vegas.

The story of migration I must have heard most deeply, growing up—piecing it together, only slowly, over the years—was the one of my own parents, coming to England just before the forces of globalism turned everything on its head. I can see my mother, neat in her English blouse and skirt, reciting the lyrics of Brooke and Shelley at the Cathedral and John Connon School in Bombay, and being rewarded by Carmelite sisters with playing cards of the Virgin Mary, which the girls swapped, she told me, as eagerly as I and my friends did "Soccer Stars"; even now, any Jehovah's Witness who comes to her doorstep, eager to convert the dark heathen within, will be greeted by a knowledge of the Bible more formidable than his own.

I can see my father too, graduated from the Doctor Antonio da Silva High School in Bombay, coming over to England two years before she did—three years after India won her independence—to the "dreaming spires" that both of them had read of in Arnold's *Scholar Gypsy*, sent there by the beneficence of the South African industrialist Cecil Rhodes, who believed that to be born an Englishman was to be awarded first prize in the lottery of life.

The one common link between my parents was the English history and literature in which they had been schooled, the one shared inheritance in a country as divided as Jerusalem; although both of them had grown up in the same city and gone to the same college, regional differences would have kept them apart in a world cut up into Hindu and Muslim and North Indian and South and caste and subcaste.

When she was in her teens, my mother told me much later, she impressed my father (also in his teens, though already a professor) by reciting some lines of Tennyson; and on the last day of every school term, tears would run down the cheeks of the girls at Cathedral as they sang of England's "green and pleasant land" and were ushered forth into the world.

The setting of Blake's Jerusalem could never have been quite what the girls expected, if ever they took the boat to England, but the shock must have been many times greater when Britain became a suburb of the International Empire. The one thing "convent-educated" Indians were not prepared for, surely, was an England made up of Islamic Fundamentalists (and of settlements like Glastonbury, where flaxen-haired kids sport names like Sita and Krishna and Ganesh); according to the British Tourist Authority, the national dish of Britain now is curry (having triumphed, I assume, over doner kebab and pizza), and the most popular flavor ordered from Domino's Pizza in the U.K. in 1994 was tandoori chicken. What seemed most to upset people like my Indian friend was that so many of the people in England now looked a lot like him.

To an English-born outsider like myself, the spicing of England was all to the good: the island has grown stronger and darker, like a mug of lukewarm water in which 1.7 million Indian (and West Indian) teabags have been left to steep; the Earls you meet these days in London are from Trinidad, and the *Times* will inform you, without apparent rancor, that there are more Indian restaurants in Greater London than in Bombay and Delhi combined. Insofar as Princess Diana was taken to be an avatar of the New England, it was not just because she brought "American" values—health clubs and Prozac and McDonald's and talk-show therapeutics—into the mainstream, and not just because she upended the traditional order by allying herself increasingly with the rival, new aristocracy of the celebrity culture; but also because she was linked, romantically, to a Pakistani doctor and an Egyptian film producer, and visited a debutante friend, Jemima Goldsmith, who'd married the captain of the Pakistani cricket team.

Yet those who'd always looked up to a certain England (brought to them, often, by homesick "Oxford men" abroad) were left not knowing where to turn. Recently, a friend told me, the readers of Sri Lanka, always eager to keep up with the latest in English letters, had asked the British Council to send them some voices of Young England. Ever sensitive to the niceties of racial diplomacy, the British had sent Hanif Kureishi (half-Pakistani) and then Caryl Phillips (born in the Caribbean). No, the Sri Lankans said, clearly disappointed: send us a *real* British writer (in other words, someone who looks like the people who held us down).

My Indian friend, though it sounds too perfect to be true, had run away from home and come to England in the hope of making it as an actor, and one evening I went to see him in a play in the West End, on the Strand, just across from India House. It was a piece written by one of Britain's most distinguished playwrights, drawn from his boyhood years in India, and yet it followed the pattern of almost every English account of India: a young Englishwoman is haunted by some doglike, "Englished-up" Indians who keep her in a constant state of sexual agitation. One of the actors on stage had actually played a judge in *A Passage to India* and a magistrate in *The Jewel in the Crown.*

Chelsea is "my favorite part of London," says one Indian character, who loves Tennyson and Macaulay; his next sentence is, "I hope to visit London one of these days." The play turned on a series of such witticisms—"I cannot be less Indian than I am" and, "Oh, I thought you'd be more Indian." Next to me, an Irishman lectured his pretty young Asian girlfriend on the hazards of multiculturalism in her native Malaysia.

After the curtain, I went to the nearby Opera pub to meet my friend, his makeup rubbed off and his fancy dress (if not his accent) put away for the night. "I know you're not going to like me saying this," he began (casting me, perhaps, in his private drama as a hypocritical Englishman), "but this is a very, very racist place, and it's getting worse with all this political correctness. It's just another kind of fascism, another way of putting you in a turban."

He'd had difficulty finding parts, I assumed, and in desperation, he confessed, he'd accepted jobs reading Kipling's works for Books on Tape (where his face didn't interfere with his Royal Shakespeare Company voice). Once he had "swallowed my pride and played a racist magistrate telling a black to go home." Even in this play, he said, they'd wanted him to wear a turban—till he'd pointed out that, post-polo, an Indian was far likelier to be wearing jodhpurs.

"It's getting to the point where they only let you play the parts you know," he complained. "It's like South Africa: we're all getting ghettoized." He blamed some of it on the Jews: "And I feel really angry after we fought to save them in the last war, and now they're turning on the Indians." What made it worse, though, were the other minorities. "The notion of a colored minority is a myth, because the Jamaicans hate the Trinidadians, and they both hate the Indians. But no one's letting on."

He would have been bitter anywhere, perhaps, but mobility had given him more people to blame and the chance to turn every decision into one of race.

"The one good thing about England," I said, to try to change the subject, "which almost redeems it, is the sense of humor."

"English humor is so cruel," he said, and he sounded so deeply shipwrecked that I didn't know how to answer.

But soon the curtain came up again, and he was telling me how he'd just gotten a call from one of Gandhi's grandsons, at the Nehru Centre, asking him to participate in a special reading. "Here it is, the bloody centenary of Tennyson, and the only ones celebrating it are the Indians! The only ones who care: don't you think that says something?"

I said very little, maybe because I felt he wanted only a confirmation that would compound his various agonies, and he turned on me, bitterly, with, "You're so English!" ("English" now meaning formal, cold, reserved.) "If there's one thing I don't like about this country—and there are many things I love, otherwise I wouldn't be living here—it's that they don't admit to their feelings. They keep them all inside."

He paused to take a breath, a sip of his beer, and to give me a genuinely warm and forgiving look.

"I mean, I love things here—like village cricket and going to the pub" (the very two elements a lonely English expat in Paris had just singled out for me). "But everything depends on who you know, who you went to school with—all that kind of thing. And of course, the other Indians here I really don't have very much in common with. They're from East Africa, they don't know anything; they're all Bangladeshi restaurateurs. They don't even know how to say 'Ramayana.'"

I didn't know how to say "Ramayana" either, so I kept quiet: there was nothing I could say if the place where he belonged was, almost by definition, the one where he didn't want to be and the place where he wanted to be was, almost by definition, the one that wouldn't have him.

"I should let you go," I said finally, since I knew where the conversation would go, and I had nothing to contribute to it.

"How terribly English of you," he snapped before releasing me, "saying you want to let me go because you want to go yourself."

One summer's day in England, I went to the cricket grounds at Headingley, in Leeds, to see the fifth and final day of the first Test match between England and the West Indies. Only six other people got off the train with me at the tiny country station near the grounds, and all of them, I noticed, were of my parents' age or older. Perhaps this was because England had lost to Australia, to India, and to Pakistan recently, and hadn't, in fact, beaten the West Indies on British soil in twenty-two years, winning exactly four of their last forty-four matches against their Caribbean subjects. It's the unemployment in the Caribbean, the old people were saying as we walked toward the grounds, and, besides, all the competitive fire's gone out of England; there's a special value placed on success if you grow up in one of those poor countries.

Around me in the stands, most of the plastic seats were unoccupied for this climactic day (because of the recession, said the men with rolled-up brollies); so few had shown up the previous day that everyone in attendance had been given free tickets to return today. Now I saw a few men in ties, scattered here and there, following the action on Walkmans, and two others dressed from head to toe as Ninja Turtles (or "Hero Turtles," as they are ineffably known in Britain).

The players on the pitch, as I'd never seen before, had chalk on their faces, so they looked like Burmese village girls, and the ads around the grounds advertised "Daewoo"; one of the spectators nearby muttered about one of England's players being "very patrician" and was quickly told, "Actually, not so patrician: he grew up in the East End, and his father used to stand on the street selling birds. The trouble was, they were homing pigeons."

On the radio, the famously articulate Old Etonian announcer, who had just dined with the Queen, was murmuring like a tributary of the Thames about "handsome strokes" and "cultivated cricketers" and shots pulled out "like a silk handkerchief being removed from a top pocket."

So much of it was like the England I'd grown up with, watching the regal West Indians effortlessly thrash the combined Oxford-and-Cambridge team in the University Parks: the redbrick buildings grouped together under chill gray skies, the hand-operated scoreboard and the puddle on the pitch, the intermittent clapping as batsmen returned to the pavilion after "ducks" or bowlers completed "maiden overs" with their "googlies" and their "Chinamen." In one part of the stands, a small band of merry West Indians was playing barbershop ditties, and as the match began to go against them started to sing, "Please, God, Please" ("I think," said one of the fans around me, "it's a West Indian rain dance or something."); before the match had begun, I gathered, the Yorkshire Club president, Sir Lawrence Byford (once Her Majesty's chief inspector of constabulary), had reminded the assembled throng that the West Indian lads should be treated "with the respect they are entitled to deserve" and had issued a stern headmasterly caution that "bad behavior and abusive language have no place in a cricket ground."

Now, though, as England began to close in on an unexpected victory, its fans struck up a beery, cheery chant of "God Save Our Pring"—a reference to their hero, Derek Pringle, an English player—and at the end the "man of the match" was given a jeroboam of champagne. In the national jubilation that followed, the one thing that was not so often mentioned—and more obvious to a visitor, perhaps—was that the main reason England had prevailed was that six of its eleven players came from the colonies—including those in Africa, the subcontinent, and, in fact, the Caribbean ("much the most orthodox and secure of the England batsmen," according to the *Daily Telegraph*, had the newly typical English name of Mark Ramprakash). The one time in recent years England had fielded a team without any colored players—their style was a little languorous, the gentlemanly arbiters of cricket had suggested—it lost a five-day match before the third day was over.

This was not so much to say that the Empire had reversed direction as that the very sense of what direction it pointed in was somewhat by the by; the same day that a "pitifully small" crowd showed up at Headingley, more than 60,000 had packed into the Wembley arena to watch the London Monarchs take on Barcelona in the "World Bowl" championship of the newly popular American football league in Europe. There were cheerleaders and marching bands and cartoon characters performing somersaults, and the crowd, said the *Times*, was full of "youth and keenness" as well as "almost universally wearing some form of Monarchs merchandise." When the Monarchs held up their trophy, the entire stadium turned into a field of Union Jacks, and the players (most of whom were American) gamely ran around the stadium collecting and waving the English flag. It was as fine a celebration, a British sportswriter said, as ever seen in Wembley, and for a while England was back on top of the world. Not the dangerous plaything of hooligans (as soccer could be), not the polite diversion of gentlemen (as cricket occasionally was), American football had seemed to save the English from themselves.

*

The next time I saw my Indian friend happened to be in Los Angeles, at one of the Bombay Palace restaurants now reproduced around the globe. He had come to America in search of a new life, I guessed, and I was reminded, sadly, of how the unhappiest people I know these days are often the ones in motion, encouraged to search for a utopia outside themselves, as if the expulsion from Eden had been Eden's fault. Globalism made the world the playground of those with no one to play with.

As my friend began talking, I felt I was hearing exactly the same lines as before, in Cambridge; it was as if he were perpetually conducting a discussion (an argument, really) with himself, or with someone who said nothing in return. "I see so much hatred in England now," he said, as if to explain his presence in L. A. "Maybe it's just because I'm more aware of it than I used to be, but I know bloody well I speak better English than they do, and the English won't accept that. The English hate me for being more English than they are; they want you all to conform to some image they can patronize. But because I know more about English literature than they do, and because I believe in the good old notions of fair play and decency, they can't stand me. I should have won an Oscar for the roles I've played in real life."

The sentences went round in circles, much as he did; he'd lost track of where he was, I felt, playing an Englishman while he cursed the English, fleeing an India that was surely his great calling card in England.

"You see, I grew up with all these notions," he continued—tucking into the hottest food the waiter could find, his voice as sonorous as Gielgud's—"I used to pick a line of Shakespeare, and my great-uncle could always give me the next one. I think it was from there that I got my love of English literature, and the buildings, the history, all that. The men who raised me believed in all the Victorian values."

But Victoria, I wanted to say, had died almost a century ago, and I wondered how many of these memories had actually grown out of my friend's nostalgic accounts to Englishmen. "When I was a boy," he went on, "my aunt used to bring me a cable-knit sweater every year, handmade, from Dehra Dun; now I'd do anything to get a cable-knit sweater. It's funny: I suppose the only people who believe in the old values anymore are a few old fogies writing for the *Daily Telegraph* and talking about the loss of the country they love. So I find myself agreeing with the people I want to hate."

Just as I was beginning to despair, he surprised me with a shaft of self-knowledge, and I thought how deeply Indian he sounded even in his affirmation of Englishness (so assertive, so earnest, so passionate even; besides, few Englishmen would have been caught dead talking so warmly about the Beeb or the *Times* or the Marylebone Cricket Club).

"Whenever things fall apart," he said, and I was touched again, unexpectedly, "I turn to India. Indian restaurants, Indian faces, Indian news." But he couldn't go back, of course, until he'd made it as an Englishman, and I couldn't imagine many Englishmen wanting to be told by him what "Englishness" really was. America was a desperate last resort.

"The Indians living in England seem to me to embody all the worst qualities of England, to do with greed and undereducation," he said, "and none of the best. Maybe it was never really like that, but I always felt that England stood for something, that there were ideals there." In the made-for-export version, I thought, perhaps cruelly; in the never-never England "before the war" that both of us could idealize because we'd never seen it.

"I left England," I said, maybe only to provoke him, "because I felt that, having gone to the 'right' school and college, I had no incentive to do anything; I could have been a homicidal maniac, and still, I felt, I could always get a good job."

"Then why didn't you stay?" he responded to this unkindness, and I realized that what I should have said was that anything can be a source of resentment in England: the details are neither here nor there. What colonialism had given me was the chance to grow up so close to the heart of Empire that I could never be enthralled by it. But that wasn't what he wanted to hear.

"I can't help thinking they've changed the rules on me," he said, and again I felt as if he were talking to himself. "They taught me to believe in one set of values, and I do; and now it's a completely different England."

Indeed it is, and the old, simple relation of dreamer to dream has been shaken about in the Global Age, as if by a hyperactive child in the heavens. When I got off the plane at Heathrow on a recent trip, it was to find the London cabs swathed in ads for Fujitsu and Burger King and the billboards in the tube stations advertising "Afro-Caribbean" hair treatments and an all-black production of *Antony and Cleopatra* (on my next trip, they were advertising a production in which Cleopatra was played by a man). The laundry list in my little hotel had a special box for "Arab Gown" (and spelled "college" with a "d"); in the Yellow Pages, a place that still bore the name of an Anglican church now advertised itself, impenitently, as a "Temple of Fitness" where you could "work off thy last Supper" with "our 100 American state-of-the-art machines."

Every myth (as the great fashioner of them, Wilde, explains in his parable of Dorian Gray) has a power to hang on long after the reality has shifted, and Little England would surely uphold old notions of "Englishness" long after Great Britain had reached out to the larger world; the country I'd grown up in greeted me in the tabloid headlines, such as, "He's Found the Chink in Chang's Armour," or the fire notice in my room—not far from a laminated card offering direct-dial service to Häagen-Dazs—warning, "Do not prejudice your safety by stopping to collect your personal belongings" (in the event of a conflagration). Cities face the same choice that celebrities do when measuring their shadows—they can either play to the cameras or turn their back on them (do a Norman Mailer, you could say, or a J. D. Salinger). England had unapologetically chosen the first course, marketing the Royal Family for all it was worth and encouraging bagpipers to play outside the Dunkin' Donuts parlor in "Theatreland." In the Keats House Museum you could buy a teddy bear wearing a sash that says, I AM A R♥MANTIC.

To me, again, much of this was welcome. No one but an American is likely to deny the appeal of American culture, and I can still remember, as a child in Oxford, sitting transfixed before Hanna-Barbera cartoons or Lucille Ball, not because they were American but because they were better and more vivid than anything else on TV (and later, in adolescence, finding images of possibility and hopefulness in Henry Miller or the Grateful Dead that simply weren't available in England); anyone who's grown up on Wimpy bars and greasy "transport caffs" can appreciate how life in places like Oxford was made unimaginably more pleasant by the advent of first Baskin-Robbins, then McDonald's, in the late Seventies, offering clean and dependable places in which to eat that were neither cheap nor expensive. Again, in fact, like America, England seemed to have been invigorated by its visitors from abroad, and it never seemed a coincidence to me that many of Britain's proudest new traditions—the Globe Theatre, *Granta,* and the modernized Oxford colleges—had been rescued by energetic "Yanks."

England now looked, as most places do, more American, more European, more Asian—more everything but its old self—and that meant that the food was better, the culture was livelier, and the grudges were buried under a new glossy sheen; everything, including the colors, was richer than before (to the point where London had even managed to "rebrand" itself as a city of young lovers whose "Cool Britannia" styles were drawing kids from around the Continent). To some extent, the island was being forced to grow less insular, more tolerant to a whole world streaming into it (the Empire in reverse), and anyone who wanted to say, as Nancy Mitford had not untypically done, "Abroad is unutterably bloody and foreigners are fiends" had to do so now sotto voce.

Nobody, of course, is entirely smitten with the place where he was born. By chance, my own family had ended up following the very course of empires, from India in the last days of the British, to England as it was falling under the spell of America, to America itself, in the mid-Sixties, when the American century was at its zenith, and the psychedelic California in which we eventually found ourselves was suddenly on every screen. Later, again by pure coincidence, I would move to Japan just as it was buying up Rockefeller Center and Columbia Pictures, in the late Eighties, and becoming what looked to be a new center of gravity.

But for my parents and for me, such movements carried very different meanings, I think. It wasn't so much that they were born in India and I in England as that they knew they came from India (albeit a British India), whereas I always felt I came from nowhere. Our worldviews didn't clash so much as they didn't overlap: my parents knew where they belonged, what they believed, and where their allegiances lay, and they remained unchanged in this for all their lives (in thinking that India was home, and Pakistan was an enemy, and Macaulay and Churchill had been enemies to India); after fifty years of living in the West, they still, quite rightly, kept their Indian passports.

I, by contrast, lacked their furies and felt I'd inherited none of their enmities. I had no tradition to protect, I felt, and I reveled in those like Theodor Adorno, who said, "It is part of morality not to be at home in one's home." Instead of their passions, I was more prone to a floating dispassion; and instead of their fierce sense of right and wrong, I had a more unanchored, relativistic sense. "Perhaps there is an advantage in being born in a city like Monte Carlo, without roots," says Brown, the suitably anonymous character in Graham Greene's *Comedians* (having seen his "unknown brother" Jones die along the international road), "for one accepts more easily what comes."

The biggest difference between me and my Indian friend, as well as those of my parents' generation, I came to feel, was that I'd never had a strong sense of departures (or arrivals); as a member of a mobile, global generation, I'd grown up without a sense of a place to come to or from which to leave; and whereas someone like my Indian friend was caught in the space between two worlds, as between mother and father in a custody battle, someone like me, I figured, could (for worse as much as better) fit in everywhere. My friend had a map made up of clear divisions; mine was a shifting thing in which everywhere could be home to some extent, and also not home. My sense of severances was less absolute, and although I could visualize the partings in the old stories—the boy at dockside, carrying the hopes of his family across the seas, perhaps not to see them again for years—I knew I could get anywhere very soon, and nothing was final.

It was many years, then, before I could understand the spells that distance could create, in an age when people really might not know whether they would ever return and separation had a special force. It was many years before I could see pictures of my father, proud in his Indian formal wear, president of the Oxford Union, and realize that he was flanked on every side by the kind of Englishmen that an Indian might have dreamed of, in Bombay (one would go on to become editor of the *Times*, one deputy prime minister; one would become head of the Liberal Party; another, the steady sage of the BBC). I imagined his family gathered around the crackly transistor radio in the small flat in the Bombay suburbs, listening to their distant hero on the World Service broadcast, opposing such notions as "This House refuses to take itself seriously," and I realized that by going halfway through the open door, he had allowed me to walk out of it on the other side.

One day, when I met my Indian friend in New York, it was to find that, somehow, and unexpectedly, he'd set up house within his dreams: he'd met a highly eligible young Englishwoman—well-born, beautiful, intelligent, sincere, and highly successful—and this very picture of the blushing English rose had consented to be his wife. Now, as he spoke, in his Old World cadences, of the "human sufferings" and privations of an India he'd scarcely seen, she sat, quite literally, at his feet, eyes filling with tears at the thought of all he'd been through. Her father, I was not surprised to hear, was a domineering imperial type, still administering his own corner of Empire in the East; she was guilty, anxious to atone, a vegetarian.

Her eyes came to life as she spoke of the possibility of visiting her new in-laws, in the place her husband had worked so hard to flee; he said Hawaii sounded preferable.

A little later, when the romance was over, she would say that he was a hypnotist, another dark sorcerer from the East come to ensnare this young Englishwoman out of Forster; he had tried to turn her into an Indian woman, she complained, expecting her to walk six paces behind him and do up his shoelaces. "Come now, my dear," he had said, "what is this, *Othello?* In Thatcher's England?"

But he had made one mistake that no shrewd Englishman would ever make, and that no Englishman of the old order would forgive: he had faked a ruling-class pedigree.

"I said I'd gone to Winchester," he told me, a little defiantly, when I saw him next (down on his luck again and sad), "because I *felt* I'd been there. I remember, when I was fifteen, a man in Singapore telling me, 'You're my little Wykehamist. You talk like a Wykehamist, you act like a Wykehamist, you believe, like a Wykehamist, that manners maketh man.'

"I thought of myself as an Oxonian," he said, a little plaintively, "because Oxford is the home of lost causes."

*

Perhaps the last time I had contact with my Indian friend came after a long absence. I had happened to call him to tell him of a death in the family, and he, fumbling for words on the international phone lines, had left a message on my answering machine in which he reached for a quote from Christina Rossetti, then lamented that he couldn't quite summon the right words from Eliot, and then concluded, in his antique voice, "Look after yourself, dear boy," with a resonance that sounded theatrical and emotional both, India and its version of Great Britain.

When I saw him a couple of months later, though, he was playing the same tape as before, over and over, as if some mechanism had got stuck somehow, as if in the process of emigration he'd got caught in a revolving door, unable quite to come through to the place he'd set out for.

"Of course, if you talk with a thick Indian accent, they'll love you. But if you're middle-class, and have some sense of decency, they feel threatened. The working-class white hates a middle-class Indian much more than he does a working-class Indian with a thick accent and Cockney slang.

"Oh, I don't know," he finally said, turning the tape off at last. "I suppose I just miss an England that is built on elegance and love of language and love of literature, instead of money. Maybe I'm kidding myself, maybe it never existed. Maybe Bernard Shaw was right in saying 'Patriotism is the last refuge of a scoundrel.'" I didn't have the heart to tell him that the quote came, in fact, from Samuel Johnson.

Lidia Torres

Three Keys

From *The Massachusetts Review*

I inherit three skeleton keys,
a thick metal ring
tied in a bow at the end.

These keys cannot lock
the bare rooms with quiet
ghosts of three brothers.

I call them at night,
the rusted metal ringing
in my pocket. My brother answers, tapping

the conga skin with the tips of his fingers,
lightly, not to wake my sister
in the room next door dreaming

of my father. In her dreams,
he is counting beds, readying rooms.
Another brother taps the clave's beat.

The last brother answers by barely scraping
a güiro. Then we are all
in the same dream, alive and dead.

There is the palm tree you wanted.
The mangos are so low,
they graze your fingers

when you try to reach them.
Limes among roses, orchids.
Even the roots bear fruit

in our garden. The scent
of guavas. The tapping
and scraping of the trío.

Bryant Keith Alexander

Standing at the Crossroads

From *Callaloo*

Standing at the crossroads, tried to flag a ride,
Standing at the crossroads, tried to flag a ride,
Ain't nobody seem to know me, everybody passed me by.
—*Crossroad Blues*

I am the fifth child of seven children, the fourth boy of five boys. I was born into a social experiment that my parents called a family. In spite of the dynamic social interaction that goes on in a large family, I grew up a very private kid, constantly demanding his own space, his own place, his own identity—separate from my brothers (the athletic brother, the talented brother, the handsome brother, the younger brother). I always felt that I was at a crossroads between who I was and wanted to be and who they were, my biological brothers and my cultural brothers—and the directions that their lives were taking them.

The house that I grew up in was located on a corner lot in the center of our neighborhood, at a crossroads between Simcoe Street and 12th Street. All the local kids flocked over to our house. My mother used to say, "with seven kids you're bound to attract a lot more." Our yard was the place to be. We had pecan trees and mulberry trees, a fig tree and a pine tree. We had a big front porch, an area for football and a dirt basketball court. This was the main attraction. Guys from around the neighborhood would come with their attitude and bravado, fighting over who would be shirts or skins. Sporting their new Converse tennis shoes, these guys would walk into our yard talking a whole lotta shit, who would win, by how many points and who would make it to the NBA. These Black guys performed the pageantry of youthful dreaming and the ritual of growing up. I watched the fellas from the side window, one of two in the living room of our house. I would watch them, young Olympians in the prime of their manhood—calling up the dirt, swirling in dust clouds of hopes and dreams. Their bodies were caked with a mixture of sweat, dirt and tenacity. The basketball court was a crossroads, a passage into another time, another space, a ticket to another place.

The other window in the living room looked out the front. The house that I grew up in was located across the street from Syrie Funeral Home. During the evening I would often look through it and see the pageantry of death and the ritual of saying good-bye. In the distance I could hear the mournful wails of those feeling grief. I could see the old men sipping from a bottle of courage near the dumpster. I saw children doing what children do—some playing games, others engaged in solemn social banter. I saw people looking silently, longingly into the distance, standing at the crossroads of their memories and their reality.

On September 7, 1994, I drove from Carbondale, Illinois, to Lafayette, Louisiana, to attend the funeral of my brother Nathaniel Patrick Alexander, who had died from complications with AIDS three days earlier. Family members and friends asked why I didn't fly, but I needed the time. In my informed confusion I thought that if I delayed getting there I could somehow suspend time. During that eleven-hour drive I crossed real and imagined borders, traveling down a road that took me to painfully familiar places: The day he told me he was gay. The day he introduced me to a partner. The day he called me and said, "Are you coming home this summer?" The day I helped him move home. The day I found out he had AIDS. The day he said, "I'm sorry I let you down." The day he said, "I love you." The day he died.

As I pulled into Lafayette, I reflected on another special day. After a name calling episode with some of the local boys in which I was the focus of their pro-masculine anti-sissy juvenile male posturing, my brother sat me down and said, "I see me in you. We are so much alike. There are many versions of being a man. Find the one that is best for you that does not cause harm to others. Be who you are, what you are, how you are, and to shit with them." I was 13, he was 17. I enter my parents' house at 10:30 p.m., and I am immediately surrounded by family, minus one. I navigate myself through childhood memories and put to rest sibling rivalries. I greet my sisters, my older brother, his wife and children. I talk to the other older brother on the phone; he was incarcerated in the local jail for drug dealing. He was feeling the pain of his absence in that time of family grief. I hold a strained conversation with the younger brother who, since dropping out of high school, finds it difficult to talk to me, his graduate student-teacher-older-brother.

The next day my family arrives at the funeral home early for a private viewing of the body. This is the first that I have seen my brother in months. He looks thin and ashy. Surprisingly, I find myself more angered than sad. I am angry at his carelessness. I am angry that as a Black man he carried himself recklessly through the world. I am angry because his hair is combed forward instead of backwards. I am angry because he is wearing a plaid jacket that even he would not be caught dead in. His skin is darkened. His eyes are deep. The clothes are draped over his body like they are hanging on a rack. His eyes are closed, and there is a slight smile on his face, a glimmer of recognition, but no real acknowledgment. I miss him. I miss seeing the me in him. This is not the brother that I fought with for years, the brother who helped me to cross over into being.

Later that evening I saw faces from my past, all older, a little grizzled. I have not seen many of these faces in years; as the resident family recluse and all around shy-guy, I retreated from the neighborhood years before and busied myself with high school, then college, then graduate school and then teaching. Many of them hesitate when they see me, an adult version of the child memory, the face in the window. Then almost predictably they comment, "You look like him." "You sound like him." "You act like him." It is an attempt to recreate him. It is a form of celebration and renewal. I smile uncomfortably and welcome them. I see a number of my brother's friends, gay men who float in on a trail of tears. I know many of them. We greet. We hug. We kiss, and as gay men we stand at the crossroads of our lives. We look at each other, searching our faces for some sign, for some assurance, for a denial, for escape.

During a novena, a repetitive chanting of prayers, I step out. While standing outside of the funeral home, I realize that I am engaged in the pageantry of death and the ritual of saying good-bye. In the distance I can hear the mournful wails of those feeling grief. I can see the old men sipping on a bottle of courage near the dumpster. I can see children doing what children do, some playing games, others engaged in solemn social banter. I am looking silently, longingly into the distance, standing at the crossroads of my memories and my reality. I look across the street at an empty lot where my childhood house used to stand, long removed. I hear the faint sounds of brothers and sisters fighting and laughing. The trees are still there, but the grass has long grown over the arena of boyish dreams, where Black boys performed the pageantry of youthful dreaming and the ritual of growing up in the swirl of dust and clouds of sweat.

In the distance leaning against the pecan tree, I see a figure. Standing there is the memory of a boy named Donald, one of my childhood friends, a basketball player—a titan of the court. Now, he is a shadow of a man, frail from drug and alcohol abuse. The tree holds him up as he sips a bit of courage before he begins to cross the road to pay his respects. As he approaches me, I see that his skin is darkened and ashy, his eyes are deep, the clothes are draped over his body like they are hanging on a rack. He conceals his bottle as he pulls up his pants. I stand there dressed in a tailored suit, manicured fingers and designer glasses. When he crosses my path, he hesitates. Our eyes meet. There is a glimmer of recognition, but no real acknowledgment. I mourn the loss of Donald. I mourn the loss of my brother. I mourn the loss of young Black men and youth-filled dreams.

I am standing. I am standing at a crossroads between my brothers: the married brother, the dead brother, the jailed brother, the dropout brother. I am standing at the crossroads between my biological brothers and my cultural brothers. I am standing, looking through a window to another time onto a dust basketball court, seeing young Black Olympians in the prime of their manhood perform the pageantry of youthful dreaming and the ritual of growing up. I am standing at a crossroads of my life as a Black gay man living in the age of AIDS. I am standing at a crossroads looking through the window, seeing myself engaged in the pageantry of death and the ritual of saying good-bye. I am standing at the crossroads between Simcoe Street and 12th Street, between my childhood home and the funeral home, between boyish dreams and adult realities. I am standing at a crossroads—looking, reflecting, remembering, moving and being moved, but standing still at an intersection in space and a breach in time.

Aimee Nezhukumatathil

Speak

From *Chelsea*

If the Hopi say *ripi*
to mean *notch*, then
for them, *serration*
is "ripiripiripi." I want
to speak like that, fill
your ears and hands
with wet stones, turquoise
and smooth, as if
they had been tumbled
in the mouth of a macaw.

Larry McMurtry

Death of the Cowboy

From *The New York Review of Books*

The death of the cowboy as a vital figure has been one of my principal subjects, and yet I'm well aware that killing the *myth* of the cowboy is like trying to kill a snapping turtle: no matter what you do to it, the beast retains a sluggish life. The cowboy has long since been absorbed into the national bloodstream, but is no longer quite so front-and-center in the popular culture. The Marlboro man is a last survival of the Western male in the heroic mode. In Marlboro ads the West is always the mountain West, the high, rich country that runs from Jackson Hole around to Sheridan, Wyoming, where the Queen of England sometimes goes to buy her racehorses. The West of those ads is the familiar, poeticized, pastoral West—the Marlboro men themselves need to do little other than light up. Perhaps they swing their ropes at a herd of horses that are thundering toward a corral.

Horses only, mind you—never cattle. The image of horses running is perhaps the most potent image to come out of the American West: cattle running produces, to most eyes, a far less appealing picture. The fact is, cows are hard to poeticize—even longhorns. They tend to seem ugly, stupid, and slow, which they are; images of cows are unlikely to loosen the pocketbooks of smokers in Japan or elsewhere where the Marlboro man and his horses are seen, and they are seen everywhere. No image out of the American West is so ubiquitous, and they are images that are entirely male—Marlboro country is a woman-free zone. Sometimes there is a cabin in the snow, with a wreath of smoke coming out of the chimney. The running horses may be making for this cabin. But if there is a woman in there, cooking for her man, we don't see her: we just see the rugged male, riding the high country forever.

Few cowboys, though, smoke Marlboros. The image is rural but the consumption is mainly urban. One reason for this is that the Marlboro man is so commanding an image that the dusty, slightly lumpy real cowboys don't feel they can aspire to it. The mere fact that the real cowboys have to wrestle smelly cattle all day removes them from the world of godlike horsemen. The level of romanticization needed to sustain the Marlboro image is extremely high: it needs the prettiest country in the whole West, plus horses, to keep it working.

Another indicator that the cowboy myth is gradually being absorbed into suburban culture is the current smoothing out of country music. Garth Brooks, who will soon have sold more records than the Beatles, is at the head of this trend. His songs are music for the suburbs and the freeways, songs to be listened to in the cabs of the newer, more expensive pickups; it is genteel music, domestic music, as opposed to the loner's music of someone like Hank Williams.

What the Western experience has demonstrated perhaps more clearly than any other is the astonishing speed with which things can change. There were so many buffalo—fifty million, by some estimates—that no one could really envision their disappearance, yet it took barely twenty years to eliminate them. Similarly, the cowboys who went north up the plains to the Yellowstone couldn't quite at first imagine that the unfenced purity of the Great Plains would be fenced and cut into ranches in less than half their lifetime. A young cowboy of 1866 saw the virgin land as one great expanse, stretching all the way from Mexico to Canada; such a cowboy would have had to be very prescient to imagine that most of that land would be cut up and fenced before he was even middle-aged. But many cowboys lived to see that happen, and it left them with a confused, unhappy, bittersweet feeling, unable to forget the paradise they helped destroy. They could never either recover it or forget it. Some may have realized that they themselves were only insignificant pawns in the economic drama of the West.

The giants of finance had already begun to look at the West with a hungry eye, and would soon begin to use their might to shape it to the needs of business, a shaping which first required the elimination of both the native people and the buffalo, who were occupying what was thought to be good farmland. Though it was easy enough to despoil the West, it turned out to be not so easy to despoil it profitably. For one thing, little people such as my grandparents began to trickle in, settling their sections and quarter sections, getting in the way of more visionary schemes.

I have said that my father studied cattle with the same fascination with which I study books, but now that I've thought back on it, I'm not sure that's true. He studied cattle practically, with a view to herd improvement, or to detect signs of illness in his cattle. What interested him more, on both the intellectual and emotional level, was grass. To the extent that he had a religion, it was grass, a religion whose grandeur and complexity were worthy of him. He was born and lived his whole life on one of the great prairies of the world, on the shore of a sea of grass that stretched northward into Canada, and he retained a religious feeling about grass to the end of his life. He recognized, from walking on it and contemplating it all his life, that the world of grass was multiplex. He envied his neighbor the oilman, rancher, and philanthropist J. S. Bridwell, who had the financial resources to successfully fight the two local enemies of our grass which were the bane of my father's life as a cattleman: mesquite and prickly pear. Mr. Bridwell had the money to bulldoze the mesquite off his land, the result being that his land—separated from ours only by a wire fence—looked like a paradise while ours looked like a hell. Even to the uneducated eye our grass was clearly less robust and less varied than his. The reason was obvious: we had mesquite and he didn't.

Not that we didn't fight it. Whenever a space appeared in a workday unexpectedly, my father would attack the mesquite with spade, axe, grubbing hoe, and kerosene can, pressing a struggle so hopeless that I could never understand why he did it. At best he could only hope to drive the trees back a few yards, and for a short time at that. Within a year or two they would always regain whatever territory he had wrested from them. The mesquite was as implacable as the Comanches had been, and far more resilient. My father couldn't hope to win, and he didn't win, but he kept fighting.

I expect I must, in part, have developed my notion of character from watching my father struggle against the mesquite. Character came to mean struggling on in the face of hopeless odds: in that attitude lay the vital stubbornness of the pioneers who refused to acquiesce to the brute circumstances they were faced with daily: the hostile natives, the often unresponsive land, the destructive elements—flood, drought, fire. Some of your children might die, your livestock might starve, the toil to be toiled might be beyond your strength: but at least the land was yours, if you could just hold it. Some could, some couldn't.

My father, I believe, always felt a little hamstrung by his own sense of duty. His brothers left and made modest fortunes in the Panhandle; he stayed home, took care of the old folks, and worked all his life with very limited acreage, which he was only partially able to supplement with leaseholds scattered all over the county. Though historically minded, to a point, he nonetheless romanticized the possibilities that existed to the north when his brothers left home; for all their efforts, none of the nine McMurtry boys got very rich in the cattle business, or any business. They prospered but their prosperity didn't approach that of the legendary Texas rich.

Studies had been available from the 1940s—indeed, from the turn of the century—that showed clearly enough that the range-cattle business had never been a particularly good business. It had depended from the first on overgrazing, with the subsequent and almost immediate deterioration of the prairie ecosystems on which it was based. These conclusions were drawn very early and were clearly stated by the Department of Agriculture in its yearly handbooks. But my father didn't like the Department of Agriculture; he saw it as creeping socialism. Studious though he was about the cattle business, he probably didn't read the department's conclusions, which were, in the main, sound. Instead, he stayed in debt for fifty-five straight years, attempting to profitably raise the wrong animal—the Hereford cow—on land that had been far better utilized by the animal that had been there to begin with: the buffalo.

Herefords and Angus and other English or continental stock were lazy grazers, and were also ill adapted to severe winters, but the English who began to pour money into the Western cattle business in the second half of the nineteenth century wanted them anyway, and got them; never mind that the cattle died like flies in the high plains blizzards and merely stood around listlessly during the blazing summer.

In a sense the whole range-cattle industry, source of a central national myth, was a mistake, based on a superficial understanding of the plains environment. As Richard Manning cogently points out in his recent book *Grassland* (1995), 50 million buffalo were replaced by 45 million cattle, to the ultimate detriment of everyone's home on the range. Now the plains are so overgrazed—the public lands particularly—that should a major drought occur, the potential for a new Dust Bowl is great.

What small cattlemen such as my father got, in place of fortune, was a life that they loved. Seen historically, they were in conflict almost from the first with farming interests. Like most cattlemen my father recognized that running cattle was an indulgence, economically; he would have made more money farming. But it happened that he liked raising cattle and hated farming, though even as a young boy, I often heard him predict that our land would be farmland someday—and farms are lapping at its borders even as I write.

Looking back on the more than forty years during which I have been involved as a writer with the American cowboy, I wonder if part of what kept me interested was the tragedy, the inherent mismating of beast and place, which was always woven into it. The twenty-two years when I was involved with the ranch exposed me regularly to a small but representative group of cowboys and cattlemen—the men we worked with. This little bunch contained all the types that one finds up and down the range country. There were a couple of ranch owners whose holdings were roughly comparable to ours. There were three or four cowhands who were just that, cowhands, men who didn't own an acre of land and never would. These ranch hands were well into middle age; they were not very competent, drew small wages, and lived in single rooms behind the larger ranch houses; their fates were sealed. They had no wives, no visible women.

Then there were two or three extremely competent cowboys who did all the most complicated work; they were smallholders, owning a few cattle, leasing a pasture here and there, which we helped them work. Shared labor is the norm in the cattle country; few ranches can afford to employ all the help they might need. The work exchange is virtually universal.

And then there was a foreman or two, men who managed sizable ranches for absentee (or indolent) owners; the foremen customarily owned no land themselves, though it was the custom for the ranch owners to let them run a few head of cattle, as a bonus for their industry and trustworthiness.

There, in essence, you have the ranching West: smallholders, foremen, top hands, and just hands. Even the more prosperous ranchers were smallholders, really, men with ten or twelve thousand acres, not a vast range in country where it can take thirty-five acres to support a cow.

Occasionally, in this mix, would be an old cowhand, too old to be very active but respected for work done in earlier years and still capable of performing small chores—loading the vaccinating needles, keeping the branding fires stoked, carrying the bucket in which calf fries, mountain oysters (calf testicles), were collected. These old-timers are kept active as long as possible out of a sense of decency, kept a part of the work, because if an old cowboy can't work what would he do but wither and die? So it was with my father. When arthritis and fatigue slowed him to the point where he couldn't move fast enough to get out of the way of a gate or a running animal, the ranchers he had worked with much of his life became reluctant to call him to help them work cattle, for fear he would injure himself; but he had been a highly respected man and they were reluctant to relegate him to an old man's chores. Once it became clear to my father that his neighbors were right—that he was an old man who, for all his skill and experience, would mostly get in the way—he was bitter for a few weeks and then lay down and died.

The tragedy of my father's life effort, and that of many ranchers up and down the West, was that, despite skill and hard work (application, my father called it), they could never really get ahead. At best they held their own, living off credit, struggling, working, seeking a method that would improve their chances. My father read constantly in the literature of the range—the literature, and the science too—hoping to discover some new approach or technique that would allow him to improve his cattle or his land.

The statistical literature on Western ranching, available even when he was a boy, told the story plainly enough. The experts knew early what percentage of Western land had already been ruined. They also knew something about the cycles of Western drought, flood, and winter severity. They knew, in short, that the odds were heavily stacked against the smallholder in the West who was dependent on cattle alone. I don't think my father ever found his way to these statistics—perhaps he didn't want to know them. He wanted very much to make the cowboying life last, and by dint of shrewd planning and very hard work, he did just manage to make it last his lifetime. But tragedy was woven into the effort anyway. He had limited acreage and was raising the wrong animal; he was only able to stay in business because he lived most of his life in an era of cheap credit. Like most smallholders in the West he knew quite well that if a really bad year came—drought or flood—the elements alone might crush him.

I was born in the Depression, only a year after the great dust blizzards that Woody Guthrie sang about. Times got better during World War II, which didn't keep all the people I grew up with from being Depression-haunted. I derived early the sense that solvency was a precarious thing. Now and then I heard talk about so-and-so, who had gone under. I didn't really know what going under meant, but I knew that the prospect of it was never very far from my father's mind, or the minds of his peers in the small-ranch country. People went under, and that, apparently, was the end of them.

From the age of three until I left for college I was sometimes constantly and always frequently on horseback on the land. Day after day I was out there under the sky, a partial nomad, working in fenced country but still much freer spatially than city kids. I spent enough time directly on the land, beneath that sky, to understand that the elements were a lot more powerful than myself, my father, or any of us. I was once knocked down by a steer in a lightning storm so intense that the white light made the animal invisible, obliterated by brightness, as if an X-ray were coming toward me.

I've also seen conflicts between men and animals escalate into terrible, Dostoevskian violence, men beating stubborn cattle with fence posts, fleeing bulls knocking over pickups and even, once, a large cattle truck. All this is unexceptional in Western ranch life.

What struck me in the cattlemen, my father most particularly, was the intensity of their desire to make it last. No Indian ever wanted to call back the buffalo more intensely than they wanted to call back the open range. The same land that the Indian longed to see filled with buffalo the cattlemen wanted to see filled with cattle, moving north, though in fact the real open range lasted almost no time. Barbed wire, the invention that was to slice it up, was invented scarcely five years after trail driving began. But in the minds of cattlemen and also in movies, the open range survives still, an Edenic fantasy of carefree nomadism in which cattle are allowed to follow grass wherever grass grows.

The notion that all flesh is grass is one that would have pleased my father; it would, I expect, please all cattlemen, herdsmen, drovers, men who follow grazing animals over the land, seeking the grass that nourishes them. Such men, pantheistic by nature, resolutely reject anything that smacks of the modern world: its politics, its art, its technology. What they accept, at a profound level, is the cycle of nature, in which men and animals alike are born, grow old, and die, to be succeeded by new generations of men and animals. Recycling of this natural sort does not bother men who live on the land; some even resent the fact that modern burial practices retard the process. The notion that they will soon again become part of the food chain doesn't bother them at all.

It is usually when one is in one's sixties that one begins to wonder whether the customary yardsticks by which success is measured have any relevance at all. My father, as he neared the end, counted himself lucky that he had owned a few good horses in his life and had sustained a good name through seventy-six years. Though he enjoyed great respect, and the love of his family, in his last years he often expressed to me his conviction that reality was more than a little cracked. Somehow life hadn't really added up; his works and days hadn't been a harmony, as he supposed they might have been for his brothers and other cattlemen who had accumulated more land and raised better cattle. In the end the two or three good horses seemed to mean more to him than anything he had done with cattle or the range. The winds of futility blew through like northers. What had it all been for?

When I would try to argue against my father's sense of futility he would sometimes cheer up a little, reminding himself that he had his children, he had his good name, and there had been those two or three horses. He could not really hand his children a viable tradition—ranching had by then become an avocation for oilmen, lawyers, insurance men, and other nostalgic city dwellers who wanted, somehow, to make contact with the land again.

Once he was too old to wage war against them, the mesquite soon began to sweep over the old prairie. On the last day of my father's life—I'm told by my son, who was with him—he slowly drove around the hill down at the home place where his parents, William Jefferson and Louisa Francis, had stopped some ninety years before, enticed by water, by that fine seeping spring. The next morning my father lay down in the kitchen and died. The hired man who found him and woke my son merely said, "Jeff's gone."

I now think it's likely that a lot of my writing about the cowboy was an attempt to understand my father's essentially tragic take on his own—and human—experience. He was not, day to day, an unhappy man; he was accessible to jollity, joking, dancing, laughter, fun—but still the tragic mien was his and I suspect it was because he saw too clearly the crack, the split, the gully that lay between the possible and the actual. He had attached his heart to a hopeless ideal, a nineteenth-century vision of cowboying and family pastoralism; such an ideal was not totally false, but it had been only briefly realizable. It was an ideal he himself could never realize, but it had been kept alive, though trivialized and cheapened, by the movies and pulp literature. It had even been kept alive by my own writing, about which he had a decided ambivalence, though I believe he had a better opinion of it than his last living brother, Joe McMurtry. Uncle Joe came up to me just after my father's funeral and said in a kindly spirit that he thought I ought to consider going into another line of work, since, in his opinion, I had been going downhill as a writer since my second book.

The frequent presence of my father in my thoughts and memories recently suggests that as we begin our long descent toward the country we won't be back from, our memory seeks to go back to where it started. *In My End Is My Beginning*, the title of a now forgotten book by Maurice Baring, suggests a notion that is itself an important filament in the emotions of older people, even if all it means is that as one is ending it is good and proper to think about one's beginning in order to gain at least a fleeting sense of the whole.

Phebus Etienne

A Ride to the Wedding

From *Callaloo*

I said goodbye to another piece of childhood,
watching the bride, pretty in organza bows and orchids.
She was billowed in joy, not like the morning
when she finally opened the door after I had knocked
for an hour, fearing she had overdosed. The woman
who had offered me a ride to the church turned up
the air conditioning in her apartment. I groped
for small talk as she rubbed her brown shoulders,
and leaned forward on the couch
to finish her cigarette, a tall can of beer.
She grabbed her wrap, walked into her kitchen,
stirred sugar into her ice water.

On my way to her bathroom,
she directed, "Don't sit on my toilet!" I obeyed.
We trailed the speeding limousine
ribboned in turquoise and she complained
about having cramps. When she asked me how I got
to her house, I said I took a cab. Six blocks
in heels was a long walk in the heat. She'd never

take a cab in this town, she ranted. She *hated* Haitians,
especially the taxi drivers. Using what
was left of her middle and index fingers,
nubs without fingernails,

she found a rhythm and blues station
on the radio. I pulled the tulle on my hat
closer to my eyes and hoped it wasn't
a Haitian who maimed her. Maybe I should have said
that our chained relatives could once
have been heading for the same auction block.
Maybe her peoples' ship docked in the Caribbean
where the captain sold my ancestor as he waited
for the end of an autumn storm.

But she did not want to hear me link us.
I didn't say that sometimes we drink
poor man's soda, sweeten our ice water, too.
I hid myself, as if defending what I am.

E. Ethelbert Miller

Fathering Words

From *Obsidian II*

I am a poet with a particular perspective on reality.
—Mahmoud Darwish

I must have been ten or twelve when my father told me he could have left my mother. I never thought about how this simple remark shaped my life as a writer until many years later.

It was 1969 when I made my decision to become a poet. I was a student enrolled at Howard University in Washington, D.C. My parents had sent me off to college to become a lawyer and to achieve the distinction of being the first college graduate in the family. I was constantly reminded of my responsibilities, and they included primarily watching whom I associated with and not running with the wrong crowd. When I informed my mother and father that I wanted to be a writer it was a conversation that fell on deaf ears. I was told to get an education and not be distracted by foolishness. Art, I gathered according to my parents, was foolishness.

It was difficult to explain to them that I was suddenly a witness to the Black Power Movement that was exploding across the country and changing the consciousness of the entire black community. To be a writer, following the King assassination of 1968, was as important as pursuing any other profession. The black community needed artists as much as it needed doctors and lawyers. So, for a young college student like myself, reading the works of Amiri Baraka, Sonia Sanchez, Norman Jordan and Don L. Lee was part of a catharsis that redefined and strengthened my commitment to my community.

However, I could not embrace the general black community without first grasping the dynamics of my own household. My father's decision to stay and raise a family was a lesson in black love and responsibility. If I were to become a writer I would have to approach my craft the way my father raised me.

How can one talk about the art of writing without mentioning the word love? The decision to write must be linked to a love of language and to the freedom of expression. Living in the United States, it is often too easy to take our basic liberties for granted. History, like our blackness, serves as a constant reminder that the African American struggle for liberation comes with a price. I didn't know this when I started out on my own journey to become a poet. I thought one simply created work, found a publisher and had a literary career. Even while some of my early poems contained references to revolution, I did not see my art overthrowing the American government. I was aware that it could and did have an effect on many of my friends and often strangers who became familiar with my work as a result of a public reading.

I thought poetry, black poetry, could raise the consciousness of black people. I felt that if the "beautiful ones" could just see themselves their lives would be different. Little did I know that when my father told me he could have left my mother that he was attempting to raise my consciousness. In his own way he was warning me not to take things for granted, that one's world could easily and quickly change. He was also saying in his own way that he loved me. Being a quiet man it was often difficult for him to express his emotions, especially those linked to the heart.

My father, Egberto Miller, worked and supported a family consisting of three children. He survived the South Bronx. When he died in 1987, I had been writing seriously for over sixteen years. Little did I realize that his passing would result in my new awareness of what it meant to be a writer. I discovered almost by accident that I could reclaim my father's life, I could interpret it and elevate it to heroic heights. I could use language to explore memory and celebrate myth.

The need to discover the singular voice, to understand the dreams and frustrations of a black man living in this century, is a task I now embrace like a parent holding a newborn. What I have written about my father has helped shed some light on those black men who we see going to work early in the morning and coming home late at night. These men are not invisible, they are responsible for us having a community. As a writer I must learn what they have to teach. In my conversations with other male African American writers such as Alexs Pate I have learned that I am not alone. There are other poets, novelists and playwrights who have accepted the responsibility of correcting the stereotypes that have buried the aspirations of African American males. Our art is now part of the national dialogue on race and family. We have entered a new period of reconstruction. Such events as the Million-Man March of 1995 simply draw media attention to an important social movement within our community.

As a writer, the act or process of creation is not divorced from the task of raising a family. What we desire as fathers is nothing different than what we might advocate as political leaders or social activists. Our exploration and articulation of values on paper as well as our daily instructional advice to our children is part of an equation which is integral to black survival. The equation is private as well as public. There are no borders of separation. As a writer one immediately is confronted with the realization that one is a refugee; and this status, so prevalent in our world today, carries with it the awareness that one is not homeless but instead embarking on a journey in search of freedom. How do we keep our families together? What dreams do we have of refuge or shelter?

Despite the odds, my father succeeded in raising his children in America. As a writer, I am equally optimistic that I can contribute to a body of literature which will provide the foundation for a new America. I must reclaim the ground beneath my feet, for my children and myself. I must reaffirm the importance of blackness in this world. It is the reason I write, it is the reason I look to my father's legacy for strength.

Adrienne Su

My Middle Kingdom

From *Prairie Schooner*

It has happened again. My guests are sitting back, well-stuffed and tipsy. I have pulled off a proper Chinese dinner, from the crackling pan of pot stickers to the whole steamed fish, and I'm trying not to look surprised.

Someone asks, "Where did you learn to cook?"

I fidget, then say a bit too fast, "From my mother."

It is not exactly a lie. My mother spent much of my childhood preparing meals both Chinese and Western, and sometimes I helped wrap the wonton or toss the salad. Most of the time, however, she cooked while I played or read, and when dinner was ready, I came to eat it, usually with a book in hand.

"From my mother," however, is still the correct answer. It evokes images of a daughter and her pioneer mother in a '70s Atlanta kitchen, then the mother as a girl in a '40s Shanghai kitchen with *her* mother, and so on—generation after generation of women handing down culinary wisdom, from Chinese antiquity to this afternoon in 1998, as I stand in my Cape Cod kitchen, scrubbing mussels that are about to meet their maker in a bath of sherry, ginger, and fermented black beans. Perhaps it goes all the way back to a man, the Song Dynasty poet and gourmet Su Dongpo, whom some of my relatives like to claim as an ancestor, and after whom a famous dish of braised pork, *Dongpo Rou*, was named.

Such notions suggest that the dinner that has just been consumed is the real thing, not some washed-out American version of ginger beef or phoenix-tail shrimp, because I have genetic license to prepare it properly.

This is how I used to feel about my Chineseness in general, that it was passed down biologically, like the color of my hair and eyes, and that I had a kind of automatic passport into Chinese society, should I ever wish to join it. Although I had been born in Georgia Baptist Hospital, couldn't speak Chinese, and did not set foot in Asia until I was nineteen, I had grown up in a community that considered me Chinese, so I thought I was. My parents had become U.S. citizens before I was born, but they did not mind being called "Chinese" or even "Oriental"; they had grown up in China and tended to use the word "American" to mean "white American." If someone referred to Chinese food as "exotic," it was fair enough, because once upon a time, mashed potatoes had been "exotic" to *them.*

For the children, however, the terms used to describe us suggested that we were not American. I think it was sometime after we had reached our adult heights and weights that it first occurred to us to wonder what that meant we were, what "Chinese" meant. From the way people treated us, we could gather this much: We were math-and-science whizzes; we played musical instruments well; we valued hard work; we were soft-spoken and studious. Also: We weren't the best literature students; we were not creative; we bound women's feet; and we ate dogs.

People also assumed that in a Chinese restaurant, we knew what to order. That was perhaps the one respect in which they were right.

I grew up in suburbia, at a time when the women were shifting from being full-time housewives to being mothers with outside careers. They tried to maintain pristine homes and happy families while working forty hours a week, invariably for less than they were worth and far below their creative and intellectual potential.

Like each family's neat green lawn, menus were predictable from house to house: spaghetti with sauce from a jar, iceberg-lettuce salad perked up with dressing from a bottle, chicken baked with breading from a box. Convenience was the culinary cutting edge, and a kid's lunch bag did not meet the schoolyard standard unless it included a vacuum-sealed juice pack or at least an individual bag of chips—proof that their mothers had better things to do than wash thermoses and distribute potato chips into sandwich bags.

My family depended on these standbys just like our neighbors, but we also had a second set of standbys. These included Cantonese roast pork, which my mother made in quantity and froze; dried *somen* noodles, which we boiled up in canned chicken broth with sliced Napa cabbage; and a pantry full of pickled vegetables made by my aunt, who often visited from Savannah. Also, we had Chinese-American family friends, addressed by my brother and me as "Aunties" and "Uncles," who turned up with homemade spring rolls, fried noodles, and whole fish ready for steaming. One Auntie became known to us as "the snail lady" for her plain steamed buns, sprinkled with sesame oil and scallions, that were coiled like big white snail shells. Another brought trays full of homemade meat dumplings, ready to freeze, boil, or panfry.

My mother, who was raised in a Shanghai house with a cook, had learned how to cook in America, because it was expected of her, and because she was hungry. Thus her culinary knowledge, Eastern and Western, came from books written in English, and from the cooks among the Aunties.

My parents' friendships with the Aunties and Uncles dated back to the early 1960s, when one couldn't buy tofu or wonton wrappers in Atlanta. They had made their own tofu then, starting with mail-order soybeans and plaster of Paris. They kneaded and formed their own dumpling and spring-roll skins; they sprouted mung beans at home. These were the opposite of convenience foods; these were the foods they craved and would go to great lengths to taste again. They did the work not because they enjoyed it or wanted to save the planet, but because they were hungry.

As a teenager, I knew I wanted to be a writer. I read and wrote without considering the genre barriers that would trouble me later: stories, poems, essays, a try at a young-adult novel. In my bedroom, the world seemed to be emerging on blank sheets of paper, and I couldn't wait to enter it.

Later, in college up North, I began studying Chinese civilization and learning Mandarin from scratch, out of two personal hungers, one for a body of knowledge less Eurocentric than the one offered in high school, one for stories that might give gravity and purpose to my poetry and fiction.

It seemed that Chinese history was something I should know, especially since it seemed to contain my family's history. I thought that if my writing were to have urgency and moral weight, it would address—or at least possess awareness of—what my predecessors had experienced during the Chinese civil wars and wars with Japan, the Great Leap Forward, the Cultural Revolution, and other twentieth-century upheavals. In 1979, when I was twelve, my father had made his first trip back to his hometown in Fujian since 1949—a fact I liked to cite at school because it made the teachers gasp. I watched my father pack a suitcase with mountains of ball-point pens, neon Frisbees, and bright skeins of wool. Why is he taking such common stuff? I wondered, and tried to imagine a country without pens.

With the snippets of information my parents had given, quite casually, over the years, I formed a foggy picture. The Japanese had invaded when my father was a youth; when I asked what he had seen, he had said neutrally, "Atrocities." My mother, as a girl in Shanghai, had stepped over the frozen bodies of the Asian and Caucasian homeless. My father had once had a brother, who died young from an infection that would be easily treatable now. My mother's family had had a beloved dog, who, left in the care of friends when the family fled for Taiwan, died apparently of a broken heart. My father's family, when insects got into their rice, spent all day picking the insects out rather than waste the grain. And one day, when our basement flooded, my mother was forced to take all her Chinese dresses out of their storage bags: custom-tailored *qipaos* in muted blues, pinks, reds, and yellows, ruined by water, signifiers of a whole other life.

Wanting the full picture, I studied Chinese history, literature, mythology, thought, and language, and just before my junior year in college, got what I thought I needed most, a scholarship to study in Shanghai for a year.

That fall, I moved into Fudan University's Foreign Students' Compound, a severe, heavily guarded complex containing dorms, classrooms, and a dining room for foreigners and a handful of government-appointed

Chinese roommates, who kept tabs on us. It should not have been surprising that the dining room served Chinese food three times a day, but it seemed a fabulous treat to me. Back in Cambridge, the best approximation of Chinese food in the dorms had been the occasional stir-fry that happened to contain soy sauce and a few snow peas. Real Chinese food in college was reserved for dates and night-before-the-exam takeout. There was something novel and indulgent about having it all the time, and unlike most of my classmates, I didn't get lonely for another kind of food for many weeks.

My first real Chinese conversation in Shanghai took place near the university, with a fruit vendor.

"Where are you from?" the vendor, a middle-aged man, asked.

"America, but my mother's family home is in Shanghai," I said.

"Ah, you've come back," he said, filling a newsprint bag with yellow pears. He smiled, revealing black gaps between his teeth. "Welcome home."

"Thank you," I said and paid him.

Back in the compound, I followed all the guidebook warnings and washed and peeled the first pear carefully. It was firm and juicy and peeled easily, but when I cut into it, it revealed itself to be rotten inside. The next pear was rotten, too; so was the next. Every pear was rotten, and later I realized I had also paid triple the normal price.

All over China that year, I seemed to get the equivalent of rotten pears. "She doesn't really know how to use chopsticks," someone commented at a dinner table. "You write like a foreigner; what's wrong with you?" a teacher asked after reading an essay I had written in elementary Chinese. "You aren't a real foreigner," my Chinese roommate sneered, "but you aren't a real Chinese person, either." At the entrances to foreigners' hotels, guards gripped me by the arm until I produced my passport, after which they cowered; I don't know which reaction troubled me more. White American tourists looked through me, even while I conversed with them in their own English. Travel was a nightmare of standing in long lines and arguing with reluctant clerks. My foreign classmates, also frustrated with the Communist bureaucracy and their own physical and psychological isolation, railed bitterly against the Chinese, and I railed with them, yet felt evil and divided for doing so.

The country that had held such mythical stature in my mind annoyed me more than it moved me, and welcomed mainly my dollars. I might as well have gone to Hungary or the Soviet Union. The neighbors back in Atlanta had been using the wrong terms all along. Nothing about me was at home in China.

What did move me was the private unrest of students who were beginning to stage protests, protests that would eventually build up to the cataclysmic one in Tiananmen Square in 1989. I could see History beginning to happen, even feel it in the streets sometimes, the same kind of History I was trying to grasp so that I might understand my parents' past lives. I could see why the contemporary literature, which disappointed me by being short on interior life, was political; *life* was political. I watched and listened; I met many relatives for the first time, and gave them pens and stockings.

Nevertheless, stories rarely came from firsthand sources; mainly, I got them from my parents in letters and over the phone. Among our elders were a man who had been arbitrarily exiled to decades of poverty and loneliness in the countryside, a woman who was abused throughout her old age by cruel stepchildren, a woman whose husband had destroyed her psychologically after taking a young second wife. . . . All of this seemed to matter in a way that my own experiences—biking with my best friend to the Seven-Eleven for an Icee or attempting to teach my rebellious Welsh corgi to heel—seemed banal, unnecessary even.

In the spring of 1988, having traveled to several regions and becoming fairly fluent in Mandarin, I left China with the intention of telling the stories I now knew about the place, the impersonal ones of official corruption and crackdowns on political dissent as well as the personal ones of my own family's trials during the various revolts and revolutions.

Shortly after scenes from the massacre in Tiananmen Square flashed across our television screens, I graduated from college and took my first job and apartment, in New York City. Because the job was entry-level and in publishing, I was poor and likely to remain that way. I was writing poetry with sureness and ease, but to give expression to what I had recently learned, and also in the hope of making some money, I began writing a novel as well. Mornings before work, nights after work, and sometimes during lunch hour at work, I worked on chapters about a Chinese family that gradually reveals its shattering personal history to a visiting American relative. (*The Joy Luck Club* came out around this time; its success suggested that people were willing to listen to such a story, and gave me a greater sense of urgency.)

In the meantime, I had to figure out ways to stretch my sorry paycheck, most fundamentally by learning to cook. Although I had perhaps one frying pan and could not tell a raw chicken breast from a raw pork loin, I had hope. My apartment was a furnished sublet with a kitchen full of saucepans, dishes, and utensils, along with a bookshelf jammed with cookbooks. I began to cook from the apartment's fading Time-Life *Foods of the World* series and the other volumes that the owners had accumulated over the years, mainly classics like *The Joy of Cooking* and *The New York Times Cookbook.*

It turned out that I was as interested in cooking as I was in eating, and I wanted to know about every regional food covered by Time-Life, plus any regions they had missed. I tasted the real things at some of Manhattan's cheapest restaurants, many of which were around the corner. The Indian restaurants on Sixth Street, the Polish diners on First Avenue, and the Vietnamese noodle shops in Chinatown each offered entry into a universe of food. These places taught me things about cooking that I couldn't have learned from books. They were about styles of eating, which offered some insight into people, who must have been shaped by the same ecological forces that shaped their cuisines.

Each new dining experience, however humble, sent me into another flurry of culinary research, generally in bookstores, "ethnic" groceries, and Greenmarkets. When I wasn't writing, I was cooking, from whatever cuisine had most recently crossed my path. Friends and acquaintances, living on takeout, offered themselves up as guinea pigs.

What mystified me was that my Chinese dinners invariably got from them a stronger, more visceral response than any others, even though I knew very little about cooking anything at all. Perhaps, I thought, people saw me as an authority because I ought to be; they couldn't see beyond my Chinese face that I had not grown up peeling fresh water chestnuts at my grandmother's side. They had a notion of my mother and me sitting before rows and rows of perfectly wrapped wonton, as the torch of Chinese home cooking was handed on, and preferred not to imagine that the kitchen of my childhood was just as likely to feature my brother and me heating up a frozen pizza just in time to watch a rerun of "Three's Company." So, even after I became a competent cook, I tried not to hear praise for my Chinese cooking because I knew I was a fraud: In the same way that I had learned to speak Chinese in a classroom in college, I had learned to cook Chinese from books written in English, just like any other flatlander.

I don't know exactly how and when I realized that the novel I was writing was doomed. Maybe I was preparing a few chapters to send out, or maybe I was simply stepping back and taking an honest look at last. All I remember is that one day, after two or three hundred pages had piled up on the desk and my already-poor eyesight had further declined from staring at computer screens day and night, I saw that the whole thing, even with the moment of insight here and there and the reasonably competent writing, was a hoax—and not in the way that a good novel should be.

My characters were facile constructs, made by an American writer projecting convenient, usually virtuous, personalities onto Chinese people. The cousin who teaches the American a thing or two about eating a balance of hot- and cold-element foods for health was just a device for transmitting what I had found interesting about Chinese medicine. The solemn grave-sweeping that takes place during Qing Ming actually takes place to open a narrative into recent family history, a history that I never actually heard any Chinese person relate. And the enormous sense of struggle and history that eventually gives the American character a sense of her identity as a Chinese American was totally fake, a carrot held out to the American consumer, who hungers for an identity, preferably exotic, that goes back farther than two hundred years.

I had to admit it before I dragged the effort out any longer. This was not the story that mattered to me. It was someone else's story, that of relatives I neither knew nor understood, and I did not have the personal stake in it that would make it ring true on the page. I had missed the point about the American character, whose real story was taking place back home, with jobs, parents, siblings, boyfriends, and friends. The Chinese stories I did possess were sketchy and delivered haphazardly in English by my mother, father, and other dear people in my life, such as my aunt from Savannah, who told me how the first silkworm eggs were smuggled out of China (in a woman's tall hairdo). "Facts" like this gave me a bit of authority in the schoolyard, but they hardly made me Chinese.

In fact, I was guilty of the very crime that others had committed every time they looked at me and saw a grandmother with bound feet or a Welsh corgi roasting on a spit. It was the offense one of my Atlanta neighbors had committed shortly after I returned from Shanghai, by suggesting that I study in England in order to experience a culture different from my own. In writing the novel, I had taken these misguided assumptions to heart and adopted, for the story's duration, a *faux* Chineseness that would allow me to tell the more exciting story, because it was too hard to find the revelatory aspects of my own, hopelessly peaceful, suburban life.

I do not remember this realization as devastating. It was, in fact, a relief. There had been so many compelling individual stories and such a preponderance of facts and characters that the undertaking had become impossible to control. I was glad to be free of the unwieldy, sprawling project. While poetry was not marketable like the Great Chinese-American Novel, it had remained true for me, perhaps because of its lack of marketability, perhaps because of its lack of (often misleading) narrative. Each poem I wrote, whether it was about Apollo and Daphne or an empress or Tompkins Square Park or The People's Park, contained a kernel of personal truth. And a good poem, unlike my narrow-minded novel, could be read several ways, so that each reader could come away with something different.

I suppose I must have closed the notebook in which I had organized the pages of that moribund epic, sat back, and poked around the kitchen for something to eat. What about my Chinese cooking? I wondered. Is that fake, too? Am I just a Kraft Macaroni & Cheese kind of girl?

Resigned to the novel's demise, I viewed it with detachment. I had written hastily, for fear of quitting, but I had taken the time to be accurate with food references: boiled meat dumplings for Beijing, soupy shrimp dumplings for Suzhou, fried oyster cakes for Xiamen, deep-fried carp and braised fava beans for Shanghai. I had consulted authoritative cookbooks as well as my parents and my China journals for proof of authenticity, and I had prepared many of the foods in the cookbooks for the fun of it. I had thought back to the gifts of "the snail lady," the steamed fish and drunken chickens of various Aunties, the powerful bitterness of bitter melon, and the gleaming red strips of roast pork being basted in the oven. I even knew a little about chicken-slaughtering because my father had described it to us as one of *his* teenage chores when we complained about having to sweep the carport or wash the dog bowl.

The only thing that worked about my failed fiction was the food, and the reason was obvious. I was knowledgeable—and I cared—about Chinese food long before I ever set foot in Asia (or even learned the names for most of the dishes). My attachment to it was honest, cultivated at the dinner tables of childhood. Food had been the only aspect of daily life that truly set my family apart from our Southern neighbors, and thus food was the only thing that really made sense to me when I lived in China.

Perhaps, then, my Chinese dinner parties were not entirely fraudulent. Quite possibly, my Chinese culinary education had nothing to do with cookbooks, mine or my mother's, but with our eating of the stuff in America, whether in an Atlanta restaurant, the kitchen of an Auntie, or our own home. And similarly, my literary territory had far more to do with the elements of my own childhood than with the "heritage" I had tried to collect in language labs and on the road. My parents' sketchy anecdotes were more "authentic" than my superficial encounters with the actual people involved in the anecdotes. It was the force of narrative within my immediate family that mattered, not the hard facts. Some stories, like some recipes, are mine, and some belong to others. This is how I have learned to place before a gathering of hungry friends a platter of *Dongpo Rou* and to accept credit for understanding its spirit, but to keep my hands off the story of Su Dongpo's or any other life, except those that have honestly touched my own.

Opal Palmer Adissa

Oath Taking

From *MaComère*

used to be
the word spoken
lived like the multi-colored butterfly
that hovers over a nectar-laden tree

every word
was a nail
driven with force
into wood
to say it was to make
it come through
and if perhaps
you didn't value what you spoke
the priestess would come around
hold up her mirror
to help you remember
the spirit of the words

and every time
you moved a hand

jerked a neck
or stretched from your rib-cage
a sharp nail-stabbing pain
would remind you
not to speak lightly
your words would reflect
from the mirror that was your soul
you would know then
the consequences of speaking idly
you would be reminded
that speaking
is a noble act
a gesture of respect
that we insignificant beings
offer to the life force

Kate Krautkramer

Walking

From *High Plains Literary Review*

When we get out of the car, I notice that Marguerite's shoes match. This is a rarity, the first time I've seen it. In the middle of winter I have often seen her in a "pair" of shoes—one a dingy blue flat that we would have called a boat shoe in high school, the other a Chuck Taylor Converse All Star high-top sneaker at least two sizes too big. At first I thought Marguerite was old and absentminded; sometimes she wears two unmatched lefts or two unmatched rights. When I got to know her better, she started telling me about her shoes. Her feet are wide, so she prefers men's sizes. Sometimes she wears whatever she can find at the thrift store. Whatever she has, she wears until they are worn out. Once, in January, she told me she thought it would be best to wear socks and nothing else because she could get better traction on the ice that way. Today Marguerite has on a matched pair of sturdy Reebok running shoes that I have never seen before; she's dressed for an occasion.

The three of us and the two dogs begin up Greenridge. Evelyn is sure that I will be "bored out of my head" spending the day with two old ladies; we giggle about this. She knows that I love to be outside and to walk.

She also knows my name, though she almost never says it. She knows I am a poet, and she knows where I live, just down the street from her. I've told her that I once lived in Africa, but she is perhaps unimpressed or doesn't remember. Rarely do Marguerite and Evelyn ask me about my life, and never do they ask anything personal. It seems, in fact, that we have little in common, yet we walk all day and never stop talking.

On our way up Greenridge, Marguerite and Evelyn point out a hill where they used to ski. With a long piece of grass hanging from her mouth, Evelyn explains how their mother, Louise, made them skis. "She took boards and planed them down in front. Then she shaped the noses on them. She stuck the noses in water, then put them in the kitchen stove and bent them as far as she wanted. This took a while. Sometimes they caught fire, and she'd stick them in a pail of water. When they were done, she fastened leather straps about midway on the skis, then melted paraffin on the bottom so as they'd slide."

Marguerite is quieter, but she sometimes tells a story too. She tells about her brother Bill, who married Mildred. "Oh, Mildred lived up here on Greenridge. Bill knew she was in school, so one day he climbed up in a tree that hung over the path where she walked on her way home. He always said he just happened to be in that tree, then happened to lose his balance just as she happened to be walking by. He happened to fall on the ground right in front of her." Marguerite pauses to look and see that I am getting the gist of the story, then says, "Shortly after that, they just happened to get married."

Marguerite is eighty-four years old, and her sister Evelyn is eighty-three. I met them walking near the small town of Yampa, Colorado, where we all live. I grew up thirty miles away in a resort town, Steamboat Springs. I went to college, went around the world on a boat, lived and taught in Africa, went back to school, and moved to Idaho to write a thesis. I fell in love with an old friend, a forest ranger, and somewhat reluctantly moved back to Yampa. When I was growing up, Yampa was a place we hardly thought of. We drove through it.

When I moved back to Routt County with John, I didn't know what I would do. Fresh out of the world of fast-talking poets, writers' workshops, performance art, and film, I was accustomed to lively discourse, literary criticism, and hours of yoga. I was no stranger to the mountains of Colorado, but I had no idea how my lofty poetic consciousness would be filled. Further, all of my grown life I had been moving, always traveling and always with thoughts of where I would go and what I would do next. Moving home with the intent to stay was a radical life change. I hardly knew how to begin or end a day in a place knowing that I would be there indefinitely. I had always been a renegade, a gypsy.

When I moved to Yampa two years ago, I began to take walks on Eagle Rock, a short county road that goes up Greenridge, the long mountain east of Yampa. Greenridge, an offshoot of the Gore Range, rose here at least twenty-five million years ago as part of the Laramide Orogeny and Park Range Fault-Block. Morrison Creek defines the eastern side of Greenridge, and the Yampa River flanks the mountain's western edge. Eagle Rock Road crosses the Yampa River about one half mile from the town of Yampa (population four hundred). From my house to the second cattle guard on Eagle Rock Road and back is about five miles; a round trip is a ninety-minute walk. It was here that I met Evelyn and later Marguerite and learned that they had been walking in the mountains around Yampa since the 1920s. When I walk with them, I silently calculate. Evelyn was fifty-four years old when I was born, seventy-two when I graduated from high school. It seems at once impossible and comforting that Evelyn and Marguerite have been walking here longer than I have been alive.

Evelyn is a handsome woman. She stands about five feet tall, even with a decided lean to the left. Her body is hard and compact; when she wears tight knit slacks to work in the yard or to walk in summer, the bulge of her thigh muscles shows through the blue or yellow polyester. Evelyn's face is leathered; wrinkles reach deep around her eyes and mouth. In summer her face and smooth hands turn the color of walnut shells. A willful shock of Evelyn's white hair occasionally escapes her headwear. I have never seen her without either a hat or her wig, an old blondish swab she attaches to her head with thick, obvious bobby pins. Under her wig or hat, Evelyn's blue eyes jig. When she tells a story, when she stoops in her yard picking dandelion heads to fry for supper, when she stands at a pasture gate counting new calves, Evelyn's vivid blue eyes are telltale of the joy and good humor that seem always to accompany her.

Marguerite's eyes are the same blue but harbor a less playful tone. Her face is more rugged than Evelyn's. She had four children and a husband and worked hard ranching her whole life; the years testify through her face, which is square and framed by loose dark-gray hair. Marguerite's hands are gnarled and usually black from loading coal or ash into or out of her stove. Marguerite is less talkative than Evelyn and more forgetful but equally strong in body. Evelyn claims that Marguerite, whom she refers to as "Poochy" or "Poodle," is also more surefooted, more agile. Marguerite glances sideways at Evelyn when she says this, at once thanking her for the compliment and casting an eye of weathered love and admiration on her sister.

There is no explanation for how my simple interactions with Evelyn and Marguerite became endearing. We would meet out walking and talk about our dogs, the weather, and the turning seasons. There is no explanation for how familiarity sometimes turns to love. After I had known her more than a year, Evelyn gave me some trimmings from an elk her nephew "Sonny" had shot. She said her dog was too old to eat them, it might upset his stomach, but maybe my dog would like them. I took the bloody bits of meat home in a bucket, at once horrified at the stench and amazed that I had somehow become friends with Evelyn. A few days later I returned the bucket with a little loaf of banana bread, and Evelyn invited me into her house.

That was when Evelyn first showed me photographs of her family and the house where they used to live on Greenridge. On one wall was a photograph of Marguerite and Evelyn and their brother as little children, all of them sitting in a wagon. We leaned across Evelyn's old organ to get a good look. Noticing the organ and the piano opposite, I remembered to ask Evelyn about the next time she was going to play at church. I had heard that she sometimes played accordion and mentioned that I would love to see her play. Her eyes lit up, and she laughed, "Really?"

"Yes, really," I said.

To my surprise, she dug the accordion out from behind an old striped sofa with claw feet. While she strapped it on, she explained that Mrs. Bolton, whom she used to work for, helping with the sheep, had bought the instrument for her from Montgomery Ward. She taught herself how to play. Before she began, Evelyn leaned down and addressed the dog, who looked up at her with mischief: "Now, Bobbie, you be sure to sing along." She started pumping the accordion back and forth, then stopped to turn on the organ, which she set to play a samba backbeat. She adjusted her accordion, concentrated a moment to get on the beat, and with an immense grin on her face performed a medley of familiar songs, including "High Hopes" and "Let the Sun Shine In." The songs went on for ten minutes or more while Bobbie sat at Evelyn's feet and howled with the music. Evelyn's fingers poked with decided precision at the buttons on the accordion, keeping the beat even as she lifted her chin to the ceiling, closed her eyes, and wailed and yowled along with Bobbie, her face flushed and happy.

Almost a year later, I met Evelyn and Marguerite walking together on Eagle Rock Road. It was June, and we talked about how the wild iris had been replaced by lupine and how the aspen trees had lost their spring green and settled into the rich color of summer. Marguerite told me she had been hearing coyotes singing around her ranch every night. Eventually, the conversation came around to how beautiful it used to be this time of year on Greenridge, and, with little forethought, we made a date to go up to their mother's old house. Although the sisters rarely ride in cars, they agreed it would be easiest if I picked them up and we drove to the Rossi place, thus avoiding walking on the highway. We'd park the car on the ranch and walk from there.

Marguerite and Evelyn are locally famous for their walking. When they were young and lived on Greenridge, Evelyn and Marguerite would often walk to Yampa or nearby Phippsburg and back to their house on Greenridge, a round trip of about twenty-two miles, in a day. They walked to parties and to teach Sunday school. The sisters taught together and so would make the trip to Yampa and back at least once a week, and according to Evelyn, they thought nothing of it.

Once I met Evelyn on Eagle Rock in August, and she told me this was the time of year she had once walked to Trapper's Lake and back in one day. I called her a liar. "No, I wouldn't lie to you," she said. "I know it's a long way. It's fifty-one miles, but I did it. I started at midnight, and I didn't stop until I got home about seven o'clock the next night." I told her that I was really impressed, so impressed in fact that she was my hero. I told her I was going to get her a great big letter and sew it on her chest, an "S" for "Super Evelyn." She chuckled and said, "Or you could just get me an 'E,'" and then by way of explanation, "for idiot."

In recent years, the sisters have taken to camping. Marguerite's son, David, called "Sonny" by everyone in the valley who has known him more than a day or two, rigged some old shopping carts for his mother and aunt. The shopping carts are not the grocery-store kind that require pushing from the back; they are the taller variety that can be pulled along behind the shopper. The old women pack a few things in these carts, and off they go without maps. "I wouldn't know how to read one if I had one," Evelyn told me once. "We just decide where we want to go, and why, we go there. Then, when we want to, we come home."

No other explanation seems to be required, although Evelyn often expounds on how she loves to sleep outside, loves to hear the frogs in the evening and the birds in the morning. In the summer she sleeps in a little bed she has made up in the shed outside her house. She shows me this bed one day, pointing out the tin roof and explaining how she savors the sound of the rain on the roof, especially when it is so close to her head. There is childish delight in her face when she points to the bed and says, "When I sleep here, it's almost like camping."

It is a town pastime in Yampa to talk and worry about Evelyn and Marguerite. When they go camping, they have no particular destination and no set time to return. They sometimes walk together or alone all day. I've seen them on roads or crossing meadows miles from town. Their particular forms and gaits have become distinctive and dear to me. Marguerite walks slowly, usually with her hands joined behind her; her back is humped at the top, and she carries her head quite forward from her body as she walks. Evelyn's steps are livelier, but Marguerite never falls behind. In summer, Evelyn's silhouette is easy to pick out because of the sunbonnet she wears to shade her face. This is actually two hats, a straw hat with a stiff brim over which is pinned the more decorative but faded, old-fashioned calico bonnet. Evelyn ties the thing on her head with the bonnet's strings. The ragged edges of the straw hat have been kept from fraying by brown postal packaging tape stuck around the circumference of the brim. Evelyn has a slight limp, and she leans obviously to the left as she walks. Both Evelyn and Marguerite are tiny, maybe five feet tall and 110 pounds each, but their strength shows in their persistent strides.

So I was not reluctant to take them on the walk to their former home. I picked them both up at Marguerite's house, the house where she moved with her husband, Carl, over thirty years ago. Carl has been dead for several years; Evelyn once showed me his place in the Yampa cemetery, which is about two miles from town on another county road, suitable for walking in the spring when Eagle Rock is too muddy. She also showed me the place where Marguerite will go when she goes, her name already carved in stone beside Carl's. I assume Evelyn will also be buried here somewhere near Marguerite, as she was never married and never cared to be. As we make our way out the gate, Evelyn does concede that Carl was a good man, then adds as a sort of disclaimer, "as far as men go."

After two or three hours of walking, we come near to "Mam's place." When I ask them why they always say Mam's place and never Pap's place or Mam and Pap's place, Marguerite and Evelyn answer in unison, "Because it was hers." Their mother inherited some money when her mother died; with that money she bought the 160-acre ranch here on Greenridge. Since Pap was often away hunting, I gather Mam did much of the work on the ranch as well.

When we catch sight of the house, the women are silent. I look on, incredulous at the view and the thought that they actually had lived here. Although not in good condition, the house is standing. The setting is pristine, idyllic. The front door opens on a sprawling meadow. The back is skirted by aspens. Beyond the meadow we can see Yampa nestled by the river and beyond that the Flat Top Mountains under a lumpy quilt of clouds. In less than a moment, I know why there is a kind of melancholy longing in their voices when my friends speak of this place. Columbines bob their heads in the aspens' shade. Everything is still but for a few mosquitoes and a slight breeze through the tall July grass. The moment seems to go on as far as we can see.

Finally Evelyn speaks out about the house, a big two-story building with a porch most of the way around the second floor. "Don't that porch look like arms just saying welcome?" she says. "When I see that house it just always seems to be saying, 'Welcome. This is your home.'"

We push open the door to look inside. Paper is peeling off the walls and ceilings, cobwebs dangle from rafters, and the floor is covered in droppings of bats and mice and chipmunks that have taken the house to be their own. There's an old stove quietly disintegrating in the corner and a rusted broken shovel in the middle of the floor. It's dark inside. I can't guess what Evelyn and Marguerite are thinking.

Even though we agree it isn't safe, Evelyn and I go up the stairs. She shows me her room, where light now pours in the square that was once a window. We open the door that used to let out onto the porch but now opens only onto air and a few dying boards sticking out of the house. We wave at Marguerite, who is standing in the grass below.

After a few photographs, we lunch at an old table behind the house. While we eat, Marguerite and Evelyn argue about where the bunkhouse was and where Mam kept the chickens and where the garden had been, who planted it, and what had grown in it. Marguerite remembers when her old pig, Rosey, named after the woman who had given it to her, got into the bunkhouse, ripped open a feather bed with her snout and hooves, and was eventually found fast asleep in the feathers.

When I am with these women, I spend a lot of time trying to remember exactly what they say. I listen, and while I am entranced by them, there is no explanation for my being so charmed. In many ways Marguerite and Evelyn are the epitome of ordinary, but they are also extraordinary in ways they could not even have planned. I like them because they are old and I will undoubtedly learn something from them. I like them because they are unself-conscious (although Marguerite and I have more than once discussed her distress at the "whiskers" she has grown with old age). I enjoy them because they are honest and, like me, they walk. But mostly, because they have been here all their lives, they exude a purity, a strange, old purity, that has come about not because of discipline or intent but in spite of age and perhaps in spite of the aging process itself.

Evelyn and Marguerite do talk about wrinkles and whiskers and pain. They never complain, but neither do they pretend that they will never die. Last year I made some calls for Evelyn (who does not have a telephone) concerning her coal stove. She was afraid that she would no longer be able to get big "lump coal" and that she would have to convert her old house to electric heat. When I informed her, after talking to a representative at the mine, that lump coal would be available for at least ten more years, she sighed audibly before she laughed and said, "Well, then, that will do it." She has told me that she is not afraid to die, and I believe her. When I listen to Marguerite and Evelyn talk, I begin to see how I might come to the end of my own life, should it be long, with satisfaction, maybe even in peace. I begin to see that, yet it remains unfathomable to me that they (or I) will die.

For lunch Marguerite has two raw "weenies," three slices of white bread, and a 7 Up. Aside from a long-sleeved shirt tied around her waist, this lunch in an old bread sack is the only baggage Marguerite has for the trip. Evelyn and I fish our lunches out of our backpacks, and we all share. I have some of Evelyn's Lay's BBQ potato chips, and she has some of my chocolate raisins. She tries to toss one in the air and catch it in her mouth, tries a few times before she decides she is too old to do this trick anymore. Then, because I am sitting in front of her on the ground, she gets the idea to throw the raisins up so I can catch them in my mouth. It turns out that we are a good team, and Evelyn takes such obvious satisfaction in this game that I catch raisins in my mouth until I am more full than I care to be, she and Marguerite laughing out loud through the whole act.

While we are eating, Evelyn tells about a little bear the family had when the girls were young. Evelyn and Marguerite's father, Pap, was a government hunter. He killed mountain lions, bears, coyotes, anything that might be threatening to stock or people. The baby bear had been caught in one of Pap's traps.

Pap brought the bear home because he couldn't stand to let the little fellow die, and the cub was kept as a family pet for more than a year. Evelyn recalls the day a man from a zoo in Louisiana came to take the bear away. "I couldn't stand it. That bear loved us, and we loved him. We fed him, hugged him, and slept with him. Then here comes this fella from Louisiana, puts him in a cage to take him away. Long as I live, I'll never forget it." When she gets to this part of the story, Evelyn puts her face very close to mine and nearly yells. "That bear cried, 'Maa! Maa! Maa!' so sad like I couldn't stand it. I ran inside, put my head under the pillow, and bawled and bawled." She looks like she's going to cry again until she lets her face relax, sighs, and stretches, signifying the end of lunch.

We stand a few moments in the meadow and take pictures of the Flat Tops. Although their tabled-off appearance gives them a subdued look, they are the highest mountains in this part of the country. From our vantage point, we can see their whole wildness and splendor as well as the tranquil pasture lands and our houses in the valley.

Our next destination is "the big tree." Marguerite and Evelyn argue as to its exact location, but as we fumble along guessing, we eventually see it in the distance. I'm amazed. It is a ponderosa pine, not common to this area, and it is indeed immense. As we approach, they tell me it was big when they were young; in fact, it seems no bigger now than it was then. Evelyn points out a branch that has fallen to the ground, saying that the branch alone is bigger than most trees around here. I snap a photo of the sisters; standing abreast in front of the tree, holding hands, they show how large the trunk is. The three of us, reaching around it, could not touch fingers.

When I tell them that ponderosas smell like butterscotch, Evelyn and Marguerite don't even consider that I might be fooling; they plunge their noses into the old bark. The ancient tree does give off a sweet odor, but only faintly. The women are unsatisfied, so we make our way to the other, smaller ponderosas, the great tree's offspring, sniffing each one. When Evelyn puts her nose to a tree, her hat hides her entire face, but she's determined, stands there breathing in and smelling. Finally she puts her cheek to the tree. "Well, I never knew any tree could smell just as fine as a batch of cookies baking in the oven," she says, looking satisfied and thankful.

We debate about which Greenridge destination to visit next. Every place on Greenridge is a place, I learn as they talk. "We could go right to the Nelson place, or we could go to the Brown place," Marguerite says.

"Well, either way, when we get off Mam's place we'll have to cross the Wright place," Evelyn answers. I spend the rest of the day trying to figure out the boundaries of the various places and their significance to Evelyn and Marguerite.

We decide to head for the Nelson place. This is where Marguerite lived with her husband and parents-in-law when she was first married. There is a large house standing on a hill, and this house is probably still inhabited, although no one is home at the moment. There is a steep gravel road that might be passable by a good vehicle with high clearance. There are two barns filled with odds and ends of old machines, tools, scraps of leather, and buckets of rusted nails and screws. The windows are broken; cobwebs hang from every place a cobweb can hang. On the way out an overgrown driveway, we spot some rhubarb. Marguerite tells us she planted it there years ago. We each pull a piece, and the sour taste is refreshing as we suck it from the red stalks.

On a hill behind the house is an old graveyard. It takes a few minutes, but eventually we spot the fence surrounding it. Inside the fence is hardly different from outside. Serviceberry bushes, lupine, sagebrush, and rye grass cover the stones. We push the plants away carefully to find the stones for Carl's parents and for a little girl, Mattie Louise, who was born dead. I look to Marguerite for an emotion, but she is matter-of-fact. "Named for her grandmothers," she says. "My mother's name was Louise; Mattie was Carl's mom." The date on the stone is 1948.

Unable to squelch my curiosity, I ask quietly, "Did you know? I mean, did you know she was dead inside you?"

Marguerite tells me no, she hadn't known, although in retrospect it seems that she ought to have felt it stop moving. She even offers that the baby had likely been dead in her for a long time, that the poor thing's flesh was tender and soggy, almost came right off the bone when you touched it.

Even if this is more than I had wanted to know, I am not surprised by Marguerite's frankness. Both Marguerite and Evelyn remember particulars from the distant past even when they cannot remember what happened last week or yesterday. Marguerite offers this detail of her dead child not to shock me or to shame me for having asked. She tells me simply to explain. As we leave the little cemetery, Marguerite does not look tired or sad or even sentimental when she states, "This may be the last time I come here."

She says it almost without regret, and as the old women lead me up the hill, now bound for the Brown place, I keep the practice of guessing why I've become so fond of them. Part of it, I decide, is because they speak plainly, say what they mean, and offer most interactions with a sense of humor, even mirth. But there is more.

Nothing bad has ever happened to me in my life. My father's parents were dead before I was old enough to remember them; my mother's parents are still living. My parents are living and married, to each other no less. I've never been accidentally or deliberately pregnant, never lost a brother or sister. My friends who have passed away have been either not close enough to really make me feel the loss or old enough that it seemed they had lived full lives. I've traveled all over the world, often alone, and never been stabbed, shot, or otherwise mortally threatened. Certainly I've had my share of romantic heartbreak, and I was once attacked and bitten by an Ethiopian monkey. But those seem almost trifles compared to what misfortunes might befall any given person in a lifetime.

Evelyn and Marguerite both worked hard. Marguerite worked a ranch and raised children with Carl for many years. Evelyn worked for a ranching family, looked after children and sheep, and spent one summer trapping muskrats. But I would not say that their lives have been particularly unfortunate. Of course, they have lived through the deaths of their parents. Marguerite outlived her husband and also buried the stillborn girl, Mattie Louise. Evelyn and Marguerite had two brothers who are both now dead. But it is not only bearing the loss of loved ones that concerns me. These women have also gone from young to old. They have wrinkled faces, and their skin has the transparency of old age; Evelyn has almost no hair. They've outlived vanity for the most part, yet they are honestly attractive and strong. They've lived and walked in the hills. They talk of the past with relish, but equally do they enjoy the present, always bringing attention to common and beautiful things, listening to insects, smelling chokecherry blossoms, laughing at an old crow scolding from the branches of a cottonwood. Nothing they've encountered in their years has made them bitter, and I follow them around like a little child after sugar.

It is already late in the day, but we decide to walk up to the Brown place. This is where Marguerite lived with Carl after they left the Nelson place. A thin layer of clouds relieves us from the afternoon sun as we make our way, waist deep in grass, across the fields. We cross a little creek and lose each other, happily calling out in a copse of high skunk cabbage.

Before we get to the Brown place, we come upon a huge field ablaze with yellow daisies. Because of the long oval leaves, this plant is called mule's ear, but Marguerite scoffs at the dazzling field and calls it rosin weed. She says Carl would roll in his grave to see his hay meadow covered in the flowers, and she gives an indignant snort.

At the Brown place there is a house, a schoolhouse, two barns, a lot of fence, and an ice house, all in various stages of decrepitude. In the schoolhouse, Evelyn explains how just a few years ago they slept here when they were camping. When they woke up, their sleeping bags had perfect squares of snow that had fallen through the chimney hole in the roof.

We go to the house. The windows are missing, and the roof has caved in, gray boards sticking up out of what was Marguerite's kitchen. This is where her children were born and where she poses for me. She stands by an aspen tree in which she carved the words to an old song fifty, maybe sixty years ago. The poem can no longer be read; it has turned into indecipherable scars. She and Evelyn try to remember the words—"This old house once knew my children, this old house once knew my wife"—but we won't get all the lyrics until a few weeks from now, when Evelyn will pull out her old record player and play the song for me on a scratched 33.

I'll give her and Marguerite copies of all the photographs I took the day we went up Greenridge, and as she has done four or five times now since I have known her, Evelyn will stand, throw her arms out wide, and declare with a certain vigor, "I love you!" and wait for me to come hug her. We will argue about whether or not she is allowed to pay me for the photos.

We are friends. Evelyn and Marguerite have let me in on a secret, but it's not a secret I could relay or even fully understand. It is a secret I must repeat to myself as I walk around Yampa, as I walk around in the ironies and paradoxes, all the mountains, the flowers, the seasons that become familiar and somehow become a life. When I come close to the end, perhaps I will know how to say audibly what Evelyn and Marguerite have passed on to me.

Shuffling our way back down the mountain in fading light, Marguerite suddenly admits that she cannot remember my name, even though she heard Evelyn say it just moments before. Evelyn scolds her: "It's Kate!" And without pause, in unison they begin to sing a song I loathed as a child but now, in vain maturity, love the sound of perhaps more than any other.

"K-K-K-Katy, beautiful Katy, you're the only g-g-g-girl that I adore. When the m-m-moon shines over the cow shed, I'll be waiting by the k-k-k-kitchen door."

They sing it twice through, and I try to absorb the moments and hide my tears. This is a time, a trip I will keep in my hopelessly sentimental heart for a very long while. Marguerite and Evelyn might think nothing of it. The walk we made that day was a walk they made hundreds of times in their lives. Yet their love of the places we visited was clear and uncommon.

When we get back to the car, it is almost eight o'clock, and we figure we've walked about fifteen miles. The dogs hop in the back and flop down in contented exhaustion. I drop Marguerite off at her house first; then, after a stop at the post office, I drop off Evelyn. Our partings are unceremonious. When I get home, I cry.

This is always the case at the end of a journey. When the airplane lands, when the train wheels squeak to a final stop, when I park the car in the garage after a cross-country mission, there are always tears. Whether these tears are about relief or thankfulness or whether there is simply no other appropriate action to express the simple yet great pleasure of coming home, I'm never sure.

That day I had another familiar feeling, a feeling that I forget over and over, for as surely as I end some travel, I determine to begin another. Perhaps, like Evelyn and Marguerite, I will live in this valley for a long, long time. And maybe, if I am lucky, I will still be grateful, even stunned and joyful, to hear the coyotes howl and the crows scold and to walk from one place to another just noticing things. The feeling I had that evening after we finished our walk on Greenridge was the same feeling I've had after returning from months in Southeast Asia, years in Africa, or a week in the Utah desert. It is knowing that I went a distance in order to discover what I already knew. The task is to keep that discovery at the front of my thoughts, to know that Evelyn and Marguerite are out in the hills around Yampa, making it home again and again, by walking.

Kyoko Mori

Suffering

(at the Art Institute of Chicago)

From *Crab Orchard Review*

In the small upstairs gallery where the centuries
change, the doorway behind me flickers with

the orange and gold light from the haystacks.
The swirling blue sky that embraces the drinkers

as they tip their glasses and the yellow
island turning into geometric plains

of pure color are only a few steps
around the corner, but I am walking

toward the dark bronze sculpture cast in 1907
by Brancusi. It is a bust of a child who

leans away from the light, eyes closed, head
shaved, the sharp bone of the jaw pressed

against the right shoulder. Cut off
a few inches below that shoulder, what

remains of the arm resembles a wounded
bird or a plucked fruit—an object

far beyond consolation though it is cradled
against the tender skin of the throat. The left

ear tilted up into the empty air, the child strains
to hear some music that will never come.

The right ear turns inward, tries to burrow
into the dark place between the muscle and

the bone where the warmth of our own skin can
only fail to comfort us the way a lover's

might. The sculpture is called "Suffering." Do
you remember it? We paused a few seconds here

before moving further into our century where,
hand in hand in front of the Cornell boxes, we

peered into the small squares of light. The same
paper ballerina is still poised in mid-leap

across the bottomless well of blue shadows.
The white owl stares, back-lit and formidable

among seashells and fungi. Alone in a quiet
gallery, I push the button that lights up

the boxes. It is a small gesture of hope,
trust, or curiosity—this simple wish

to see. The green parrots, the blue hotels,
the mysterious maps and timetables—they

cannot assuage our suffering except in
the way a sudden color flashes across

our memory like a stubborn Morse code.
I am out here in the mid-century

before our birth, my fingers tapping
the light switch to send you a message.

On the other side of the glass, our favorite
birds are beckoning. As surely as we are born

into suffering, we are meant also for this.

contributors

Opal Palmer Adissa, originally from Jamaica, is a professor at the California College of Arts and Crafts, and the author of four collections of poetry and the novel *It Begins with Tears.*

Ai is the author of *Vice: New and Selected Poems,* winner of the 1999 National Book Award for Poetry, and five other poetry collections, including *Cruelty, Killing Floor, Sin, Fate,* and *Greed.* She teaches at Oklahoma State University and lives in Stillwater, Oklahoma.

Bryant Keith Alexander is assistant professor of performance and pedagogical studies in the communication studies department at California State University, Los Angeles. His work appears in *Callaloo, Text and Performance Quarterly, Theatre Topics,* and other journals and edited volumes including *The Future of Performance Studies* and *Communication, Race, and Family: Exploring Communication in Black, White, and Biracial Families.* He is currently working on a collection of essays tentatively titled *Performing Culture, Performing Pedagogy, Performing Identity.* Bryant lives outside of Pasadena with his partner, Patrick, their dog named Prissy, and Peanut, the cat.

Sherman Alexie is the author of the novels *Reservation Blues* and *Indian Killer* and three collections of poetry. He also wrote the screenplay for the movie *Smoke Signals.* He lives in Seattle.

Julia Alvarez is the author of *In the Name of Salome, In the Time of the Butterflies* (a National Book Critics Circle Award finalist), and *How the Garcia Girls Lost Their Accents.* Currently, she is a writer-in-residence at Middlebury College.

Robert Antoni is the author of *Divina Trace*, winner of the Commonwealth Writers Prize for Best First Book 1992, and *Blessed Is the Fruit*. He has published fiction in numerous periodicals including *The Paris Review, Missouri Review, Parnassus, StoryQuarterly, Ploughshares*, and *Conjunctions*. He has received a National Endowment for the Arts Fellowship and a James Michener Fellowship, and he holds an M.A. from the Writing Seminars at The Johns Hopkins University, as well as a Ph.D. from the Writers' Workshop at the University of Iowa.

Fred D'Aguiar is a poet and the author of *The Longest Memory*, which won a Whitbread Award in 1994. His third novel, *Feeding the Ghosts*, was published by the Ecco Press. He lives in Miami.

Phebus Etienne was born in Port-au-Prince, Haiti, but grew up in East Orange, New Jersey. She studied at Rider University and New York University and has worked most recently as a teacher. Her poems have appeared in *Poet Lore, Mudfish*, and *Caribbean Writer*.

Ifeona Fulani teaches writing in New York City. She is the author of the novel *Seasons of Dust*.

Henry Louis Gates, Jr., heads the African-American studies department at Harvard University and is the author of the memoir *Colored People*. He lives in Cambridge, Massachusetts.

Pico Iyer is the author of five previous books, including *Video Night in Kathmandu* and *The Lady and the Monk*. His most recent work is *The Global Soul*. He lives in suburban Japan.

Kate Krautkramer's essays and stories have appeared in the *North American Review, High Plains Literary Review*, and *Seattle Review*. She lives and writes in northwest Colorado.

Chang-rae Lee is the author of the novels *Native Speaker* and *A Gesture Life*. He is director of the MFA creative writing program at Hunter College in New York.

Larry McMurtry is the author of twenty-five books and currently runs a bookstore in Texas.

Jaime Manrique was born in Colombia. His first book of poems received his country's National Book Award. He's the author of several books in Spanish. Among his books in English are the novels *Colombian Gold, Latin Moon in Manhattan*, and *Twilight at the Equator*; the volume of poems *My Night with Federico García Lorca; Sor Juana's Love Poems*, cotranslated with Joan Larkin; and the memoir *Eminent Maricones: Arenas, Lorca, Puig, and Me*. He also teaches in the MFA Program at Columbia University and frequently reviews for Salon.com and *The Washington Post Book World.* In 1999, he received a grant from the New York Foundation for the Arts in Fiction and a John Simon Guggenheim Fellowship. Forthcoming in 2001 is *Tarzan,* a new book of poems.

E. Ethelbert Miller is the author of several collections of poetry, including *Where Are the Love Poems for Dictators?* and *Whispers, Secrets and Promises.* He is the editor of *In Search of Color Everywhere.* His memoir, *Fathering Words: The Making of an African American Writer,* was published in spring 2000.

Kyoko Mori is the author of five books: *Shizuko's Daughter, One Bird, Fallout, The Dream of Water: A Memoir,* and *Polite Lies: On Being a Woman Caught Between Cultures.* She was born in Kobe, Japan, in 1957 but moved to the United States in 1977, where she earned a B.A. from Rockford College, an M.A. and a Ph.D. in English/creative writing from the University of Wisconsin, Milwaukee. Mori is currently a Briggs-Copeland lecturer in creative writing at Harvard University. Her awards include the Best Novel of the Year from the Wisconsin Council of Writers for *Shizuko's Daughter,* the editor's choice from the *Missouri Review* for the poem "Fallout," and a Book of Distinction citation from the Wisconsin Library Association for *Polite Lies.* Her novel, *Stone Field, True Arrow,* is to be published in September 2000.

Walter Mosley is the author of twelve books and has been translated into twenty-one languages. His publications include the nationally best-selling Easy Rawlins mystery series; the Socrates Fortlow stories; the blues novel *RL's Dream;* and the science fiction novel *Blue Light.* His most recent book is the nonfiction *Workin' on the Chain Gang: Shaking Off the Dead Hand of History.* Forthcoming in spring 2001 is *Fearless Jones,* a novel.

Aimee Nezhukumatathil was born in Chicago to a Filipina mother and an East Indian father. She is a fellow at the Wisconsin Institute for Creative Writing and is the winner of the *Atlantic Monthly* Student Writers' Competition in poetry and an AWP Intro Award in creative nonfiction. She holds an MFA from Ohio State University.

Nicholas Samaras won a 1997–98 National Endowment for the Arts Poetry Fellowship. His first volume of poems, *Hands of the Saddlemakers,* was a Yale Series of Younger Poets selection. His second book, *Survivors of the Moving Earth,* was published by the University of Salzburg Press. He lives and teaches in Florida.

Adrienne Su, author of the poetry collection *Middle Kingdom,* is visiting poet-in-residence at Dickinson College in Carlisle, Pennsylvania. Her essays have appeared in *Prairie Schooner, Saveur, The NuyorAsian Anthology, Girl: An Anthology,* and elsewhere.

Diane Thiel's book *Echolocations* has received the 2000 Nicholas Roerich Poetry Prize from Story Line Press and will be published in November. Her work appears in *Best American Poetry 1999*, the *Hudson Review*, and *Poetry*. Her writing guide, *Writing Your Rhythm*, is to be published in spring 2001. For more information, you can visit her website (www.dianethiel.net).

Lidia Torres lives in Brooklyn, New York. Her poems have appeared in *Hayden's Ferry Review* and are forthcoming in *Bilingual Review/Revista Bilingue.*

Derek Walcott, winner of the 1992 Nobel Prize in Literature, was born in St. Lucia, Windward Islands, the West Indies, and has maintained a permanent residence in Trinidad for over twenty years. His poems have appeared in *The New Yorker, The Kenyon Review, The New York Review of Books, The Nation, London Magazine, Antaeus,* and other periodicals. Mr. Walcott divides his time between his home in St. Lucia and New York. During the academic year he teaches at Boston University.

Lois-Ann Yamanaka is the author of a book of poetry, *Saturday Night at the Pahala Theater,* the novels *Wild Meat and the Bully Burgers, Blu's Hanging,* and *Heads by Harry,* as well as a young adult novel, *Name Me Nobody.* She is at work on her fourth novel, *Father of the Four Passages.* Yamanaka is the recipient of the Pushcart Prize XVII and XIX, a National Endowment for the Arts Creative Writing Fellowship, the Asian-American Studies National Book Award, a Carnegie Foundation Grant, the Elliot Cades Award for Literature and National Endowment for the Humanities Fellowship, the Asian American Literary Award, and a Lannan Literary Award. Born in Ho'olehua, Moloka'i and raised in Hilo, Pahala, and Keauhou-Kona on the Big Island in Hawai'i, she lives in Honolulu with her husband and son.

credits

"Oath Taking" by **Opal Palmer Adissa** originally appeared in *MaComère*, vol. 2, 1999. Reprinted by permission of the author.

"Charisma: A Fiction" by **Ai**. Copyright © 1999 by Ai. Published in *Poets & Writers Magazine*, vol. 27, issue 1, January/February 1999. Reprinted by permission of W.W. Norton & Co.

"Standing at the Crossroads" by **Bryant Keith Alexander** first appeared in *Callaloo*, vol. 22, no. 2, 1999. Reprinted by permission of Johns Hopkins University Press.

"The Toughest Indian in the World" by **Sherman Alexie**. Copyright © 1999 by Sherman Alexie. First published in *The New Yorker*, June 21/28, 1999. Reprinted by permission of the author.

"Planting Sticks and Grinding Yucca: On Being a Translated Writer" by **Julia Alvarez** first appeared in *Zoetrope: All Story*, vol. 3, no. 4, Winter 1999. Reprinted by permission of the author.

"My Grandmother's Tale of How Crab-o Lost His Head" by **Robert Antoni** was first published in *The Paris Review*, no. 152, Fall 1999. Reprinted by permission of the author.

"A Son in Shadow" by **Fred D'Aguiar**. Copyright © 1999 by Fred D'Aguiar. First appeared in *Harper's Magazine*, vol. 298, no. 1786, March 1999. Reprinted by permission of the author.

"A Ride to the Wedding" by **Phebus Etienne** was published in *Callaloo*, vol. 22, no. 2, 1999. Reprinted by permission of Johns Hopkins University Press.

"Precious and Her Hair" by **Ifeona Fulani** was first published in *Black Renaissance/ Renaissance Noire*, vol. 2, no. 2, Summer 1999. Reprinted by permission of the author.

"Rope Burn" by **Henry Louis Gates, Jr**. Copyright © 1999 by Henry Louis Gates, Jr. First published in *The New Yorker*, August 23/30, 1999. Reprinted by permission of the author.

"The End of the Empire" by **Pico Iyer**. Copyright © 1999 by Pico Iyer. First appeared in *Harper's Magazine*, December 1999. Reprinted by permission of the author.

"Walking" by **Kate Krautkramer** first appeared in *High Plains Literary Review*, vol. 15, nos. 2/3, Fall/Winter 1999.

"The Volunteers" by **Chang-rae Lee**. Copyright © 1999 by Chang-rae Lee. First published in *The New Yorker*, June 21/28, 1999. Reprinted by permission of the author.

"Death of the Cowboy" by **Larry McMurtry**. Copyright © 1999 by Larry McMurtry. First appeared in *The New York Review of Books*, vol. 46, no. 17, November 4, 1999. Reprinted by permission of Simon and Schuster, Inc.

The excerpt from *Señoritas in Love* by **Jaime Manrique** appeared in *Global City Review: Laughing Matters*, no. 11, 1999. Reprinted by permission of Painted Leaf Press.

"Fathering Words" by **E. Ethelbert Miller** first appeared in *Obsidian II: Black Literature in Review*, vol. 13, nos. 1/2, Spring/Summer 1998–Fall/Winter 1998–99. Reprinted by permission of the author.

"Suffering" by **Kyoko Mori** first appeared in *Crab Orchard Review*, vol. 5, no. 1, 1999. Reprinted by permission of the author.

"Pet Fly" by **Walter Mosley**. Copyright © 1999 by Walter Mosley. First published in *The New Yorker*, December 13, 1999. Reprinted by permission of the author.

"Speak" by **Aimee Nezhukumatathil** first appeared in *Chelsea 67*, 1999. Reprinted by permission of the author.

"No Countries but the Distance of the World" by **Nicholas Samaras** first appeared in *The Kenyon Review*, vol. 21, nos. 3/4, Summer/Fall 1999. Reprinted by permission of the author.

"My Middle Kingdom" by **Adrienne Su**. Reprinted from *Prairie Schooner*, vol. 73, no. 4, Winter 1999 by permission of the University of Nebraska Press. Copyright © 1999 by the University of Nebraska Press.

"Family Album" by **Diane Thiel** was first published in *The Dark Horse*, Autumn 1999. Reprinted by permission of the author.

"Three Keys" by **Lidia Torres** was first published in *The Massachusetts Review*, vol. 40, no. 2, Summer 1999. Reprinted by permission of the author.

Excerpt from *Tiepolo's Hound* by **Derek Walcott**. Copyright © 2000 by Derek Walcott. Reprinted by permission of Farrar, Straus and Giroux, LLC.

"Ten Thousand in the Round" by **Lois-Ann Yamanaka** first appeared in *Conjunctions: Crossing Over, 1999*. Reprinted by permission of the author.

publications

Black Renaissance/Renaissance Noire publishes essays, fiction, reviews, and artwork that addresses the full range of contemporary black concerns. Subscribe by mail: Indiana University Press, Journals Division, Black Renaissance/Renaissance Noire, 601 North Morton Street, Bloomington, IN 47404-3797. Subscriptions are $33 for individuals and $65 for institutions.

Callaloo, the premier African-American and African diaspora quarterly literary journal, publishes original works and critical studies of writers of color worldwide, including a rich mixture of fiction, poetry, plays, interviews, critical essays, cultural studies, and visual art. Subscribe by email: jlorder@jhupress.jhu.edu, fax: 410-516-6968, phone: 800-548-1784, or mail: Johns Hopkins University Press, Journals Publishing Division, P.O. Box 19966, Baltimore, MD 21211. The subscription options are as follows: print for individuals ($35.50); print for institutions ($86); online to institutions ($77.40); both print and online ($111.80). Postage is as follows: U.S. (free); Canada/Mexico ($9); outside North America ($18.35).

Chelsea is an eclectic independent literary magazine, publishing fiction, poetry, nonfiction, book reviews, and art, with an emphasis on freshness, translation, and the avant-garde. Domestic subscription costs for individuals are $13 for one year, $24 for two years; for agencies, $18 for one year, $34 for two years. Foreign subscription costs for individuals are $16 for one year, $30 for two years; for agencies, $21 for one year, $40 for two years.

Conjunctions is a biannual literary journal devoted to publishing innovative contemporary fiction, poetry, and plays. Subscribe by phone: 914-758-1539; website: www.conjunctions.com; or mail: Michael Bergstein Managing Editor, Conjunctions, Bard College, Annandale-on-Hudson, NY 12504. Subscriptions are $18 for one year and $30 for two years.

Crab Orchard Review is published twice yearly under the auspices of the Department of English, Southern Illinois University, and features the best in contemporary fiction, poetry, creative nonfiction, interviews, and book reviews. Individual subscriptions are $10 for one year; $20 for two years; and $30 for three years. Please contact Crab Orchard Review, Department of English, Southern Illinois University, Carbondale, IL 62901-4503.

The Dark Horse is a Scottish-American poetry magazine edited by the Scottish poet Gerry Cambridge and publishing poems, interviews, polemics, essays, and in-depth reviews. Subscribe by mail: Jennifer Goodrich, U.S. Assistant Editor, 70 Lincoln Ave., New York, NY 10706. A subscription of three issues is $18.

Global City Review publishes twice a year, spring and fall. Each pocket-size issue includes stories, essays, drawings, interviews, memoirs, poems, plays, and performance texts, on any and all subject matters, here and abroad. Subscription options are as follows: individual (one year $14, two years $25); international (one year $20, two years $35); institutional (one year $30).

Harper's Magazine aims to provide its readers with a window on our world, in a format that features highly personal voices. Through original journalistic devices—Harper's Index, Readings, Forum, and Annotation—and its acclaimed essays, fiction, and reporting, *Harper's* informs a diverse body of readers of cultural, business, political, literary, and scientific affairs. Offering a distinctive mix of arresting facts and intelligent opinion, *Harper's Magazine* continues to encourage national discussion of topics not yet explored in mainstream media. An individual subscription in the U.S. is $21. Call 1-800-444-4653 or try the website (www.harpers.org).

Founded in 1986, the **High Plains Literary Review** is designed to bridge the gap between commercial magazines and literary quarterlies. *High Plains Literary Review* has published award-winning nonfiction and fiction from around the world during its fourteen-year existence. The magazine places a very special interest on publishing works of western writers. Subscribe by mail: High Plains Literary Review, 180 Adams Street, Suite 250, Denver, CO 80206. Subscriptions ($7) per issue, ($20) per year.

The Kenyon Review, an international journal of literature, culture, and the arts, publishes the work of emerging and established writers alike in fiction, poetry, and nonfiction, including interviews, book reviews, and works in translation. Subscribe by phone: 740-427-5208; or mail: The Kenyon Review, Kenyon College, Gambier, OH 43022. Subscription options are as follows: one year ($25); two years ($45); three years ($65); sample copy ($9). Subscribers outside the U.S. add $8 per year for postage.

MaComère is the refereed journal of the Association of Caribbean Women Writers and Scholars (ACWWS), devoted to scholarly studies and creative works by and about Caribbean women in the Americas, Europe, and the Caribbean diaspora. The current price for a single issue is $20 for institutions, $15 for individuals. Email macomere@jmu.edu or visit the website at www.macomere.com for further information.

Based at the University of Massachusetts, Amherst, **The Massachusetts Review,** which celebrated its fortieth anniversary in 1999, is a quarterly of poetry, fiction, the arts, and criticism by writers established and promising, regional and international. Subscribe by mail: The Massachusetts Review, South College, University of Massachusetts, Box 37140, Amherst, MA 01003-7140. The subscription options are as follows: one year ($22); two years ($34); three years ($52). Subscribers outside the U.S. add $8 per year for postage.

The New Republic. Subscription rates for the USA: one year (48 issues) for $39.99, two years (96 issues) for $74.97; Canada: one year (48 issues) for US$64.99 (includes postage and GST); International: 1 year (48 issues) for US$79.99 (surface delivery); International: 1 year (48 issues) for US$159.99 (airmail).

The New Yorker is a weekly magazine dedicated to ideas. It is timeless and immediate, energetic and thoughtful, serious and funny. *The New Yorker* is about good writing, a point of view, and a deeper understanding of the world. To subscribe, contact The New Yorker, Box 56447, Boulder, Colorado 80322-6447, or telephone (800) 825-2510 (United States) or (303) 678-0354 (outside the United States).

The New York Review of Books reviews books and serious literary, cultural, and political articles. Subscribe by mail to: The New York Review of Books, 1755 Broadway, 5th Floor, New York, NY 10019-3780. Subscription costs are $58 for one year; $109 for two years. Biweekly, except for January, July, August, September, and December, when monthly.

Obsidian II publishes literature of the African diaspora. Subscribe by mail: North Carolina State University, Dept. of English, Box 8105, Raleigh, NC 27695-8105. Subscription per issue ($10); per year ($22); and two years ($37).

The Paris Review is published quarterly. A one-year individual subscription is $40; two years, $76. Please address letters to The Paris Review, 46-39 171 Place, Flushing, NY 11358 or try the website (www.parisreview.com).

Poets & Writers Magazine, a trade journal for creative writers, publishes profiles of contemporary authors, essays on the creative process, and grants and awards information. Subscribe by mail: Poets & Writers Magazine, P.O. Box 543, Mount Morris, IL 61054; phone: 815-734-1123; or email: www.pw.org.

Prairie Schooner is published quarterly in March, June, September, and December. Subscriptions are $22 for one year; $38 for two years; $50 for three years. Single copies are $7.95 (Nebraska residents add sales tax). The rate for libraries is $25 per year. Special rates for bulk orders. To subscribe, call 1-800-715-2387.

Zoetrope: All Story is published quarterly. Subscription rates for one year are $20 within the United States; $26 within Canada and Mexico; and $40 for other foreign countries. Subscription rates for two years are $35 within the United States; $46 within Canada and Mexico; $70 for other foreign countries. Subscription rates for three years are $50 within the United States; $65 within Canada and Mexico; $100 for other foreign countries. Zoetrope: All Story, 1350 Avenue of the Americas, 24th Floor, New York, NY 10019. Fax: 212-708-0475 Website: zoetrope-stories.com. Single copies can be obtained in bookstores and at newsstands. Call Eastern News Distributors at 800-221-3148 for more information.